THIN ICE

Also in this series

Other books by Desmond Bagley

MICHAEL DAVIES

Thin Ice

A Bill Kemp Thriller

HarperCollins*Publishers*

HarperCollins*Publishers*
1 London Bridge Street,
London SE1 9GF

HarperCollins*Publishers*
Macken House, 39/40 Mayor Street Upper,
Dublin 1, DO1 C9W8. Ireland
www.harpercollins.co.uk

First published by HarperCollins*Publishers* 2024
1

A catalogue record for this book is available from the British Library

ISBN 978-0-00-864476-5

This novel is entirely a work of fiction. The names, characters and
incidents portrayed in it are the work of the author's imagination. Any
resemblance to actual persons, living or dead, events or localities is
entirely coincidental.

Typeset in Meridien by HarperCollins*Publishers* India

Printed and bound in the UK using
100% renewable electricity at CPI Group (UK) Ltd

MIX
Paper | Supporting
responsible forestry
FSC™ C007454

This book is produced from independently certified FSC™
paper to ensure responsible forest management.

For more information visit: www.harpercollins.co.uk/green

*In memory of
Ken and Wanda*

*And for the other 'boys' –
John, Patrick and Nick*

I am persuaded that the people of the world have no grievances, one against the other. The hopes and desires of a man who tills the soil are about the same whether he lives on the banks of the Colorado or on the banks of the Danube.

Lyndon B. Johnson

In skating over thin ice, our safety is in our speed.

Ralph Waldo Emerson

PROLOGUE

We had exchanged barely ten minutes of conversation in the café; now Anna Stern was dead.

From where I lay in the snow, I could see the policemen swarming around her body, half an anxious eye on the far bank of the river as they covered her with a tarpaulin and hefted her onto a stretcher. Some strands of vivid red hair poked out from under the canvas and one arm hung limply to the side, her bright yellow windcheater smeared with mud. The clash of vibrant colours had been impossible to miss when she strolled into the café, and had been just as my informant described. Here, under the watery winter sun, I didn't need binoculars to confirm her identity. There was no mistaking her then and there was no mistaking her now, even on such short acquaintance.

I wondered how Anna Stern had wound up dead beside the freezing shallows of the Danube less than twenty-four hours after meeting me. More selfishly, but more alarmingly, I wondered if the two things were connected.

Four officers took a corner of the stretcher each and, glancing warily behind them, carried Anna's body up the short slope towards the tree line. The front pair hoisted their load onto the bank, about three feet higher than the pebbled foreshore, where another two policemen grabbed the handles and pulled. As Anna Stern disappeared into the darkness of the little wood, I felt a shiver run down my spine.

A few nervous officers swept the pebbles for any vestiges of evidence before clambering after their colleagues into the safety of the trees. From my first arrival on a spit a hundred yards to the north, it had taken less than three minutes for the scene to be cleared. Aside from some disturbed snow that could easily have been caused by wild animals, it looked as if no one had ever been there.

I switched my attention to the opposite side, where heavy fortifications along the river's edge prevented any living creature from making it to the water. High above where a tributary split off from the Danube, the crag was topped by a grey citadel, much older than the barricades and barbed wire. I racked my brains to picture the reference book I'd been studying the night before but I couldn't call to mind the name of this medieval pile. I picked out its most unusual feature, however: a tiny stone watchtower perched on a crag of its own, the subject of countless myths across the centuries about imprisoned maidens and the like. Why the Czechoslovakian authorities had deemed it necessary to add a handful of new towers, complete with searchlights and artillery, was beyond me. For some reason their Soviet masters didn't trust the build quality of the original stonemasons; never mind that the fortress had stood for seven hundred years unconquered. Then I reminded myself that this was a different mentality altogether: the modern monstrosities were there to keep people in, not out.

I glanced at my watch and decided to give myself at least thirty minutes before trying to move. Almost immediately I adjusted my plan as a shard of ice under my belly melted into chilling wetness that penetrated the outer layers on my torso and numbed the skin on my chest. There was no way I was going to be able to stand another half-hour of this, even with the sun beating down on my back. I knew that once my protective clothing had been breached I would feel the cold much more quickly and I didn't want to sink into hypothermia. I'd be willing to risk a Czech sniper rather than freeze to death.

I gave it five more minutes then reassessed my situation. There was still no sign of any interest from the eastern side and I reckoned it couldn't be much longer before the police convoy left the scene, presumably taking Anna's body back to Vienna. By the time I'd extricated myself from the snowbound spit and retraced my steps to the car, concealed down a hiking path that was hidden from the main track, the police would be long gone. I had no idea what I was going to do then but a large part of me didn't care. I hadn't signed up for a lethal mission and nobody could blame me if I simply got on a plane and flew back to London that afternoon. The prospect of a warm fire and a large whisky seemed inordinately appealing to me right then.

I threw one last glance across the river at the fearsome communist fortifications on the other side and began my backwards crawl through the snow towards the undergrowth. I had shuffled less than fifteen feet when the cocking of a gun behind me stopped me dead.

'I suggest you stay exactly where you are, Herr Kemp.'

PART ONE

High Citadel

ONE

I'd been feeding the ducks and was running in from the garden to reach the ringing telephone when I tripped on the back step and fell headlong against the Welsh dresser in the kitchen. The lump on my forehead that began to emerge almost instantly put me in a distinctly grumpy frame of mind, even as I picked up the receiver and barked into it.

'Kemp. Who is this?'

The voice on the other end of the line was oily, in spite of my abruptness. 'Mr Kemp. We haven't had the pleasure.'

'Who is this?' I repeated.

'Oh, you don't need to know my name, Mr Kemp. Let's just say we have mutual acquaintances.'

Besides the evasiveness, there was something about his tone that I found grating. The accent was an attempt at cut-glass upper-crust but there was no disguising the hint of Thames estuary about the vowels. I'm certainly no snob about such things: it's the deception I object to. I wondered if the persona was as much of a sham as the voice.

'I'm sorry. I don't play games,' I said, and was on the verge of hanging up the phone when the voice burbled again.

'Even with a life at stake?'

I hesitated. It was just another part of the game, I knew, but it was one I couldn't ignore. I put the receiver to my ear again. 'Whose life?'

'One of those mutual acquaintances I mentioned, Mr Kemp. A certain young lady by the name of Leotta Tomsson.'

Leotta! What the hell did this have to do with Leotta? The last time I'd seen her she was repacking a vast trunk of unsuitable clothes which she'd brought with her from the Caribbean to take to the medical school where she intended to spend the next few years learning to become a doctor. In the few months between her arrival in England and the start of the university term I had invited her to stay with me in Devon and we had enjoyed a delightful summer of boats, bucolics and bed – though not necessarily in that order. We'd parted sadly but tenderly, agreeing that both our futures would be easier if we went our separate ways, and as far as I knew she was halfway through her second year of study. Apart from the occasional non-committal letter passing in each direction, that had been it. Now her name was being dropped, with lethal implications, by this mystery man on the end of an anonymous call.

'What are you talking about? What's this got to do with Leotta?'

'You're interested now, aren't you?'

I felt the anger rising in my throat. 'Who the hell are you?'

'Listen to me, Kemp.' The tone had changed: the oiliness had given way to abrasiveness. 'You'll get another call in a few days' time. This one is simply to give you fair warning, and to let you know that we're serious. Deadly serious.'

'Cut the melodramatic claptrap and tell me what this is all about.'

The oiliness returned. 'Insults are hardly going to help Miss Tomsson, now, are they? But what might is your cooperation, so be a good boy and do what you're told.'

'And what exactly is that?'

'For now, you wait. And no police. We'll be watching.'

'How do I know Leotta is all right?'

'You don't. You'll just have to take my word for it.'

The line went dead.

I stood with the receiver to my ear for a good thirty seconds before slamming it furiously back in its cradle and thumping my palm against the side of the Welsh dresser, where my head had made contact only minutes before. The bump was aching badly now so I went to my make-shift medicine drawer under the sink and fished out a couple of headache tablets, which I washed down with a handful of water scooped from the tap. I sat heavily on one of the wooden chairs surrounding the table and stared vacantly out of the window at the Devon country-side. Dark clouds threatened the mouth of the river and an icy January blast blew in from the still open back door so I got up and pushed it to. The ducks would have to fend for themselves. Then I sat back down and thought hard about the phone call.

I couldn't make sense of any of it. Who was my smarmy interlocutor with more menace than real information? What was his connection with Leotta – and why had he deemed it necessary to involve her at all? That bit I could probably answer: it was an easy way to get me to fall into line. But why me? And what line?

His instruction had been not to involve the police. I guessed that was more for effect than down to any real concern on his part. After all, what would I say to the boys in blue? That I'd received an anonymous phone call offering some vaguely threatening eventuality that might or might not happen to someone I'd last seen in person eighteen months ago and who was now, as far as I knew, studying medicine two hundred miles away? They'd give me five minutes of their time, maximum, before dismissing me as a paranoid crank.

More to the point, if he was serious and they did have Leotta squirrelled away somewhere while they watched my next step, then any approach I made to the authorities could be highly detrimental to her health. I'd experienced enough of that kind of brutality on my trip to Australia a year before and it was a chance I wasn't prepared to take a second time.

On the other hand, there was no way I was going to sit around watching the river slowly ice over and waiting for the phone to ring.

There seemed to be a simple solution to my dilemma: I needed to talk to Leotta.

I found the number for her hall of residence in my address book and dialled. I knew she was sharing a floor with about a dozen other students and it was pot luck as to who would pick up the phone – that's if anyone was around to pick it up at all. At this time of day it was quite likely that everyone was safely tucked up in a warm lecture theatre, being bored witless about anatomy or pharmaceuticals or whatever passed for the latest knowledge in medical school circles. Even if someone did answer my call, I would have to persuade them to go looking for Leotta in her room, then wait while they found her and she made the long trek back to the shared telephone.

After fifteen rings I hung up.

For most of the rest of the day I paced the house, turning over options and going back to the phone every hour to try again. At five, someone answered.

'I need to speak to Leotta Tomsson. It's urgent.'

The girl at the other end sounded bemused. 'Leotta? I haven't seen her for a while.'

Something inside me heaved alarmingly. 'What do you mean, "a while"?'

'I don't know – a few days, maybe? Listen, mate, don't shoot the messenger.'

I realised I might be sounding more than a little over-wrought. 'I'm sorry. What's your name?'

'Melissa. Who are you?'

'Melissa, I need your help. My name is Bill Kemp.' I hesitated while I considered the best way to frame my relationship with Leotta – not to mention my current predicament. 'I'm an old friend of Leotta's and I need to speak to her urgently. Is there any way you could check her room for me? Please.'

Melissa sighed heavily. 'All right. Hold on.'

I heard the noise of the receiver being placed on a solid surface, then footsteps as Melissa wandered off. In the background I could hear a door banging, some indeterminate voices and a loud laugh – the casual sounds of a communal place of accommodation. Life was going on as normal. I hoped that was true for Leotta and that my anonymous caller was nothing more than a sick practical joker.

The wait was interminable. I checked my watch several times and began to wonder if Melissa had forgotten her errand. More than five minutes later she was back.

'She's not in her room. There's no reply when I knock.'

'Lectures must be over for the day. Does she often stay out after classes are finished?'

Melissa had clearly had enough of the conversation. 'I don't know, do I? I just live on the same floor as her. I'm not her social secretary or anything.'

'I'm sorry. It's just that this is really important. Can you remember when you last saw her?'

'No.' She paused. 'Monday, maybe. I can't remember.'

Two days. I needed to find out if anyone else had seen her since then.

'How should I know?' Melissa was decidedly irritated.

'Could you ask around, perhaps? See if anyone else on your floor has seen her?'

'No, I couldn't. I don't have time to go chasing around after Leotta Tomsson. She's a grown-up. She can look after herself.'

For the second time that day, the line went dead.

I toyed with the idea of calling straight back and having another go at buttering up Melissa, or leaving it for half an hour and seeing if someone more helpful might pick up the next time I called. In the end I decided that relying on a third party was likely to prove unsatisfactory and that positive action was required.

I threw some overnight belongings into a bag and pointed the car inland.

TWO

The medical school featured a huge, imposing frontage of brown brick with white stone highlights picking out the portico and window frames. With a set of steep steps leading up to the main entrance, where vast wooden doors stood forbiddingly closed, it looked like the headquarters of a government department devoted to secrets and subterfuge. I hoped to find Leotta Tomsson somewhere inside.

The drive north had been tedious and wearying and had taken much longer than I expected. Although the expansion of the M5 motorway was continuing, there were still large chunks that were too ill-formed to make much difference to a journey time to or from the southwest. It was an improvement on the old A38 but not by much: its daytime popularity had been vastly underestimated by the engineers who had been creating it for more than a decade and it was already looking seriously underpowered for its future needs. Even in the middle of the night, with little traffic on the stretches of triple carriageway, it was hard work.

It was with mundane thoughts such as these that I forced myself to occupy my mind as I drove through the early hours. The alternative was to spend my time wondering and worrying about Leotta and that was too inconclusive to provide any comfort.

The cold seeped in around the drop head hood of the Stag and I soon regretted not taking the time to fit the hard top before setting off. The good people at Triumph had come up with a truly enjoyable machine for touring in summer climes, but the dead of a midwinter's night in rural England is hardly the time or place for a luxury convertible. Even with the heating on full I could feel the chill creeping into my bones. I reached across to my shoulder bag on the passenger seat and extricated a scarf, which I draped as best I could around my neck.

Two hours in, I stopped at a rest area and broke open the flask of hot coffee I'd brought with me. The ham sandwich I'd made was limp and unappetising but I ate it anyway: I couldn't be sure when I might next be able to find food and breakfast seemed a long way off. Despite the freezing temperatures, I got out and walked around the deserted rest stop, slapping my hands against my arms and willing the blood in my legs to keep circulating. My breath blew out great clouds of vapour and I remembered the billows of smoke I used to create when I was a regular cigarette addict. It was moments like these that I missed the filthy habit the most.

By the time I pulled up in the car park outside the front of the medical school I was cold, hungry and thoroughly miserable. What made it worse was the fact that I had arrived in the middle of the night: it would be several hours yet before anyone turned up to open the building. There was nothing for it but to hunker down in the driver's seat, wrapped in all the clothes I'd brought with me, and wait.

With Leotta firmly in the forefront of my mind, I slept fitfully amid hazy dreams of Caribbean mansions, copper-gold skin and swarthy hijackers. I half-woke on a number of occasions, disturbed by a fox or a rabbit in the shrubs nearby. Long before there was any light in the sky, a caretaker shuffled across the car park towing a metal bucket on wheels, rending the early morning darkness with an incongruously loud rattle. I stirred and watched him glance in the direction of my car but if he was curious he didn't act upon it. He wore a set of dark overalls and a flat cap that made him look like a caricature of a northern factory-worker and he dragged the clattering monstrosity across the tarmac before heaving it up the steps to the big front door. He took his time about searching in the pockets of his overalls for a huge bunch of keys, from which he picked out one and inserted it into the lock of the door. With one more look towards me, he picked up the bucket and disappeared inside.

If I'd got out of the car and approached him civilly, it was just possible I might have persuaded him to let me in for a warm and a cup of something restorative but for starters I was not feeling particularly civil and in any case I had my doubts that he would be prepared to welcome an unknown visitor in the dark at that ungodly hour. It was far more likely that I would find that hulking slab of oak slammed unceremoniously in my face. Besides, no students would be arriving for a good while yet and it would be simpler all round if I could catch Leotta before she went inside. That way we could keep things private, away from the prying of any classmates. All I really wanted was to see her in person and know that she was safe.

If she didn't appear at the medical school for classes that morning, I had another plan up my sleeve: once office hours began I would go inside posing as a relative with important family business and ask the school administrator for directions to her accommodation block. I hoped the fact that I already knew her address would convince the resident officialdom that I was genuine and they would give me the information I sought. Otherwise I would be resorting to an A to Z and hoping that some kindly fellow student would let me in when I got to the flats.

I let a full hour pass beyond the time I imagined lectures would start. I'd watched scores of studious young people arrive at the building, mount the steps and head inside; none of them was Leotta. As the day brightened into a crisp morning, the car park filled up around me and older folk – presumably the professors and lecturers – hefted their briefcases and bags towards the entrance. At one point I worried that I might be raising suspicions so I did my best impression of an academic and got out of the car. Anxious not to miss my quarry, I headed purposefully for the corner of the building as if I were making for a side door, then lurked out of sight there while I watched the front steps. Ten minutes later I was back in the Stag, firing it up again to warm the engine and the interior. I couldn't be certain but I judged the outside temperature as below zero and there had been a heavy overnight frost that left a sparkling whiteness on the bushes and paths.

Finally I was sure that Leotta had not turned up for class that morning – at least not using the front entrance. It was entirely possible she'd entered the building another way but if that was the case then I would have to take my chances with the staff inside.

The woman behind the desk in the lobby seemed distracted. Dressed dowdily in a cardigan and woollen skirt, she was focused on a large ring binder file in front of her and barely looked up when I addressed her.

'Excuse me,' I said, putting what I hoped was a polite tone into my voice despite my chilly disposition and rumbling stomach.

'Can I help you?' she asked, then looked immediately back down at her folder.

'I'm looking for a student.'

She stopped her perusal of the paperwork and lifted

her head. 'Is that a particular student or will any of them do?'

I indulged her sarcasm with a forced smile and ploughed on. 'Her name is Leotta Tomsson and she's a second-year medic.'

She frowned disapprovingly, as if I'd made some inappropriate remark. 'May I ask how you know her?'

I had an answer freshly burnished for her. 'She's my cousin. I need to speak to her about a family matter.'

'And you've come in person to see her?' She sounded dubious and rightly so: I was lying to her face.

'I tried phoning her accommodation block but I couldn't get through to her. I thought it might be easiest just to turn up.' That much was true, at least.

'Have you come far?'

I couldn't see what that had to do with anything and I told her so. The temperature dropped a further degree or two.

'Look,' I said, openly pleading with her now. 'I know she lives at Spencer House and I can always look it up on a map but it would make my life a great deal easier if you could simply tell me where that is and how I can get there from here.'

'It's not my job to make your life easier,' she said and turned back to her file. Evidently she thought better of her obstructiveness because a moment later she glanced up again. Maybe she thought I looked desperate so took pity on me. 'I'm sorry, Mr – '

'Kemp.'

'Mr Kemp. It's just that I'm a little stressed right now.'

'I understand.'

'If you go out of the front door and turn left, Spencer House is about half a mile towards town on your right. It's a big red-brick building about six storeys high – you can't miss it.'

My smile this time was genuine.

I left the Stag parked outside the medical school and started walking in the direction she'd pointed. I was increasingly aware that I hadn't eaten since the limp sandwich at the rest stop in the middle of the night but this was more pressing. I ignored the pangs in my belly and marched purposefully towards the building I could now see in the distance.

The accommodation block bore a striking resemblance to an army barracks I'd once had the misfortune to occupy and I wondered if the interior was as stark and unwelcoming as that had been. Bare walls and exposed pipework do not make for comforting surroundings and I was damn sure that if I were a student I would need something a good deal more homely to help me work efficiently. It's one thing bedding down in a grim environment when all you need is a night's sleep; it's quite another to try and complete your academic studies in a cell.

I reached the door of the block and tried the handle. I was not surprised to find that it didn't open. The half-glazed door was reflecting the wintry daylight back at me so I leaned my forehead against it, shielding my eyes with both hands to peer inside. I could see a corridor of bare brick walls stretching away to the far side of the building, with doorways inset along its length. A few feet in and off to the right, the corridor gave way to an opening, through which I could make out a set of stairs. I guessed from Leotta's room number – 409 – that her lodgings would be on the fourth floor. The only problem was how to get up there.

I stepped away from the door and looked around. Spencer House was set back a little way from the road, with a pavement and small grassed area separating it from the traffic. The footfall of frequent residents had worn a strip into the grass from the path to the door. A few yards back towards the medical school, a bus stop was marked with a shelter containing a wooden bench and I made use of the facility while I considered my next move.

I didn't have to wait long: less than five minutes after I sat down, the door of the accommodation building swung open and a long-haired youth tumbled out onto the grass clutching an armful of books. I watched him pass the bus shelter, noting that the door seemed to be on a slow hinge and took a good twenty seconds to close, by which time he was already past me.

I would be ready whenever someone else used that door.

The long-haired boy was apparently an outlier when it came to turning up late for lectures. The next person to use the door didn't appear for well over half an hour. I was utterly chilled and completely ravenous by the time the next resident left the accommodation block. Wrapped in a heavy overcoat, she seemed a nervous type, anxiously inspecting her watch and rushing past me towards the medical school, giving me plenty of opportunity to reach the door before it shut and slip inside.

The corridor was almost as cold as outside. I didn't hang about to be challenged by anyone else who might be around but mounted the stairs two at a time to the first floor before slowing my pace and taking the next two flights more easily. When I reached the door marked 400 I hesitated to listen for sounds of activity along the hall. I heard nothing so began to make my way along the numbers, stopping when I reached 409. Behind this door, I hoped, would be an end to my worries and I'd be able to take a leisurely drive back to Devon with a weight lifted from my mind.

My knock was intended to be a balance between confident friendliness and gentle concern. It didn't matter because there was no response. I knocked again, more forcefully this time, but there was still nothing. Maybe I had missed Leotta if, as I feared, she had used a different entrance to the medical school. Or maybe she was in a deep sleep, unroused by my hammering on her door. I didn't mind going back to the school and waiting for lectures to end, if that's what it was going to take, but I wanted to make certain she really wasn't here in the accommodation block before I abandoned this line of enquiry.

I couldn't think of any other way so I stood in the middle of the hallway and shouted.

'Hello! Is anybody here?'

It took all of fifteen seconds for a door to bang open at the far end of the corridor and a dour girl in pyjamas to storm out onto the landing.

'Who the hell's shouting the odds at this time of day?'

I smiled benignly at her and checked my watch. 'It's well past breakfast time.'

'For you, maybe. I've just pulled an all-nighter to hit an essay deadline.'

I offered my apologies and took a couple of steps towards her. Immediately her eyes widened and she backed into her doorway. I halted my advance and lifted my hands in a placatory gesture.

'I'm just looking for Leotta Tomsson. I don't suppose you know where she is, do you?'

'Leotta? Who's asking?'

I repeated my lie from earlier, which the girl didn't question.

'You can't be that close as a family, then,' she said.

'What do you mean?'

'If you were, you'd know that she was out of the country.'

That shook me. 'Out of the country? What about her course?'

The girl shrugged. 'Special dispensation – that's what she told me. A symposium for high-flying medical students.'

'So she's on some kind of sabbatical?'

'I don't know about that but it's definitely been approved by the university.'

The whole story stank but I knew it wasn't this girl's fault. I'd never heard of a second-year student attending an international symposium, no matter how high-flying she might be. It all added to my sense of foreboding about Leotta.

'So where has she gone?'

She shrugged again. 'America somewhere. I think she mentioned Boston.'

I couldn't begin to put the pieces together. If someone had tricked Leotta with the prospect of a high-profile conference, it wouldn't have been hard to pick her up in a kidnap operation and whisk her away to some secret location while they used her as leverage against me. But I had no idea who might want to do such a thing – or what they wanted me to do. That was still an unknown, awaiting the next phone call from my anonymous friend. I could, of course, check in with the nice lady behind the desk in the foyer of the medical school to see if the symposium story stacked up, but if it didn't I'd be ringing alarm bells with her university that would surely be passed on to the police, and I'd been expressly forbidden to do that. A few days' absence might go unremarked but a strange man lying about being Leotta's cousin who then implied that she might have gone missing in mysterious circumstances would put the whole situation on a very different footing. I might even fall under the suspicions of the constabulary myself and I needed to remain at liberty to find out what on earth was going on. I decided to pursue my own angles without ruffling any feathers at the medical school.

'Thanks,' I said to the girl. 'You've been really helpful.'

'Have I?'

'Just one more thing. If you see Leotta, would you mind asking her to get in touch with Bill as a matter of urgency? I really do need to speak to her.'

'And you're Bill, are you?'

'Bill Kemp,' I said, and turned for the stairs.

It was another two days of dismal waiting before the next call came.

I spent the time wintering the dinghy, bringing it up from the sailing club on a trailer and storing it in the large boatshed I'd constructed at the end of the garden a few summers ago for just this purpose. I'd normally have done it a couple of months earlier at least but the autumn seemed to last much longer than usual and I'd managed to keep her in use, even taking her out on Christmas Day for a solo spin around the river mouth. The forecast now was for snow, though, so I removed the sails and patched up one or two areas of loose stitching, then derigged her, washed her down and wrapped her in a heavy tarpaulin. After picking up the boat I never ventured far from the house and left the back door open so I would hear the phone ring from the shed; but when the call finally came it was evening and I had already settled down in front of a log fire with a large shot of whisky in my tumbler.

'Nice trip, Mr Kemp?' the oily voice asked without any preamble.

I didn't even bother pretending that I didn't understand him. If I'd doubted his veracity when he told me I'd be watched, then this proved he had meant every word. Had they seen me at the rest stop? Was the medical school caretaker in on the action? Had they been keeping an eye on me as I stowed the boat against the forthcoming weather? I had answers to none of these questions and I felt at a crippling disadvantage to my caller.

'Where's Leotta Tomsson?' I said, not disguising my contempt. 'If you've harmed that girl in any way – '

'Now, now, Mr Kemp, I hope we can be a little more civilised than that. What would be the sense in me harming her at this stage of proceedings? No, I need her fit and well in order to encourage you to keep behaving so obligingly.'

I realised with a jolt that he was right: I had been depressingly predictable in my actions of the last few days and if these people – whoever they were – wanted me to do something for them, reliably and dependably, I had certainly given them the reassurance that I was likely to comply. Then again, what else could I have done?

'So – where is she?'

'You don't seriously think I'm going to tell you that, do you? I need you where I want you to go, not dashing off on some heroic mission to rescue the girl. No, Mr Kemp, Leotta's location will not be divulged to you, now or ever. If you do what you're told, on time and without any resistance, then she will be back in her lectures at the medical school before you can say *amaurosis fugax*.'

He laughed but there was no mirth in his tone.

'Of course, if you don't, then the people I've charged with looking after her have their instructions. They merely await my say-so.'

'What is it you expect me to do?' I said, working hard to temper my fury. While I awaited his answer I took a large slug from the tumbler.

'Ah, now we come to the crux of the matter. It's not hard, Mr Kemp. We're not asking you to undertake anything particularly arduous. In fact, you might argue there are some side benefits to the job.'

I could barely contain my rage any longer. 'Get on with it, man. Tell me what the hell it is I'm supposed to do.'

'There, there, Mr Kemp. It sounds like you might be getting rather agitated. Why don't you have another drink?'

I started violently. How could he know I was drinking at that exact moment? I checked the windows on both sides of the room but the dusk had turned to dark and I could see nothing but distant twinkling lights and blackness. I desperately wanted to close the curtains but I didn't dare leave the telephone.

'All right,' I said, tempering my voice as best I could. 'You've got my attention. What is it you want?'

'Very well. It's simply this: we want you to go to Vienna and collect a package.'

I listened for more but nothing came.

'That's it? You want me to pick up a parcel.'

'That's it.'

'In Vienna.'

'Your listening skills are clearly excellent, Mr Kemp. I repeat: we want you to go to Vienna and collect a package. Your flight from Heathrow leaves the day after tomorrow at ten-thirty in the morning. A hotel has been booked for you near the airport to allow you a leisurely check-in and all the details will be delivered to you first thing tomorrow. I think that concludes our business for this evening. Leotta will be grateful, I'm sure.'

I started to ask one of the many questions popping up in my brain but he had already gone.

After several minutes wrestling with the call, it finally registered that I was still sitting in plain view of the windows. If there was someone out there I didn't want them watching me a moment longer than necessary. I got up out of my armchair and wrenched the curtains closed. Then I went to the bookcase and took down a medical dictionary.

Amaurosis fugax: fleeting, short-term blindness.

It was my turn to laugh mirthlessly.

THREE

I'm not a great one for omens and I treat my horoscope with an indecently large pinch of salt but I have to admit that the journey to Vienna did not begin auspiciously.

I'd had a lousy night in a lumpy bed courtesy of my travel organiser, whose notion of what constituted a hotel differed markedly from mine: personally, I prefer a private bathroom, freshly-laundered bedding and dry towels. As for a leisurely check-in at Heathrow, the queue in the departure lounge snaked endlessly through the hall and the attentions of several uniformed staff members seemed utterly inadequate to cope with the number of travellers. I made the gate by the skin of my teeth and deposited my passport on the desk in front of a sour-looking matron who did not seem as if she would be inclined to accept any excuse along the lines of: 'It took longer to get through security than I expected.'

But it was the plane itself that concerned me most. I felt a sickening in my stomach when I saw that my BEA flight to Austria was to be made on a Hawker Siddeley Trident. Little over eighteen months earlier, more than a hundred people had died in one of these things two and a half minutes after it left the ground from this same airport. The

Staines air disaster had been the worst on British soil and, with the public inquiry's report still fresh in many people's memory, there remained plenty of controversy about the aircraft itself. Officially the crash was put down primarily to errors on the part of the crew and a serious heart defect afflicting the captain but there were a significant number of voices who felt the inquiry had been a whitewash in favour of the plane's manufacturer. Now I was about to board one of these beasts for a three-hour flight across the continent's highest range of mountains in the wake of some of the heaviest storms in years. And that was without even considering the ever-present threat of hijackers, who had been targeting European flights for months now.

To my relief, the pilot sounded healthy enough, although it was hard to tell over the plane's internal communication system, which rendered everyone – male and female – in the same blurry, robotic tones. As we traversed the northern Alps he pointed out the unusually cloud-free sky below us and I was able to pick out the geographical features to which he drew attention. I was grateful for the distraction but the rising wall of white off the plane's right-hand wingtip only reminded me that I was heading into the unknown. What Vienna held in store I could not know and dared not guess.

'Herr Kemp,' said a deep, weathered voice to my left as I emerged from the baggage hall. I turned to see a heavily-bearded man in his sixties, sporting a traditional Austrian *janker* jacket in dark grey wool and a peaked cap with a gleaming black brim.

'Yes?'

'I am requested to invite you to accompany me,' he said in strongly accented but perfectly formed English. 'This way, if you please.'

I surrendered my bag to him and followed him through the throng, glancing around to see if anyone else was taking the same path as us. I hadn't expected a welcoming committee but if my puppetmaster was willing to lay on a chauffeur at no additional expense, I wasn't about to reject the offer.

The whole thing – anonymous calls, mystery mission, smartly-dressed flunkey – could all, of course, have been an elaborate trap to kidnap me and my current journey turn out to be my last on this earth. But then, I reasoned, what possible motive could anyone have for kidnapping me? I was nobody, knew nothing of significance, had no influence in important circles and hardly fitted the stereotype of wealthy hostage with promising ransom potential. My lack of any unique qualities also made me a strange choice for whoever had employed my services, I realised, but I was not going to be able to solve that puzzle without more information, and that was something I knew was in short supply.

My uniformed companion led us out of the terminal and over to a black Mercedes parked illegally in a loading area. After heaving my bag into the boot he indicated to me to get in and I faltered momentarily – as I always do in countries where they drive on the wrong side of the road – before locating the passenger door and climbing in. Maybe I'd read too much Le Carré but I half-expected to find a weaselly man armed with a Luger waiting for me in the back seat.

There was no one.

The driver turned the engine over and eased out into the traffic leaving the airport. Drifts of snow were piled up along the gutters and fresh white flakes fell from the monotone sky. Since meeting me off the plane he had said not a single word and I began to wonder if his initial greeting had been something he'd learned by rote, unable to speak English colloquially. I put my theory to the test.

'Where are we going?'

He glanced in my direction and broke into a warm smile. 'To your hotel, of course. You will enjoy it, I have no doubt. We Austrians are famous for our hospitality.'

I had nothing by which to judge his claim but I was prepared to take it at face value. I hoped the famous Austrian hospitality might extend to supplying a little of that much-needed information.

'You know my name – am I permitted to know yours?'

He glanced again and the smile broadened. 'I am Josef.'

'And I'm Bill. Do you have a surname, Josef?'

'Aschauer. It seems my ancestors lived near an ash tree.'

I smiled back and worked some more on him. 'Are you native Viennese?'

'Since many hundreds of years,' he said, his grammatical grasp of English slipping for the first time.

'And do you have a family?'

He swerved suddenly to dodge a veering lorry and let out a string of affronted German that I took to be expletives. My knowledge of the language was insufficient to tell whether the words were separate or one of those enormous compound expressions favoured by the Teutonics. 'Excuse me, Mr Kemp. I apologise.'

'No need,' I said. 'And I've already told you – it's Bill.'

He lapsed into silence again and I wondered if he had forgotten my last enquiry. 'So – any family?'

'Oh, Mr Bill. So many questions. This will cause you trouble, I think.' The smile had vanished and he wagged a finger at me, which I interpreted as a warning to stop my probing, so I turned to look out of the window instead and soaked up my first views of Vienna.

The journey into the city from the airport was notable chiefly for its unremarkability. Like so many airports on the edge of European cities, it was served by a well-used arterial highway. This one fed new arrivals north-westwards, following the Danube valley through Lower Austria and into the suburbs. Industrial buildings and warehouses started to give way to single- and double-storey homes, which in turn became apartment blocks and rows of shops as we neared the old city. For twenty minutes Josef Aschauer drove through the falling snow, guiding the Mercedes through the slush and traffic with practised ease, until he suddenly swung the car off the main road and headed down a smaller street to the right. Up ahead I could see what I thought was a bridge.

I broke the silence. 'Is this the way to the hotel?'

'Oh no, Mr Bill. This is the way to the river.'

I was alarmed, partly by his answer but more by the studied equanimity in his voice. 'The river?'

'*Der schönen blauen Donau*. You know – like in the music. Strauss?'

'The blue Danube, you mean?'

'Yes, yes! You English call it wrong always. For us it is the Donau. I show you the beauty of Wien.'

And he did. Now talking as if his life depended on it, Josef drove us through the centre of the city, picking out opera houses, town halls, parks and monuments with all the skill of a professional tour guide – and all falling on disinterested ears. In other circumstances I would have been fascinated to learn how the huge public buildings were strung out along the Ringstrasse in the early years of the century, or about the Vienna International Centre being constructed on the far side of the Danube where the United Nations were forging themselves a second European base to match Geneva. I'd have lapped up his history lesson about the Holy Roman Empire, the Habsburgs and the Nazi Anschluss, as well as the pledge of neutrality required by the Soviets before they finally agreed to pull out of the country in 1955. As it was, while I appreciated the lecture on culture that covered everyone from Mozart and Beethoven to Sigmund Freud and Hedy Lamarr, there was only one name on my mind: Leotta Tomsson.

When Josef finally pulled up outside a huge art nouveau edifice on a wide boulevard with an elevated train track running down its centre, my head was throbbing.

'Your accommodation, Herr Kemp.'

He lugged my bag up the few steps into the lobby and waited dutifully while I checked in. Then he gave me another of his broad smiles, offered a curt farewell and was gone.

My room was an odd mixture of ancient and modern. Its bare parquet flooring and high ceiling gave it a flavour of its original *fin de siècle* splendour but its glory days were clearly behind it. Grey paint was peeling from various sections of the wall and the ironwork on the windows and doors was rusting. By contrast, the plumbing in the en suite bathroom looked bang up to date and when I flicked the handle of the shower a powerful jet of instantly hot water shot out from the nozzle in the wall above my head. I sat on the bed, testing its comfort, and found it to be softer and springier than I would have liked but the linen seemed clean enough and the room would do.

I lay back and studied the patch of discoloration on the ceiling above. I hoped it was caused by water damage long since addressed but judged that if the plasterwork were to come down it should miss my supine figure by a good two feet. As I stared, my mind wandered back to the medical school's halls of residence and I felt a familiar sickness in my gut as I thought once more of Leotta. Wherever she was, whatever she was doing, I hoped she knew nothing of the trammelled complexities that had led me to Austria, on an errand I knew next to nothing about, for a 'client' I had never met. The alternative – that she was being held against her will in some grim location by unscrupulous captors – was too horrific to contemplate.

After half an hour of fruitless mental wrangling I decided to go out. My orders were flimsy at best: to await further instructions on arrival in Vienna. Without a time-table, a map or an assignment, I was at a loose end but I had not been confined to barracks so I determined not to waste my time completely.

The desk clerk was young and efficient and spoke almost as impeccable English as Josef.

'How may I help you, Herr Kemp?'

'If I wanted to explore the local area, what would be the best way to go about it?'

'Of course. Do you wish to stay in the immediate vicinity or would you care to travel a little further afield?'

I had no idea what I was looking for in either eventuality so I hedged my bets. 'How far is the city centre?'

'It's a little over a kilometre, Herr Kemp. A nice enough walk in good weather, but at this time of year, with the snow falling, might I recommend the tram?'

I turned to look out of the front door and saw that the street outside was wet and covered in a layer of grey-brown slush. Although reasonably sturdy, my footwear was not ideal for an Alpine winter and I didn't want to spend the rest of the afternoon with damp feet from a leaking sole. On the other hand, I couldn't be bothered to return to my room for my walking boots.

'Where's the nearest stop?' I asked.

The clerk smoothed down the forelock of his greased hair and pointed towards the door. 'Turn left out of the hotel and go to the next corner. You'll find a tram stop just around to the left on a line which will take you directly into the city centre.'

I took the sheet of paper he offered, printed with a monochrome map showing the main tourist spots, and headed out of the door. As he'd directed, the tram stop was just a block away and I had to wait only a few

minutes before a tram arrived. Overhead, the cables supplying power to the whole system crackled as it rumbled
to a halt, and I followed an elderly woman with bulky
shopping bags up the two steps into the car.

For the second time that day I watched the Viennese
streets roll by. Bookshops rubbed shoulders with green-
grocers, whose wares were displayed in crates across store
frontages, while the aroma of bread or bacon would occasionally creep in from a baker's or butcher's, reminding
me I hadn't eaten since early morning. Everywhere the
architecture shouted history, from Gothic churches dot-
ting the suburbs to the neo-baroque apartment buildings
in the streets radiating out from the Ringstrasse, where
the old city walls had been torn down in the nineteenth
century.

I had obviously been paying more attention to Josef
Aschauer's lecture than I'd realised.

I dismounted from the tram at Schottentor, one of the
transport system's busier interchanges where the Alserstrasse met the Ringstrasse. I'd queried its name – 'the
Scottish gate' – with Josef as we drove through the city
earlier and he'd explained that it was derived from a 13th-
century Scottish abbey located nearby. It seemed odd to
me that the Scots should have had a significant presence
in Vienna seven hundred years ago but then history could
certainly throw up some oddities and I knew from people
I'd worked with in different countries that the Scottish
diaspora reached into every corner of the globe.

I was tiptoeing through the slushy puddles towards the
Rathaus, cursing my inadequate footwear, when I sensed
I was being followed.

Without turning around, I moved across the pavement
towards the roadway and stopped, as if waiting to cross.
On the opposite side stood the vast white frontage of the
Wiener University and when a break came in the traffic

I darted across and up its steps to the central portico. I dodged behind one of its square pillars and tucked myself back against the cold stone. My breath was rapid and I made clouds of thick steam immediately in front of my face as I counted to ten in my head. Then I peered around the corner of the pillar and watched for my shadow.

Plenty of people were hurrying to and fro, some armed with umbrellas against the snow, others with fur hats. None that I could see was paying particular attention to the university and all seemed to be in a hurry. At this time of the afternoon I figured it was likely that office workers would begin to think about heading home, especially as the weather was closing in and the dusk was casting its pall over the city. I scanned the pavement on both sides of the road but could see nothing untoward. Then again, I was no secret agent: any spycraft I might possess had been gleaned from the basic intelligence training I'd been given in the army or from my own experience in the field. My activities in the Caribbean and Australia over the past couple of years had exposed me to a certain amount of on-the-hoof improvisation in those areas but I wouldn't be any match for a specialist. If someone was following me and suspected I might be onto them, they would be much better at concealing themselves than I would be at spotting them.

It was also possible that I was imagining things. In my defence, the events of the last few days had done little for my nerves and I had found myself studying the faces of people around me – on the plane, on the tram – with added interest and caution. As the old joke goes, just because you're paranoid, it doesn't mean they aren't out to get you.

I shook off my unease and was about to resume my journey towards the Rathaus park when I caught sight of a figure in a long black overcoat and homburg reading a newspaper by a kiosk on the far side of the road. Something about his nonchalance was a little too studied, his stance a little too natural – and the homburg hadn't been in fashion for at least a decade outside of Hollywood gangster movies. As I watched, he stole an occasional glance in the direction of the university portico before returning to his unread paper.

I had found my shadow. The question now was what to do about him.

I pulled back from the corner and thought hard. The first unknown was whether my tail belonged to the people employing me or to some other outfit who'd got wind of my mission and wanted to know more. The former was more likely – that my anonymous caller simply wanted to keep tabs on my movements while I awaited further instructions – but I couldn't completely discount the latter either. And if a third party was involved, what would that mean for my assignment? With no knowledge of what it was even about, or who was controlling things, I could only surmise that another player in the game would make it considerably more complicated and perhaps more dangerous. I was anxious enough about the possibility of Leotta's having been kidnapped without the addition of another faction into the equation. My head was spinning.

After turning it over for a full five minutes I came to the conclusion that the presence of a tail made little difference to my mission either way. If it was my employer, then good luck to them: I wasn't doing anything they had told me not to do and how else was I supposed to pass the time while waiting to hear from them again? If it turned out to be another group with a vested interest, well, there was nothing I could do about that and they could fight it out with each other for all I cared. My prime concern was to stay out of trouble and get Leotta out of wherever she was alive.

I stepped out from behind the pillar, shook the dampness off my collar and headed out into the snow again.

A hundred yards down the street, where the Rathaus and the Burgtheater faced off against each other across the gardens, I stopped and performed an abrupt about-turn. I was just quick enough to catch the homburg dodging behind an advertising hoarding against the park fence so I thought I'd have a little fun. I marched straight back in the direction I'd come from, towards where the homburg was hiding, just to see what he'd do. As I reached the spot, I glimpsed him from the corner of my eye with his head buried behind the same bedraggled newspaper. I hesitated momentarily – just enough to give him palpitations – then turned away and crossed the street towards the theatre.

I noticed a sign indicating a restaurant in one of the front windows of the building and my hunger pangs kicked off again. I thought the homburg could endure a little longer standing outside in the cold and damp so I went inside and found a table near the door, from where I could make out his dark figure huddled by the hoarding, still engrossed in his reading. Every now and then he would look across the street and even in the darkening afternoon I swear I saw him scowl when the waitress came over to my table and took my order.

'Kaffee und Kuchen, bitte,' I said without taking my eyes off him. I didn't care now if he realised I'd clocked him: that was his problem. I took my time over the coffee and cake, watching as the dim daylight disappeared and the world outside was lit up by glistening vehicle and street lamps instead. I left him out there for more than half an hour before paying my bill and leaving the restaurant.

The air had turned even colder and I guessed the homburg must be frozen to the core. Refreshed by my delicious Austrian provender, I was feeling much more chipper and I wanted to lead my man on a goose chase – preferably a wild one. I started down the Ringstrasse, passing the imposing parliament building before turning the corner onto the Burgring, home to many of the city's largest and finest buildings. Museums and parks lined the street and by the time I reached the State Opera I'd overdosed on grandeur. My shadow was still with me, averaging twenty yards behind and clinging to his soggy camouflage, and I finally took pity on him at Karlsplatz, boarding a tram to take me back around the ring. He sneaked on at the other end of the car just as it pulled away and we retraced our journey in considerably warmer circumstances than the first time around. At Schottentor I dismounted and switched to another tram, heading back out on Alserstrasse towards the hotel. The homburg followed me all the way to the door and I wondered if he was billeted there or whether he'd been detailed to spend the night – or at least until he was relieved of duty – outside in the snow.

I was long past caring. I ate dinner in the hotel restaurant, ordering a bottle of expensive wine that I would make damn sure would be charged to my unknown client, and went to bed.

FOUR

We continued our cat-and-mouse shenanigans for the next three days. The mornings fell into a pattern of hot shower in the stylish bathroom followed by continental breakfast at the hotel before emerging into the cold winter light to identify my arm's-length escort and lead them on a journey to nowhere.

The first day I indulged in some shameless tourism, taking in Mozart's house, the bizarre golden monument to Johann Strauss in the Stadtpark, and inevitably the Prater – once the playground of the imperial rulers of Vienna, now simply a playground. Its famous Ferris wheel was one of the city's more unusual landmarks and I couldn't resist the association with Orson Welles's character Harry Lime in *The Third Man*. The black-and-white classic movie might have been filmed twenty-five years earlier but its sense of menace and intrigue fitted my mood perfectly. If I was currently living the movie equivalent, I would be Joseph Cotten, of course, not Welles: we're always the good guys in our own life story, after all. I watched the homburg from the warmth of my Ferris wheel cabin, hearing Anton Karas's zither playing in my head.

The second day I led him further afield, taking the tram

to Schönbrunn Palace and wandering the grounds before heading into the zoo – the world's oldest, I learned from a helpful guide. I was determined to keep the homburg on the move and in the open air if I could – I didn't want it to be an easy job for him – but by mid-afternoon I was feeling the cold myself and decided to head back to the hotel before dark.

It was on the third morning that I was hailed by the greasy-haired desk clerk, whose name I had established was Roland Wolf.

'Herr Kemp!'

I was halfway out of the door and turned back to see him waving a small white envelope in my direction.

'This was left for you early this morning.'

'By whom?' I didn't expect to get anything useful from this fishing expedition but it had to be worth a try.

'I'm sorry, Herr Kemp. I'm afraid I don't know. It was among a large quantity of mail on the desk when I arrived for my shift.'

I took the envelope and looked at my name, type-written on the front: no clues there. It bore no address or stamp so must have been hand-delivered. Someone in the hotel had to know who the postman was but it clearly wasn't the clerk.

I tore it open and drew out a small card containing three lines of typescript. There was still a slight curve in the card where it had been put through the typewriter but I was more interested in the contents than the method of delivery.

Anna Stern. Yellow anorak.
Café Central, Herrengasse.
11am tomorrow.

I looked up at the desk clerk, who shrugged encour-agingly, then I turned back to the door and marched out

into the cold. The air was crisp and dry and I relished the
thought of a good long walk. The homburg, still on my
tail, was much less likely to fancy the idea but that suited
me just fine. If he was so determined to keep me in his
sights then he could freeze and fester while he did so. I
set out on foot through the narrower, tourist-free streets
of Josefstadt, where the homburg would find it harder to
stay concealed, and headed for the city centre.

Twenty minutes later, I located Herrengasse. I could see
immediately why it had been one of the most exclusive
streets in the city back when the aristocrats lived in their
palaces fronting the medieval thoroughfare. Great Renais-
sance and baroque edifices rose from the narrow roadway,
pillared arches vying with ornate balconies for architectural
supremacy, and the frontages that had been converted to
shops were upmarket boutiques featuring high-class brand
names. Slap bang in the middle of all the finery was one
of the most ornate buildings of all: the Café Central. Occupying the corner of Herrengasse and Strauchgasse, it was
a three-storey fantasy of what an Italianate villa should be
and certainly didn't look like it belonged in this confined
setting, where its filigree stone and almost religious statuary
could hardly be appreciated from ground level. Through its
leaded windows I could see a vaulted ceiling like a chapel,
with vast chandeliers hanging at the apex of every one, and
in the centre of its main room a huge serving area encircled
by glass-fronted cabinets of pastries and cakes.

Not wanting to offer any unnecessary clues to the
homburg, I didn't stop to marvel but ploughed on towards
the Innere Stadt, for all the world behaving like a tourist
once more. I returned to St Stephen's Cathedral, which
I'd visited on my first day of sightseeing, wandered the
streets behind it to the Mozart museum in Domgasse, then
doubled back to the opera house, where I picked up the
tram back to Schottentor. I don't know what the homburg

thought I was up to but it seemed like a random selection of stops to me. On the slim chance that he might not be part of the same outfit as the rendezvous organiser, I figured it would be best to leave him as confused as I could.

I slept badly that night. Ornate coffeehouses jostled in my dreams with visions of Mozart in a homburg, reading a newspaper. I woke early, long before dawn, and dressed for cold weather. I breakfasted in the hotel dining room then approached the clerk at the front desk.

'Do you ever go home, Roland?' I asked him after the only other guest had passed through to the restaurant.

He smiled. 'Rarely, Herr Kemp. My life is devoted to the hotel.'

I couldn't tell if he was being serious but it didn't matter. What was important was that I felt I had established enough of a relationship with this young man over the past few days to be able to risk a favour.

'I don't suppose you have a service entrance I could use, do you?'

A bemused look passed briefly over his features but he quickly resumed his habitual poker face. Although admittedly rather out of the ordinary, I imagined this probably wasn't the most unusual request that had ever been put to him and he gave no further sign of curiosity.

'Certainly, Herr Kemp. When would you be requiring access?'

'Right now, if it's no trouble.'

He immediately lifted the counter beside him and silently invited me through, his hand outstretched with an open-palmed gesture. Then he led me through a doorway into a large office, where files were piled high and a telephone and typewriter stood in a nook under a stairwell. An array of coat hooks hung from one wall, each neatly labelled with a name, presumably that of an employee of the hotel. Through another door, the décor changed to something much less salubrious than the furnishings offered to the guests: here the corridor was dark and dingy, painted to waist height in gunmetal grey and above in a nondescript shade of off-white. The corridor led in one direction only, towards a large wooden door which was heavy with ironwork. Roland slid back two enormous bolts at the top and bottom of the door, twisted an outsize key in the lock, and turned the knob.

Outside, the dawn cast a dim light over an alleyway crammed with the detritus of a working hotel. Giant bins lined one side of the narrow passage, while crates stuffed with empty bottles were stacked high at the right-hand end. Looking left, an archway led to a steel door that evidently gave onto the road beyond. If the homburg was still keeping watch, I guessed he'd be able to have both the main entrance of the hotel and this service door in view at the same time from a location somewhere over near the train line but I hoped his focus might be on the lobby. In the early wintry greyness, I might just be able to slip out unnoticed, especially if I could disguise myself somehow.

I turned back to the clerk, hovering in the doorway behind me. 'Roland, this is going to sound strange, I know, but could I borrow a hat please?'

Once more, he maintained his air of imperturbability. With a slight nod, he retreated into the corridor and back into the office, emerging moments later with a rather smart-looking black fedora in his hand.

'Is this yours?' I asked.

Roland nodded again.

'Thank you. I promise I'll look after it.'

I jammed the hat onto my head, pulling the brim down to shade my face, and made for the steel door.

The street outside was busy, even for this time of the morning, and I was optimistic that a lorry delivering goods to one of the shops or hotels in the area might give me some additional cover. With the door open only a crack, I scanned the arches that supported the elevated railway, trying to spot the homburg. Some commuters were making their way towards the station a little further up the street but I could see no sinister figures lurking in the shadows and I wondered if that meant my tail had been recalled. It takes considerable resource to supply enough men for a 24-hour surveillance operation and it seemed quite possible that my clients' ability to keep an eye on me had reached its limits after three days of random chicanery on my part. I wasn't going to take any chances, however, and I lifted my collar and shrank into it as I dodged out onto the pavement, clanging the door behind me. I moved swiftly to my right, jogging to stay in the lee of a large truck that was heading fortuitously in the same direction, before swerving around the first corner I reached and tucking myself into a doorway.

I waited several minutes and checked both ways before leaving my hiding place. I didn't want to risk the main road again so I continued up the side street, away from the city centre, until I hit a crossroads. Turning left, I ran parallel to the main road, grateful that it quickly became a pedestrian-only street filled with market stalls being opened up for the day's trading. If anyone had managed to tail me out of the hotel, I stood a good chance of losing them here. In this way I dog-legged through the district before finally taking a left turn and heading back towards the city.

I thought I knew the layout of Josefstadt well enough by now to be able to hazard a guess on a route to Herrengasse that might throw off any pursuers. With plenty of time on my hands, I switched direction and reversed my journey so often that I even began to doubt my own judgement, so when I hit the south-western corner of the Rathauspark I breathed a sigh of relief. From here it was a short step to the Café Central and my assignation with Anna Stern.

I wondered what the meeting would bring.

I wanted to try a spot of reconnaissance myself and I had an hour to go before the allotted time of my appointment. Herrengasse was too narrow to be able to loiter without being noticed but I was fortunate that the doors to the large building opposite the café stood wide open. A sign indicated that this was the Palais Niederösterreich but there seemed to be plenty of footfall in and out so I strolled confidently through its arches. Ahead of me I could see another doorway that led into an open courtyard but I liked it in the shadows and from here I could keep an eye on the café across the street. The building seemed to be some kind of public office and business types were milling around, not minding me. I spotted a stand containing leaflets and wandered over to it, hoping I might find something useful. I was in luck: the stand was home to a variety of tracts, in different languages, offering visitors information on everything from historic Vienna to tram timetables. One in English even volunteered the history of the building itself and I took a moment to study it. The Palais Niederösterreich was evidently the centuries-old base for the provincial parliament of Lower Austria and featured an array of chambers, concert halls and even a chapel that – while only occasionally accessible to the public – were apparently stunning in their architecture and furnishings, from vaulted ceilings to baroque frescoes. I would have to forgo such cultural fripperies but as long as I remained in the foyer it seemed I could lurk conveniently while being able to keep an eye on the café opposite.

Anna Stern arrived at exactly five minutes to eleven.

The yellow anorak was unmissable among the navy and black overcoats of a Viennese winter. I saw her at the top end of the street and watched as she navigated the traffic to reach the front door of the café. The anorak fell to her hips and below it a grey skirt topped knee-length black boots in a fashion that wouldn't have looked out of place on Carnaby Street a decade earlier. She wore her red hair long, with a single plaited strand from each temple gathered together at the back of her head, revealing a face which, although undoubtedly classically beautiful, seemed serious, with a touch of the schoolmistress about it. *Stern by name, stern by nature,* I thought.

I let her go inside, where I could see her speaking animatedly to a waiter before being shown to a table out of sight to the right. When my watch moved around to precisely eleven o'clock, I followed her in.

The maître d' was on me immediately. I barely had time to scan the huge room but I knew roughly where she had been steered and the yellow anorak caught my eye straight away.

'I'm meeting a friend,' I said and indicated in her direction. He smiled, gave a slight bow and invited me to pass.

I walked over to her table by the window and made an instant assessment of Anna Stern. As assessments go, it was one of my more favourable, but I had learned long ago not to rush to early judgement: I'd been bitten too many times by superficial glamour concealing vapidness beneath. Anna looked smart and well-groomed, her hair neatly coiffed despite the wintry weather outside, and the anorak didn't fit the image at all. She seemed the type to go for a long, flowing jacket or cape in some plush velvet material and rich colour. The notion was reinforced by the frothy patterned blouse she wore under the coat and there was an air of the Bohemian about her. I guess I was only off by about two hundred miles.

As I approached, she looked up at me, registering no sign of recognition. Close up, her face was much softer than the glimpse I'd got on the street and there was a faint scent of melancholy about her. What I'd taken for a schoolmistress energy was actually a clear-eyed directness that I found instantly appealing. Her green eyes showed no emotion and, after a moment of comprehension, she looked down at the table again.

'Anna?' I said, and she nodded without looking up. 'I'm Bill Kemp. May I?'

Without waiting for an answer, I sat in the wooden chair opposite her and put my borrowed fedora on the window ledge beside me. We sat in silence for a minute or two until a waiter finally came over and, in the absence of any indication from Anna, took my order for two coffees. Anna seemed in no hurry to engage in conversation of any kind so I took the initiative. The suspense was driving me crazy.

'Who sent you?'

The abruptness of my question seemed to startle her and she looked up quickly.

'You don't know?' Her voice was quiet, with a light German accent, and – if you asked me to put money on it – trembling. Whether that was from the cold or from something quite different I had yet to determine.

'No, Anna. I don't know. Perhaps you could enlighten me.'

'And yet you know who I am and where to meet me.'

I dropped the bent little card I'd been given at the hotel onto the table between us. She stared at it, almost without taking it in, then looked down again.

'Who gave you this?'

'It was left for me at my hotel.'

'Where?'

I couldn't see any harm in revealing that piece of information. 'Out on the ring road. Now perhaps you wouldn't mind answering some of my questions.'

She looked straight at me now and I was sure I could detect fear in her eyes. I've seen enough terrified people to know what fear looks like and Anna was afraid. I wondered if she would tell me what it was she feared.

'Anna, I don't know who you are or how you're mixed up in all this but I need you to tell me what's going on. What do you know?'

She shook her head and her gaze dropped again to the table. She folded her arms across her and her shoulders drooped, giving her the air of a child being told off.

I let my exasperation show. 'For God's sake, Anna! You must know something. What am I even doing here?'

She glanced furtively around the coffeehouse and I lowered my voice in case she thought someone was listening.

'Anna, somebody needs to start talking. I've got nothing to go on and a friend possibly in danger. Now tell me what you know.'

The waiter arrived with a large tray containing two cups of coffee and two glasses of water. He made a big show of presenting them elegantly on the table, taking the coffee spoons and turning them face down on top of the glasses of water. He must have seen my bemused look as he launched into a little speech, in English and well-rehearsed for the unsuspecting tourist.

'Here at Café Central we always serve our coffee with water. It is intended to cleanse the palate. The upturned spoon is an example of the Habsburg etiquette: it is to demonstrate that the glass has been freshly filled up for the customer.'

I thanked him but I wanted to get rid of him. He didn't get the message.

'If sir and madam are interested, there is much history to the café. The Russian revolutionaries Lenin and Trotsky were among our clientele, and Herr Trotsky was a formidable chess player. He used to sit at that table over – '

I didn't care how rude it looked: I needed him out of the way. 'Thank you. That will be all.'

He looked deeply affronted in a way that only Mitteleuropeans can pull off properly, turned on his heel and stormed off. I turned my attention back to the mysterious creature opposite me and tried a different tack.

'Anna, you look frightened. Are you frightened?'

Her eyes twitched a little: was she trying to send me a signal? I reached across to place my hand on top of hers, where it rested on the table by her coffee cup. She made no attempt to move it away.

'Are you in trouble? You can tell me. Maybe I can help.' I didn't know how but I had to get through to her somehow. 'I'm here to collect a package. Have you got it with you?'

She shook her head again but leaned forward. 'Do you have a pen?' she whispered.

I was bewildered. Just what was going on? Why had Anna been sent to me, and by whom? And if she really was in such a state of fear, then why wouldn't she take a chance on telling me, in the hope that I might be able to help her? If she was worried about somebody following her then perhaps I could offer a little protection, as I'd tried to do for Sophie Church in the Australian wilderness a year earlier. In that instance, I probably hadn't been the world's most refined bodyguard, but at least we'd both made it out of that hellhole alive.

I reached into my jacket and pulled out a pen. She took it from me and scribbled on a napkin, below the level of the table and out of my eye line. Then she folded the napkin and tucked it under the edge of her saucer. For the first time since I'd noticed her fear, she looked directly at me and I saw something else in her eyes – strength? steeliness? passion? – which stirred a new sensation in me.

She spoke fast, but this time evenly and with a measured tone. 'Rent a car this afternoon from somewhere inconspicuous. Tomorrow morning you will take the road out past the airport and continue in the direction of Bratislava.'

'Bratislava?' I was shocked. 'But that's in Czechoslovakia – behind the Iron Curtain.'

She ignored my interruption and went on with her instructions. 'After fifty kilometres you will pass through the village of Hainburg-an-der-Donau. At the end of the village there is a stone cross – you will not miss it – where a track turns left across the railway line. Follow this to the end, by the river. I will be there at ten a.m.'

I had a thousand questions but this enigmatic beauty was not going to listen to them. She stood up, cast another fearful glance around the coffeehouse and hurried for the door. I grabbed my hat and began to go after her but the maître d' stepped into my path, smiling beatifically.

'Is sir ready to settle his bill?'

I cursed under my breath and returned to the table. Out of the window I caught a flash of yellow as Anna headed up Herrengasse in the direction she'd arrived from. From where I sat she didn't seem to have anyone tailing her but I could easily have missed them if there was. I tasted my coffee but it was tepid so I left what I hoped were enough Schillings to cover the drinks, even in a place like this, and started for the door again. I was halfway there when I remembered the napkin.

Another waiter was already clearing my table but I got there in time to fish the cream-coloured paper from under the coffee cup where Anna had tucked it. Scrawled so heavily that she had torn the napkin as she wrote, Anna had left me a different, private message, made up of a simple series of dots and dashes. I didn't need to be an expert in Morse code to understand their meaning: SOS.

FIVE

As I drove in the direction of the airport the following morning my head was throbbing again. I'd spent a vain day and night churning the conversation with Anna over in my mind and getting precisely nowhere. She did not have the package I'd been promised, she had been unable – or unwilling – to answer any of the questions I'd managed to ask in our brief exchange, and now she was leading me on a journey into the unknown, without a road map and in total ignorance of what I was getting myself into. If I'd thought obeying the instructions of an anonymous caller on the telephone was stupid enough, my actions now bordered on the insane.

The only problem was that I could see no alternative.

I passed the sprawling airport and drove on into the Lower Austrian countryside, ticking off the few facts I had in my head. Leotta was not at her student accommodation: that much I knew. But whether she really had jetted off to some high-powered conference, as I'd been told, was conjecture. I had no proof. Similarly, I only had the word of my mystery caller that she was a potential hostage, her absence manipulating me into following every order. If he was lying and Leotta was, in fact, in no danger at all, then I was doing all this for nothing. And then there was the homburg, who'd spent the best part of a week either trailing around Vienna after me – when he still had sight of me, that was – or freezing his backside off outside my hotel. Which side was he batting for, and why was he even watching me? If he was the puppetmaster's man he was doing a pretty shoddy job of staying hidden; if he belonged to some other outfit... I couldn't begin to figure out the ramifications of that possibility.

And still there was the question of why I had been selected in the first place for this damned job. Aside from some basic military training and a fair dose of common sense, I had no special skills, no secret knowledge, not even a reference from my previous employer to recommend me.

Every time I went around the conundrum, I kept returning to the same fundamentals: I had no choice but to be here because of Leotta, and now another young woman was in danger, perhaps because of me. Once more, I found I had no choice in the matter. Anna was meant to give me a package, together with instructions on where and how to deliver it. Instead, I was chasing her deep into a foreign hinterland, perilously close to one of the most dangerous frontiers in the world, with no idea of what to expect when I reached the end of the track by the river.

I'd spent most of the previous afternoon and evening doing some research. I may have had precious little control over what I was doing or where I was going but at least I could be prepared for the territory. I bought maps, guidebooks and even a German dictionary and holed up in my hotel room to work. The first thing I wanted to know was what kind of terrain I was likely to find when I got to the end of the track. That part was easy: a couple of hiking trails led in either direction along the bank of the Danube, cutting through fields and wooded patches, but at this time of year the whole area would be covered in a thick blanket of snow. I thought I'd be lucky if I even made it to the river in a hire car and I made a mental note to rent something sturdy – preferably a Land Rover or similar. I memorised the immediate area, including its hills and valleys, and folded the map in a way that left the track visible before stowing it in a plastic envelope I could wear around my neck, orienteering-fashion.

Next I investigated Hainburg-an-der-Donau, the village where I was supposed to turn off the main road by a stone cross. One of my guidebooks had a photograph of the landmark itself and Anna was right: I couldn't have missed it. I looked up its name – *Dreieckiges Kreuz* – hoping for some meaningful insight into its background but found to my disappointment that it simply meant 'triangular cross'. Standing over six feet tall and carved in bright white stone, it wasn't clear whether it was simply a wayside marker or something more elaborate, such as a religious shrine. It reminded me of a miniature of the historic Eleanor Crosses marking a route from Nottinghamshire to Charing Cross in London, erected by the grieving King Edward I to show the nightly resting places of the body of his queen on its journey from the site of her death back to Westminster Abbey in 1290. I had visited all three of the extant crosses in that chain, although Charing Cross itself was a Victorian replacement for the original. Now I had a German version to add to my collection.

So much for the geography: now for the history and politics.

I'd questioned the proximity of Bratislava with Anna in the café but I hadn't realised quite how close the Czechoslovakian city was to the Austrian border. With the exception of Berlin, nowhere else on the entire length of the Iron Curtain were the opposing parties so intimately observable to each other: residents in Bratislava could almost literally throw stones into the West, and it was easily visible from their apartments. My meeting place with Anna was designated as the border itself, where a stretch of the Danube and its tributary, the Morava, served as the only obstacle between the two global factions, the West and the Soviet bloc. Well, not the only obstacle: there was the odd watchtower, a few miles of thick barbed wire and a garrison of heavily-armed troops to contend with, which meant that the confluence of the two rivers was one of the most intensely-guarded points on the whole of the Iron Curtain. Exact numbers were hard to come by but it seemed highly likely that several hundred people had died attempting to escape communism at this strategic location since the political portcullis fell after the war. Although Austria was technically neutral, the Soviets brooked no defiance and meted out frequently fatal justice to anyone daring to flee their regimes.

As I flicked through the pages of a depressing political history book, I wondered again why Anna had selected this particular spot for our rendezvous and whether I was being lured into some kind of trap. Mulling that one over seemed pointless so I tossed the book aside, ordered a half-bottle of Scotch from room service and drank myself into oblivion.

The alarm clock woke me the next morning bleary and full of regret for drinking so much when I needed a clear head. I dragged open the curtains, forcing myself to face the bright white of a heavy overnight snowfall, and stood for ten minutes under a hot shower trying to bring myself around. Fortunately, I'd set the alarm good and early – perhaps some sixth sense had known I was going to need extra time to get ready – and I breakfasted well, partly because I didn't know when I'd be eating again and partly to soak up the alcohol in my system. Roland had kindly allowed me to keep hold of his fedora and I adopted the same subterfuge to leave the hotel out of sight of the homburg. I suspected an additional watch might have been put on the back door as I'd given him the slip the previous day but I hoped I'd evaded him once more and ducked through the streets to where I'd parked the Range Rover I'd rented from a little garage in the suburbs. Anna's instruction to remain 'inconspicuous' had meant I couldn't be fussy about my choice of vehicle. The Range Rover wouldn't have the same rugged off-road capabilities as its Landy cousin but it would have to do.

For the first few miles I kept a close eye on the rearview mirror for followers but once I'd weaved my way through the centre of Vienna, taking deliberate wrong turns and stopping and starting to confuse any pursuers, I was confident I was alone. It crossed my mind that solitude on this kind of trip might well backfire on me and that if the homburg was keeping an eye on me, he might well have proved useful in the event of my needing assistance for any reason. My sense of unease about him outweighed all other considerations, however, and I was relieved not to have a tail as I finally joined the airport road out of town. The road was surprisingly quiet once I'd left the airport behind and the snowdrifts coated the already rustic scenery in a Christmassy layer of white. I'd left plenty of time and took the drive steadily, negotiating the wintry conditions with additional care given the fogginess in my head. A bright sun was helping to keep me alert but I knew I wasn't at my best.

Almost exactly an hour after climbing into the Range Rover, I swung it off the road and bumped over the railway line onto the track towards the river.

SIX

I had begun to enjoy the relative luxury of the Range Rover's fixtures and fittings on the drive from Vienna. When I took it off the road I remembered why I loved the Landy.

Less than half a mile from the turn-off, the track veered around to the left and virtually disappeared. As far as I could see, all around was a sheet of featureless white, with a distant line of hills straight ahead and the odd tree breaking through the horizon. Somewhere between me and the ridge, I knew, lay the Danube but I was far from certain if the car was going to get me there. I ploughed through the rising drift, leaving a pair of deep ruts behind me, and hoped the low hedges on either side were marking the route of the track. I checked the map in its transparent sleeve and reminded myself of the route of the path, heading almost due north towards the confluence of the two rivers. Focusing on a point high on the hills opposite, I tried to maintain a straight line.

After another mile I gave up, pulling the car to a halt just short of a little bridge. Road signs on either side poked up through the snow and I used the dictionary to help translate: it seemed a footpath ran alongside a stream and I imagined it must be rather pretty in the summer months.

Now, in the freezing depths of winter, I didn't suppose the path would be much used. There was nothing I could do about it anyway: the Range Rover would struggle to get much further and my best bet was to proceed on foot. I turned the car onto the footpath and forced it fifty yards or so through the drift into the bushes. If it were to be discovered by some hardy hiker, I hoped they wouldn't raise an alarm about a foolish driver who'd got lost and abandoned his vehicle. I'd have to take that chance.

I tried to sweep some snow over the tyre marks where I'd turned off the track, then crossed the bridge over a frozen stream and emerged from between two clumps of trees to find an open expanse of pristine snow for half a mile in every direction. I scanned the far hills for my point of reference and thought I located it, although looking at the ridge again it now fell away at its left-hand end and I was far from convinced that what I was staring at was my original marker. I knew from the map that the track bent around to the right after the stream but I was reluctant to take the obvious route: ideally I wanted to approach the rendezvous tangentially, without giving myself away, and scout the lie of the land before charging in. Roughly straight ahead, I calculated, the Morava river would be flowing into the much bigger Danube. Somewhere on the other side, a mighty castle stood on a crag overlooking the confluence and I was surprised I couldn't see it above the trees. From what I'd read in my research, the castle was a pretty imposing presence and marked the cornerstone of Czechoslovakia's defences at this point of the Iron Curtain. I certainly didn't want to put myself within view of the armed border guards I guessed would be manning the fortress and I wasn't too keen on getting up close to the Danube itself. I decided to stay on the near side of the trees and use them as cover to reconnoitre the site.

Trudging through the thick snow proved harder than I'd imagined and I was edgy about the furrow I was leaving behind me. There was no sign of Anna – mine had clearly been the first car along the track since the snowfall – and I thought she couldn't have reached the meeting point yet. I wasn't sure if she'd be alone but I was very unhappy to be signalling my route so obviously to anyone who might come along behind me. I retraced my steps to the bridge and began using a gloved hand to brush loose snow back onto the furrow, hoping to cover my footsteps. After a hundred yards, both my hands were chilled to the bone and my gloves were sodden by the work so I abandoned the attempt at camouflage and focused instead on reaching the trees as quickly as I could. The evidence of my trail would not be visible from the path this far into the drift, I hoped, but in any case my rigid fingers would not stand any more sweeping.

I hit the tree line and slumped in an exhausted heap.

For a man travelling to an Alpine country in the middle of winter, I reflected, I had been severely underprepared for this trip. My khaki anorak could only be described as lightweight at best while my boots were old and worn. Jeans were terrific if you needed a sturdy, all-purpose trouser but were notoriously counterproductive when it came to snow: they quickly became waterlogged, heavy and uncomfortable. In the short time I'd been out in the open, I had become bedraggled and thoroughly chilled. I'd also failed to bring a flask of hot coffee, although I dug into my coat pocket to retrieve the bar of chocolate I had managed to remember. Sweetness in my mouth and sugar in my system helped revive me a little but I could have done with a complete change of clothes and a steaming bowl of soup right then.

I looked at my watch, a rugged Grand Seiko I'd bought on my return from Australia. Nothing could replace the smashed timepiece I'd been given by my first wife, which had met its end in a dark tunnel beneath the sweltering outback a year earlier, but once I'd established that little gem would never tick again I'd splashed out on a hefty beast that I reckoned would probably outlast me.

Twenty minutes to go.

From my position on the edge of this little wood I could see the bridge where I'd left the car and would be able to spot anyone approaching without being seen myself. I hunkered down inside my anorak and banged my hands against my forearms to warm them up. Then I waited.

I switched my gaze between the watch and the bridge as the minute hand ticked interminably towards the appointed hour. Ten minutes after it had passed – and a full thirty since I'd nested myself in the trees – I was seriously concerned.

Ten minutes after that I spotted the first figure.

Way over to the left, just on the periphery of my field of vision, I noticed a dark smudge move across the white snow. I leaned forward to see past the tree where I was hiding, thinking it might have been an animal of some kind, and immediately saw three more shapes, all dressed in black, moving among the bushes where the track entered the wood. Peering into the shade where they were milling about I could see several more and, beyond them, an oddly intermittent flashing of light in the trees. As I watched, it dawned on me that the figures were police officers and the flashing was the blue light of an emergency vehicle.

I dodged back into my covert and sank further into the protection of the tree. I couldn't understand how a troupe of police officers could have made it past my watch post or what they were doing there. It seemed too much of a coincidence that they happened to be at the exact place Anna had arranged with me at the café the previous morning:

surely the two things were connected. But if they were there, apparently searching the area, what had happened to Anna? Perhaps, like me, she was observing from a safe distance, waiting for the police to lose interest and clear off before moving in for our designated meeting. Or perhaps they had got wind of whatever mysterious enterprise I'd got myself wound up in and had attempted to ambush Anna – and me – in the act of... But what act? And was it even criminal?

I considered marching out into the open, alerting their attention and requesting their help. Then I remembered I had been expressly forbidden to go to the police and it was Leotta's life that was on the line if I breached that order. It occurred to me that it was even possible Anna herself was a police officer and that this whole excursion into the countryside was a set-up. But who was being set up and to what end? If I was the target of some entrapment operation, I was going to be useless to them as I knew nothing. And in any case, if she'd wanted to arrest me for something, she could have done so perfectly easily – and far more congenially – over coffee in Herrengasse.

'*Hier drüben, Oberst!*'

The deep baritone was worryingly close by and made me start. It came from nearer to me than to the group of policemen and I wondered how many other individual officers might be fanned out through the woods behind me, away from the main search. Glancing around as far as I could, I saw the man maybe thirty yards from me, deeper into the trees and facing away from me, towards the river. I guessed he was almost at the water's edge. I took a few seconds to study the thicket and, seeing no other officers nearby, took my chance.

I darted back out of the wood and cut to my right, away from the search party, keeping close to the edge of the trees and the slight cover they afforded. I wanted to put as much distance between me and the policemen as I could but the thick snow impeded rapid movement so I opted for discretion rather than speed and hacked my way towards a break in the bushes, where I thought another hiking path opened up. All the while I scanned the wood to my right, watching for other stray officers who might stumble upon me by accident. At one point a large bird – a grouse or something – erupted into the sky less than three feet in front of me, causing me to trip and crash face down in the snow but I found my feet again quickly and hurried on.

When I reached the opening I saw that it led into a low arch of trees where the snow hadn't penetrated and I figured it would be a good way to avoid leaving footprints. I had to bend almost double to fit under the branches but I worked my way through the natural tunnel and emerged on the other side straight onto the shingle foreshore of the Danube.

Even in the grey light of winter, the view was spectacular.

I shielded my eyes from the brightness with one hand, using the other to steady myself against a tree root that stuck out into the pebbles. Where I was standing, a trickle of water flowed between two sheets of ice banking a shallow spur off the main river, which was moving much faster away to my right and in front of me. Directly opposite, the Morava fed into its bigger neighbour, with a wood stretching away on its left-hand side in what I thought was Austrian territory. But what dominated the view and seized my attention above everything else was the granite fortress that towered into the sky on the Czechoslovakian side of the Danube.

A vertiginous lump of rock rose from the hillside at the junction of the two rivers, parts of it created by the elements, other sections clearly forged by human hands. On the crest behind it stood the ruins of a castle, its turrets letting through light. And all along the riverbank, as far as I could see in either direction, great thickets of barbed wire raked the ground between ramshackle steel watchtowers, each topped with a searchlight and a roofed space where tiny soldiers were silhouetted against the snowy hillside. They seemed to be only moderately interested in what was happening on my side of the river, some distance away to my right where police officers were tumbling out of the trees and onto the shingle. I conjured up an image of swarthy eastern European guards huddled around a brazier, laughing and singing folk songs while downing copious quantities of vodka, then quickly dismissed it. The fictions of the movies were just that – fiction. I suspected it was far more likely that a well-trained marksman had his sights fixed on the hapless troupe of Austrian policemen throughout their recovery operation and it was only the lack of an order from his superior that prevented him from causing carnage on the western bank.

I wanted to remain out of sight from both angles: I was as keen not to be spotted by the Austrians as the Czechs. While I had no reason to suspect that the communists over the water were even aware of my existence, I didn't want to put myself in their firing line – quite literally – for the sake of a fact-finding expedition. The Austrians, meanwhile, were supposed to be neutral in the Cold War, but I'd learned enough over the past week to convince me that nobody in this damned stupid game could be trusted completely, and I'd rather not put their theoretical neutrality to the test with me as the guinea pig. I just wanted to know why Anna's meeting point had suddenly become a hive of uniformed activity.

When she'd nominated this place, back at the café, I'd had no idea it was literally the front line of the east-west divide. I knew it was near the border with Czechoslovakia, and I guessed one of the reasons she'd selected it was its remoteness from prying eyes in Vienna, but now I wondered if she had some ulterior motive for dragging me this close to the frontier.

And where the hell was Anna anyway?

I hugged my tree and studied the vista carefully. Just across the small stream in front of me was a spit covered in shrubs and I calculated that if I could get across there without being seen – from either bank of the river – I would get a much clearer idea of what was happening downstream. I hunched low and splashed through the shallow water, breaking up the ice and diving headfirst into the snow that bordered the shrubs. From there, I could shuffle out onto the spit as far as I dared or until I could see what was going on. I hoped that any Czech eyes would be focused on the activity downriver and that my pale khaki anorak would fade into the deep snow on the spit.

I'd wriggled about thirty feet out onto the spit, keeping half an eye on each side of the river, before I realised what I was seeing. The Austrian police were working animatedly around something that was beached among the pebbles on the foreshore. The strands of red hair and the striking yellow windcheater left me in no doubt as to what that something was.

SEVEN

When I heard the cocking of the gun behind me, I froze. After the gunman addressed me using my name, I rolled over onto my back and stared at him.

'Did you not hear me clearly, Herr Kemp? I said stay where you are.'

The man pointing a Browning pistol at me was dressed in the uniform of the federal gendarmerie – the same as the men who'd been dealing with Anna's body at the shoreline. He struck the traditional pose of the policeman confronted with an enemy: legs apart in a stable stance, two-handed grip on his weapon, one eye lined up down the sights of a gun that was raised to shoulder height, a slight tilt to the head. I couldn't fault his technique but there was one thing I wouldn't have done if I were in his shoes. He was standing in full view of the communists across the river, a cocked weapon in his hand. I wouldn't have given much for his chances if he'd happened to turn it in the direction of Czechoslovakia.

For now, I was more worried about my own immediate safety than his. I'd detected a slight tremor in the accented voice and I wondered if the officer – who didn't look more than about twenty-five years old – had ever fired his weapon in anger before. I didn't want to become his first victim, shot by an overeager youngster who thought he'd bagged a prize trophy.

And that prompted another thought: how the hell did he know who I was?

I could only imagine that Anna must have told the police, or at least mentioned me to someone else who had told them. I'd have given quite a lot at that moment to understand the chain of informants that had led to my being accosted in the snowbound shallows of the Danube, within sight of the Czech border, by an Austrian police-man investigating the discovery of a dead woman. Surely he didn't imagine that I had had something to do with her death? The fact that she was my contact and had appar-ently given me up to the authorities before she died only added to the mystery. I needed answers but I wasn't going to get them lying here with a gun pointed at my head.

'I'd prefer to move, if you don't mind,' I said, putting as much sangfroid into my voice as I could muster up at that moment. 'I suspect we're both in the firing line right now.'

I jerked my head in the direction of the fortress over the river. He shot a glance in that direction, appeared to consider his options, then wagged his gun at me.

'They will not shoot from Devín Castle.'

Devín. That was the name that had escaped me from the guidebooks.

He went on, 'But let us not take any unnecessary chances. Get up slowly and go to the trees; then stop. I shall be watching you.'

As he spoke he backed away, aiming for the shrubs and keeping his pistol trained on me. He also dropped into a crouch and I guessed he was trying to take himself out of sight of the enemy troops over the water. Like my friendly copper, I was pretty sure there'd be no firing from that direction – neither side could afford an international incident at this delicate stage of the Cold War – but if this fresh-faced gendarme were to let a bullet fly for some inexplicable reason, then all bets would be off. I didn't imagine the communists would wait to verify whether it had been aimed at them before letting fly themselves and we were the only targets remaining on the riverbank.

'Don't do anything stupid, Herr Kemp.'

'I could say the same to you,' I replied, easing myself towards the stream. 'And how do you know my name?'

'I don't have to answer your questions. You are the one with a gun facing him.'

He had a point. I said nothing more as I scuttled across to relative safety and stopped. I was never one for wilfully disobeying orders when I served in the army and I wasn't about to start now, with a loaded weapon on me and an uneasy young man with his finger on the trigger.

I waited as he glanced one more time towards the fortress then executed his own little scramble to the tree line just yards from me.

'Now, quickly, onto the path and back through the wood,' he said, wagging the gun again. 'But inside you go slowly.'

I needed no more encouragement to get off that riverbank. I was as close to the Iron Curtain as I had ever been and had no desire to explore it any further. I ducked into the shade of the trees, brushing the back of my neck as snow from the branches tried to get inside my collar, and began the long crawl through the undergrowth. It seemed much further than it had coming the other way but I was complying with my orders to take it slowly and I knew there was a pistol pointing directly at my back. Away from the prying eyes of the communists, I didn't care how long it took.

I stood up straight, rolling my shoulders and stretching my arms as I emerged into the sunlight once more. I stared

across the empty space to the little bridge where the car
was hidden and ruled out any attempt at escape that way. I
would be gunned down within seconds, especially if there
were police reinforcements around. Besides, I reminded
myself, I had done absolutely nothing wrong: I had broken
no laws, I was a legitimate visitor to Austria – hell, I hadn't
even countermanded the instructions of the anonymous
caller who'd set me on this bloody path in the first place. All
I had to do was answer honestly any questions the police
might have and they would have to let me go... wouldn't
they? What would happen after that I had no idea. I was still
no closer to retrieving the package I'd been sent to Vienna
to collect and Leotta was no nearer to being rescued.

But I couldn't contemplate any of that right now. The
first thing I had to do was to extricate myself from the
misguided clutches of the Austrian gendarmerie.

I ventured a look around at my captor, who was following me out into the sunshine, the gun never moving from
me. 'Where are you taking me?'

'I told you: I don't have to answer your questions.'

'Your English is very good for a regional policeman.
Where did you learn it?'

'Stop with the questions,' he snapped and I detected
enough irritation in his voice to encourage me to acqui-
esce. 'Now go down the path beside the trees. Slowly.'

His final instruction I judged to be redundant: the snowdrifts were still piled high, although my blundering along
this route twenty minutes before had made something of
an easier trail and we were soon heading into the thicket
where I had originally seen the police tramping around.
I realised that the track from the bridge to here did not
stop where I thought it did. Instead, it continued through
the thicket and out the other side, where the police vehicles had been flashing their blue lights, and we now came
out into a clearing where a throng of officers were still

hanging about. My appearance caused quite a stir, with a few of the men reaching for their weapons, but when my young custodian stepped out behind me they stood down, clustering around me and congratulating him in their native language. He talked back to them and almost immediately one of the larger men grabbed both my arms from behind and thrust my hands together, clamping a pair of handcuffs on them in one smooth motion and throwing a stream of fast German in my direction.

'I don't understand,' I said. 'I'm English.'

'*Englisch, huh?*' The man's outsize hands grasped my shoulders and he manhandled me towards a van parked nearby. '*Wir mögen die Englisch hier nicht.*'

I didn't understand the words fully but I sensed his meaning clearly enough. I was evidently not popular in these parts. He bundled me gracelessly into the back of the van, where he pushed me down onto a wheel arch.

'Sit and no speak,' he said.

'Your English is not as good as your colleague's,' I replied with a smile, and he gave me a backhander across the right cheek.

'No speak!'

With my face smarting and barely able to move, I decided to shut up. The burly officer climbed down out of the van and struck up a conversation with two or three others, while the youngster who'd apprehended me sidled across behind them and poked his head in at the van doors.

'You will do as they ask you, please. Some of these men may not be so pleasant as I have been.'

I wanted to know what would happen next. 'Where will you be taking me?'

'Still the questions. That is not for me to decide. They are discussing it now but I think it will be a matter for the Viennese *Stadtpolizei*. You came here from Wien, yes?'

I nodded. 'But I haven't committed any crime, either here or there.'

'So you say. The *Stadtpolizei* may have a different idea.' He turned abruptly and walked away, leaving me with a view of the little group of policemen currently determining my fate. After a minute or two's debate, the large one who'd hit me returned to the van and, without even looking at me, slammed the back doors shut. A moment later, he climbed into the front seat and fired up the engine, another colleague getting into the passenger seat.

The big man twisted around in his chair and gave me a filthy look. 'No speak,' he said again, before his face broke into a leering grin. 'And happy journey.'

He slammed the van into gear and threw off the handbrake. We lurched terrifyingly and then were off down a track I hadn't noticed before, exiting the clearing on the eastern side and crashing away down a road I didn't know existed. That at least explained the lack of any sign of Anna when I first arrived and the sudden appearance of the police on the scene: they had evidently used a different route from the one I had driven.

I tried to work out where we were, keeping a rough tally of the turns we took and the direction we were travelling at any given moment, but the driver's gleeful recklessness made it hard to keep tabs. Only when we hit the main road again did I realise that we were indeed heading back towards Vienna. I didn't know if this was a good or bad thing – I'd had no direct experience of the city's police force – but if my treatment so far by the regional brigade was anything to go by, I thought I might prefer to be handed over to another authority. Besides, once I was inside a police station, I had no doubt I would be permitted the traditional telephone call, which I could use to contact the British Embassy or consulate or whatever passed for officialdom in these parts. I was confident that I would be back in my hotel room before nightfall, polishing off that half-bottle of Scotch I'd begun the night before. I could spend the evening in comfort and an alcoholic haze, contemplating what to do next. For now, my top priority was surviving the drive back to the city.

There seemed little point interrogating the two regional policemen any further. They were clearly in no mood to talk, and if they were going to hand me over to their Viennese counterparts it would be a waste of breath anyway. The back of the van had no windows so I bent low to try to look out of the front but all I could really see was two thick heads, and the lurching banged me around on the wheel arch so I gave up and leaned back against the steel side panel and closed my eyes.

Forty-five minutes of being thrown around in a metal box does no good to the body and by the time we pulled up in a courtyard somewhere within the city walls I felt black and blue. The muscles of my thighs ached from trying to hold myself steady and my arms were on fire from being constrained behind my back. On several occasions my head had banged against the side of the van as we swung around a corner or took a turn much too fast and I quickly realised that the grinning driver was a sadist. There was no reason to be hurtling through Lower Austria at such a lick and he was doing it purely to get under my skin. Needless to say, it worked.

'*Raus!*' A tall, thin man with a sallow complexion and steely eyes wrenched open the doors and barked at me. I stepped down gently from the van, only to have my elbow grabbed by the sadistic driver and yanked in the direction of a large wooden door. I just about had time to take in the courtyard, which seemed to feature a flamboyant rococo façade along the wall behind me but three sides of breezeblock completing it. I guessed an inelegant extension had been made to an original Habsburg palace at some point in its history of being occupied – probably by the Nazis during the war – at a time when architecture was deemed less important than functionality. Of course, architecture is never unimportant but philistine invaders rarely appreciate that.

I was bundled through the door by the tall man and had to blink to acclimatise my eyes to the interior. A bare-walled corridor led away, lit by overhead strip lights, with a succession of identical doors lining both left and right. The drab paint job made it clear this was a place of confinement and I guessed the doors opened onto cells of some kind.

My hotel shower and glass of whisky might have to wait a little longer than I first thought.

About two-thirds of the way down the corridor, my escort stopped and rattled some keys on his belt. He used one to open a door on the right then shoved me inside with a firm hand on the small of my back. He followed me into the room, where he patted me down before unlocking my handcuffs and pushing me again, this time to sit on a low, metal-framed bed with a wafer-thin mattress on the top.

'You wait,' he said, and left.

I didn't think I had much choice as he banged the door closed behind him and turned the key in the lock. I wondered how long I would have to cool my heels before I was allowed my phone call.

The cell was about eight feet square, painted in the same dull décor as the corridor outside only with scratch marks etched into the walls at various points above the bed and around the door. It was impossible to tell whether it was boredom, insanity or a combination of the two that had driven previous denizens of the room to inflict the damage but it couldn't have been painless: the gouge marks in some places were quite deep and, in the absence of anything sharp, could only have been made by finger-nails. High up on the back wall, a small rectangle of light

offered a view of the grey sky beyond, framed and interrupted by a series of vertical bars.

I rubbed my arms and legs to get the blood circulating
again, then stood up and began pacing the boundary of
the cell, partly to dispel any remaining stiffness but also
to stimulate my brain. I had no idea how long I would
have to wait but I wanted to get my story straight before
anyone started asking questions. I figured the truth was
about the best option under the circumstances and the
truth was that I had nothing to hide. I also had nothing
useful to offer and I just had to hope that if I emphasised
the injunction against my going to the police, Leotta's kidnappers – if that's what they were – might understand
the impossibility of my predicament. If they wanted me
to complete my mission then I needed to be on the outside of this prison cell and that meant I couldn't very well
comply with the order not to talk to the police.

Half an hour later, my theory was put to the test.

A key jangled in the door, which swung inwards to
reveal the tall officer who'd put me in the cell. Without
entering, he signalled at me to leave and indicated for me
to turn left, back towards the courtyard. I waited while
he cuffed me again, then I led the way down the corridor
until we reached a door different from the others, heavier
and made of wood rather than steel. He placed a hand on
my shoulder to stop me, then eased past to unlock the
door. It opened to reveal a short passageway leading to a
set of stone steps – about half a dozen – which turned to
the left at the bottom. He nudged me forward and I began
descending to the turning point, where a window looked
out onto a busy Viennese street at the level of the pavement. People were going about their ordinary business,
none of them casting even a glance in the direction of this
building, and I wondered if anyone in the outside world
actually knew its purpose.

Another nudge propelled me down the next dozen or so steps to a new corridor, just like the one above only subterranean. The air seemed even colder down here and the lights dimmer but that might have been my imagination running wild.

My escort steered me to the left at the bottom of the steps and I could see a passage lined with cell doors running for a long way under where the courtyard was: whoever had built this pile had made provision for considerable numbers of prisoners. We walked the full length of the corridor before I was unceremoniously shoved into a larger room at the end, where a simple wooden table stood in the centre with a chair on either side. The officer jabbed a finger at the one on the far side of the room and I sat while he took the cuffs off and left. Above my head, a single lamp hung from a point in the middle of the ceiling and in my nostrils I got the claustrophobic scent of long-standing damp.

The next man to appear in the doorway was not what I expected. He was short, wide and dressed in a well-cut navy suit and tie. He was almost completely bald, except for a few little tufts of hair brushing the collar of his jacket, and his thick-rimmed black glasses gave him the look of a cartoon villain. In one hand he held a fat cigar; the other was stuffed casually into a trouser pocket. He moved slowly but assuredly into the room, the hint of a smile twitching at the corners of his mouth. On the street outside he could easily have been mistaken for a wealthy businessman; in here, he was an enigma.

He stopped on the opposite side of the table and studied me. '*Also*, this is the man everyone is so excited to meet.'

Another Austrian with excellent English.

'I have no idea what you're talking about,' I said honestly.

'Oh come now, Herr Kemp, you are too modest. You

cannot hope to stroll about a foreign capital, meeting and
murdering spies, without attracting some attention.'

Murder! It appeared that the Austrian police really did
think I was responsible for Anna's death. But what had
any of it got to do with spying? I had never knowingly
met a spy in my life – the whole business had always
seemed dirty, dangerous and damned destructive to this
layman and I wanted nothing to do with it. My erstwhile
employer Lord Hosmer had once hinted at a job connected
to the espionage line and I had firmly but emphatically
turned him down, much to his chagrin.

'I repeat, I have no idea what you're talking about.'

'And yet you look alarmed, Herr Kemp.'

'Wouldn't you, if someone you'd never met suddenly
accused you of murder?'

He smiled and took out his pocketed hand to draw back the
other chair from the table, scraping it across the stone floor.
'There are many possible reasons for alarm.' He sat heavily
and took a long drag on his cigar, blowing the blue smoke
up into the metal lampshade. 'Yes, of course it is possible that
the alarm may originate from innocence or ignorance. However, I do not believe that to be the case in this instance. No;
I believe your alarm stems from the fact that you have been
caught – what is the English idiom? – red-handed.'

'That's a lie and you know it!'

He smiled equably at me. 'Isn't that just what an assassin would say?'

It was getting worse. In the space of ten seconds, he'd
escalated my putative crime from simple murder to assassination, with all its sinister implications and political
undertones.

'Don't be ridiculous. I'm no killer.'

'And yet we have a victim. My officers inform me that
her body was in quite a state when they recovered her
from the Donau. I won't go into details but it was most

definitely not a clean kill. Tell me, Herr Kemp, just how well did you know Anna Stern?'

I felt a surge of anger which I attempted to control by standing up and leaning over the table towards my interrogator. 'I don't have to tell you a damn thing. I'm a British subject and I demand to speak to the ambassador.'

He let the outburst hang in the air for a full five seconds before laughing in my face.

'Oh, Herr Kemp, you are most entertaining. That is such an amusing comment.'

My rage was rising. 'Under international law – '

'Ha! International law?' He seemed incredulous. 'What do you know of international law?'

'I know you can't hold me here without allowing me a telephone call and I insist that that call is made to the British Embassy.'

He moderated his voice again and spoke as if to an elderly relative. 'Sit down, Herr Kemp. Let me explain your position to you.'

I wanted to hear what he had to say so I did as he asked and sat down.

'You have come to our country pretending to be a tourist, yet all the while you are engaged in subterfuge.'

I started to interrupt but he raised a commanding hand and I stopped.

'You lead our officers on chases of wild geese around the city – '

'So that was your man?'

He ignored that and carried on: ' – wearing hats no doubt stolen from some unsuspecting gentleman.'

'I borrowed it.'

'As you wish. But you cannot deny that you have evaded us at every turn.'

'I didn't know he was a cop. And besides, I haven't done anything wrong.'

'Perhaps, perhaps. But yesterday, in a café on Herren-gasse, you met with Anna Stern.'

Now we were getting to the point. But I still had nothing to hide. 'Why would I deny that?'

'Oh, I don't know, Herr Kemp. Perhaps because she is dead.'

This was going nowhere and I had a nasty feeling in my gut that any further conversation would end up landing me in deeper trouble.

'I note that you are *not* denying it.'

'I'm not saying anything else until I've spoken to the embassy.'

He stared at me for a few seconds then took another draw on his cigar and blew it out slowly. 'Then you will be enjoying the hospitality of my officers for a considerable length of time.'

I stared back at him. 'How long?'

'Indefinitely.'

I may not have been an expert in diplomacy or the nice-ties of the Austrian legal system but I strongly suspected this was hogwash. No nation's sovereignty – and certainly none on the western side of the Iron Curtain – allowed them to detain suspects indefinitely without some hard evidence and the say-so of a judge. Throw in the fact that I was a foreign national from a nominally friendly coun-try and this squat little Napoleon hadn't a leg to stand on. My only problem was that he didn't seem to know that. It reminded me of the old saw that, if they obeyed the laws of aerodynamics, bees shouldn't be able to fly: it's just that nobody has told the bees.

'How do I know you're even a real policeman? You're not wearing a uniform.'

'Oh, this?' He indicated his crisp suit, dropping ash on the jacket sleeve as he did so. 'I have an important meeting with some politicians today and some of them get nervous around uniforms. Hitler had it wrong, you know: when you reach a certain level in the hierarchy, one doesn't need the false authority that a cap and badge confer. The force of one's own personality is enough. I don't quite understand why the Führer never realised that.'

'Well, whoever you are, you can't hold me here and you know it.'

Behind the smoke, he smiled. 'Tell me something, Herr Kemp. Who in your own country knows that you are here?'

I thought about it. Besides Mrs Larner from the village, who I'd asked to look in once or twice during the few days I was expecting to be away, the answer was nobody. And even she didn't know where I'd been heading when I set off for London in the Stag.

Napoleon continued his theme. 'As I thought. And who at your hotel here in Vienna is aware of even your name?'

I jumped on that one. 'There's Roland, the desk clerk – he's the one I borrowed the hat from. And there'll be an entry in the hotel reception log. They'll know I'm missing.'

He reached inside his jacket and pulled out a small black notebook. He clamped the cigar between his teeth and started making notes in the book. 'Roland, you say? I don't suppose you have this Roland's surname, do you?'

A wave of nausea overcame me as I realised I'd blundered. I'd given away my only remaining solid contact in this city and now I feared for his safety along with Leotta's. As for the log, that would be easy enough for someone to doctor and I doubted any other members of staff at the hotel would stick their neck out if the *Stadtpolizei* suggested it would be a good idea if they didn't. I felt the damp walls of the little room close in a fraction as my horizons narrowed.

He dropped his pencil on the table next to the notebook and reclaimed his cigar from his jowly face. 'Ah well, it is no matter. You understand my point. In the absence of anyone to verify your presence in Austria there will be no one out looking for you. The embassy is unaware of your existence and, even if someone were to start exploring the details of a certain aeroplane manifest listing a Mr William Kemp – and why should they, after all? – then they will most likely conclude that he landed in Vienna as expected, then changed his plans and perhaps went sight-seeing across Europe. After a few days he could be anywhere on the continent and impossible to find. Such an inquiry would soon be abandoned as preposterous. Now, if you are not willing to admit that you met Anna Stern in the Café Central yesterday or that you bludgeoned her to death on the banks of the Donau this morning, only metres from where you were arrested, then this meeting is terminated... for now. Perhaps a night of reflection will sharpen your recollections.'

He stood up, slammed the burning tip of his cigar down onto the table to extinguish it, and went towards the door, leaving a smouldering heap of ash and tobacco behind him. At the doorway he turned back and smiled grimly at me.

'Sleep well, Herr Kemp – if you can. We will talk again tomorrow.'

If Napoleon thought his attempt at comic-book villainy would leave me tossing and turning all night then he was wide of the mark. Despite the implications of my position and my inability to raise the alarm with the outside world, after a few minutes I found myself drifting off surprisingly agreeably. I'd convinced myself that his claims about nobody looking for me were hubristic at best and a downright lie at worst. Even the Austrian authorities wouldn't be able to conceal the disappearance of an innocent Englishman for long – and I was innocent, I had to remind myself. I juggled with the thought that this whole debacle might be some kind of set-up to land me in trouble but I swiftly gave up trying to figure out who might want to do such a thing or why. I'd heard of some less-than-scrupulous regimes trumping up charges against people they found objectionable but that was hardly the case here, and if the police tried to pin Anna's death on me then the case would have to be heard in open court, I'd have to be appointed a lawyer, and I would definitely get my call to the British Embassy. I might not be home as soon as I'd like but there was no way I would end up in a Viennese jail, unjustly convicted of murder.

Having reasoned myself into relative tranquillity, I slept.

It must have been the middle of the night when I was woken abruptly by a hand being clamped across my face. I started and tried to struggle free from the hold, which was severely restricting my breathing, but I found I could not move my arms or legs and realised I was being pinned down by three men simultaneously. Panic hit me instantly: was I being 'disappeared' in the manner of some tinpot South American dictator's way of dealing with dissidents? Or had Napoleon been given the green light by his politician friends to try something altogether more hands-on in an attempt to get me to confess to Anna's murder? I found it hard to believe that a country which lay at the heart of Europe's fragile thirty-year peace would risk its profile by applying techniques that were beyond the reach of the Geneva Convention; but then I knew precious little of the machinations of high-level international relations. Perhaps he had been right: maybe I would not even be missed by my home country.

All these thoughts and more raced through my mind in the seconds that it took the trio of heavyweights to wrap tape across my mouth, bind my hands behind my back and manhandle me out of my cell and into the darkened corridor. They moved with surprising agility for their size and kept their noise to a minimum. I quickly stopped wriggling, realising that resisting them was futile and I might only succeed in causing myself an injury, especially if they decided I would be more easily manoeuvred if I were unconscious. Instead I allowed myself to go limp, permitting them to carry me free of impediment. In this way, they took me the length of the corridor, away from the door where I'd first arrived and out of a rear entrance into a snowy alleyway. They encountered no opposition along the way and I wondered how they had not only gained entry to the building – which was clearly well-fortified – but also accessed my cell unhindered to drag me out to the street. I couldn't work out if they were themselves part of the *Stadtpolizei*, lugging me off to some mystery location away from the city to interrogate me less civilly, or a different group entirely who had some-how bypassed the police's security and kidnapped me. If that was the case, then the likelihood was that it was this bunch – or their associates – who were behind my myste-rious telephone conversations back in Devon, and if that were true then I might be one step closer to finding out what had happened to Leotta. But who the hell were they and what did they want with me?

Yet again, I found myself asking more questions than I could answer as they bundled me into the back of a black Mercedes saloon, accompanied by a thickset man with a pistol, and drove me off into the dead of the Viennese night.

EIGHT

In the darkness and silence of the sleeping city, I had no chance of following our route. At least with the police van I had been able to see out of the front window and guessed at our rough direction back into Vienna. With this driver, throwing the car around corners at breakneck speed, and my armed guard signalling wordlessly to me to keep my head down, I lost all track of where we were within the first minute and a half. We could have been heading north or east, towards the Czech border, or south towards Hungary or Yugoslavia. The only thing I was reasonably confident of was that we weren't heading west. On the rare occasions when the voices of the three men in the car spoke to one another, I couldn't identify their language but it was unquestionably uttered in the guttural nuances of an eastern European tongue.

So much for my theory about them being Austrian police.

Only once during the hour-long journey did I attempt to move, when the aching in my back from lying in such an awkward position became too much. I shifted my weight to lie on my side and began to sit up but the gunman beside me was having none of it: with a sharp elbow against my bicep, he forced me back down to my lying position and barked an incomprehensible order at me. It was a bad mistake on my part because, moments later after a brief exchange between the three of them, the gunman pulled out a handful of black material. He shook it out into a square and opened up one side to make a hood, which he roughly dragged onto my head, blocking out the last remaining light. For the rest of the trip I lay motionless, gritting my teeth through the discomfort.

With one final sweep of the driver's wheel we finally lurched to a halt on a gravel surface. The trio exchanged a few snippets of conversation, nobody seeming quite sure what their next move was, but then the gunman grabbed my arm and pulled me upright. He leaned over me and pulled the handle to open the door, letting in a blast of freezing air from a strong breeze. He pushed me towards the door and I climbed out into the cold, feeling the loose stones beneath my feet. I stood still, not knowing how far I could safely move away from the car, and waited to see what would happen next. Away to my left I could hear more voices and the driver of the Mercedes shouted towards them as if in response to a question. Then I felt large hands on me again and I was led forcibly up a slight incline towards the new voices. Seconds later the chill in the air diminished suddenly and I knew we'd gone inside. An echo suggested we were in another corridor and I was taken forwards for thirty paces before being dragged to a sudden halt.

The hood was ripped off my head and the tape from my mouth. I blinked against the strip lighting. As I found my bearings in this new environment, I quickly gathered that I had exchanged one prison for another, although the walls in this corridor were made of rough stone and the steel doors lined only one side, to my left. Imme-

diately beside me, one of them stood open and I was
invited, by gestures from the gunman standing in front
of me, to step inside the unlit cell. As I did so, I turned
to see if any of my kidnappers would accompany me but
none of them moved and none caught my eye as the
door clanged shut.

I was just starting to wonder if my eyes would ever
grow accustomed to the blackness when a woman's voice
spoke.

'What is your name, my friend?'

I jumped at the sound and let out an exclamation of
surprise. 'Who's there?'

I peered into the darkness and thought I could make
out a shadow in one corner of the room. She couldn't
have been more than ten feet away but the absence of
light was so complete that it could just as easily have been
my mind playing tricks on me.

The voice was calm and smooth, with no hint of fear.
I wondered who she was and why they had put the two
of us in a cell together but before I could ask any more
questions she spoke again.

'There's no need to be frightened.' The accent matched
those of the men who'd sprung me from the *Stadtpolizei*
and I guessed she was Czech or Hungarian: had I crossed
the border, into one of the Soviet satellite states that occupied this part of central Europe? There had been no sense
on the journey of having to stop to cross a checkpoint,
which must surely exist along this stretch of the Iron Curtain. No civilian would have been able to drive from a
neutral country into a communist one without having to
go through a whole series of document inspections and,
quite probably, close scrutiny of the vehicle itself; all of
which suggested I had not been kidnapped by civilians.
And if that were true, then my situation had just grown
immeasurably more perilous.

'I'm not frightened,' I lied, but I knew my voice gave me away. 'Who are you and why have they locked you up?'

Her tone took on a strange quality, as if she were smiling. 'Oh, they haven't locked me up.'

I didn't understand what she meant and I said so.

'You don't seem to understand very much, do you?' she said, her voice almost purring now.

'What are you talking about? Who are you?'

In answer to my question, a bright light snapped suddenly on and I was temporarily blinded again. If my hands had been free I'd have held up an arm to shield myself but, as it was, all I could do was grimace and turn my head away.

The voice came again from behind the light.

'This is tiresome. You will start by giving me your name.'

I had got it all wrong, I realised. This woman – whoever she was – was not another prisoner but an inquisitor for my captors.

'You've just sprung me from a Viennese prison. How can you not even know who I am?'

She paused. 'That is a fair question. It is because we don't know who you are that we – as you say – sprang you from a Viennese prison. Now, please, if you would answer my question.'

I thought fast. I had no idea who she was or who she was working for, but her accent and the cold walls that currently held me did nothing to ease my feeling of immense danger. The worst thing about it was that I had no idea whatsoever what this whole damn business was about.

'My name is Bill Kemp.' I figured there was no harm in at least letting her know that.

'And you are a British agent, yes?'

'No,' I said, my voice raised in alarm. 'I'm British, yes, but I'm no agent.'

'Then what were you doing meeting Anna Stern in Vienna? And what caused you to kill her?'

So this crew were mixed up in the debacle over Anna's death and, like the Austrian police, had jumped to entirely the wrong conclusion about my own involvement. I had no idea who this mystery woman was but if she believed I was working for MI6 then I was in even deeper trouble than I'd imagined. I wondered if I could disabuse her of her mistake any more easily than I had with the Austrians.

I sighed heavily. 'I was asked to meet Anna. But I didn't kill her.'

'Sit down, Mr Kemp.'

I looked around me and saw a plain wooden chair behind me that I hadn't noticed before. I sat awkwardly, my hands still bound.

'Now, who asked you to meet Anna?'

My eyes were beginning to adjust to the intensity of the bulb that was dazzling me and I could make out the woman's silhouette now against the pale wall behind her. She seemed of slight build and medium height and she was standing almost immediately behind the light, presumably to camouflage her features. I wondered what she would look like in the full glare of the beam.

'Who asked you?' The repeated question was decidedly more forceful than the first attempt and I felt a shiver run down my spine.

'I don't know.'

The voice was more chilling this time. 'I will ask you the question one more time, Mr Kemp, and then, if you do not give me a satisfactory answer, we will try another way. Now, who asked you to meet Anna Stern?'

With no answer to offer, I was boxed in and I really

didn't like the implication of what she'd said. I tried to put as much evenness into my tone as I could. 'I'm telling you the truth. I don't know who asked me because I never saw them. I only spoke to them twice on the telephone.'

The pause seemed interminable.

'Very well, Mr Kemp. Let me ask a different question. Why did you travel halfway across the continent to meet someone you'd never seen before, simply at the request of a telephone caller that you similarly did not know? You must admit it seems an unlikely thing to do.'

I readily admitted it: right now it seemed to me not only unlikely but bloody stupid. Only the thought of Leotta and her unknown whereabouts was keeping me focused and I was determined to get out of this thing for her sake, if not for mine.

'They threatened a friend of mine,' I said simply.

'How very noble of you. You must think very highly of your friend to put yourself in such danger.'

'I do – but I didn't know I was putting myself in danger when I agreed to do it.'

'And now?'

That was a damn good question. Knowing what I now knew – albeit a tiny fraction of what I imagined the whole picture must be – would I have flown to Vienna in the first place? Of course I knew the answer to that.

'As I said, I do think very highly of my friend.'

'So, let us assume that you are speaking the truth about your reasons for travelling to Austria. Please remember, Mr Kemp, I am not saying that I accept your explanation but for the sake of our discussion let us imagine that it is so. Why, then, would you do what you did to Anna and dump her body for the police to find in the river?'

'I didn't do anything to Anna. And if you can't even explain why I would have killed her, surely that adds weight to my claim that I didn't.'

'Having no explanation for it is not the same as it not having happened.'

'Look, I don't know who killed Anna or why and I'm just as shocked by it as everyone else seems to be.'

She paused again and I could see her shadow shifting behind the light.

'You would like me to believe that it is nothing more than coincidence that you met Anna Stern – whom you never knew existed until two days ago – and within twenty-four hours she is dead. Her body washes up on the banks of the Danube and you are arrested at the scene by Austrian police. *At the scene*, Mr Kemp. How else am I supposed to interpret this set of facts?'

I had long since abandoned any rationale for hiding anything from this woman. It wasn't as if I'd signed the Official Secrets Act. She might as well know everything I knew.

'I don't care how you interpret them. I'm just telling you that you're wrong. I met Anna Stern, she gave me a rendezvous point at the river, and the next thing I knew she was being carted off by the gendarmerie. I can't tell you any more because I don't know any more.'

'Why did the Austrian police think you killed her?'

I sighed again. 'You'd have to ask them that.'

There was a flash of movement from behind the light and suddenly the woman was standing over me, a pair of icy blue eyes staring coldly into mine. There was a fury in them that took me by surprise – more so than the sudden movement – and I cowered.

'I don't have to do anything of the kind, Mr Kemp. I have you to tell me what really happened. And if you continue to refuse to do so, I will resort to stronger measures.'

She took a step back and I got a good look at her now. The icy blue eyes were framed by an angular, pale face, her brow low and her shining black hair scraped to the back of her head. Her lips were thin and tight and her whole demeanour was one of controlled rage, her fists clenched and her stance like a panther's, ready to pounce. The impression was reinforced by her polo-neck sweater and combat trousers, which were all in black and hugged her diminutive figure. I couldn't help but marvel at what curious career path had led to this gothic waif interrogating foreigners in a freezing prison cell.

'I told you: I don't know any more.'

She turned and walked away, going back behind the light again. A moment later she reappeared, hefting a cudgel in her hand.

'You disappoint me, Mr Kemp. I hoped you would be prepared to give me your information a little more willingly.'

Despite the cold, I was starting to sweat. I eyed the cudgel warily as she stepped closer to the chair. 'If I had any information, I would give it to you.'

'I'm afraid I don't believe you,' she said, and lunged.

The pain as she slammed the cudgel onto my left thigh was excruciating and I screamed in agony. My first thought was that she'd broken my femur but she was cleverer than that: after the echo of my scream had died away, she kicked my foot from under me and watched as I felt the pain thrum down my whole leg. I gave two heaving sobs and forced myself to look up at her again.

'There are many parts of the body that can inflict pain in a myriad of different ways,' she said, smiling pleasantly. 'We can explore them one by one if you choose, or you can tell me who you are and why you killed Anna Stern.'

I gritted my teeth and snarled at her. 'I didn't kill Anna Stern and I don't know why I am here.'

She delayed the next blow just long enough to let me believe it wouldn't be coming. Her talent for psychological torture seemed as efficient as her physical prowess. I screamed a second time as the cudgel landed on my right thigh.

By the time my expert interrogator had finished with me, I was black and blue from my collarbone to the soles of my feet. She steered clear of my face – maybe she needed me to be presentable in the event of a public appearance – but every inch of the rest of me was subjected to a level of pain I had never experienced before. She was careful not to break any bones too, leaving me just about able to move without the remotest inclination to do so.

I told her nothing more. I couldn't: there was nothing more for me to tell. I almost thought she believed me after an hour of torture. After all, I was an amateur in this situation and who but the best-trained operatives could withstand this kind of punishment? The problem with that was that she didn't believe I was an amateur and she was merely doling out the kind of treatment any real spy would expect. For her, it would simply be a matter of finding my breaking point. As for me, I had broken long before.

As the chamber of horrors revealed each successive nightmare, I feared I might lose my mind. It did not take Sherlock Holmes to realise that she had seen Anna's body being dredged from the shallows of the Danube and, somehow, observed my subsequent arrest by the authorities. Putting the pieces together to make completely the wrong picture, she had then decided that I must have been critical not only in the story of Anna's demise but also to the Austrian version of events. Even through the fog of pain, I tried to construct a meaningful explanation for everything that had happened in the past eighteen hours or so.

My starting point was the position of Anna Stern in this whole mess. The only conclusion I could reach was that she must have been an Iron Curtain spy. What I couldn't explain was why I had been inveigled into the affair. Why had it been arranged for me – a nobody from England with no specific skills – to meet a Soviet agent in a café in Austria? What on earth could my true mission have been? And now that this agent was dead, her body discovered by unsuspecting local police officers, there was a slew of unanswered questions that would have to be faced by this non-aligned country: Anna Stern's death would have thrown a giant question-mark over Austria's supposed neutrality. If my female Torquemada was also from the Soviet side of the fence, I could hardly blame her for wanting to get to the bottom of the grisly business. I thought back to Napoleon, my squat Viennese inquisitor, and wondered if he'd had half a clue of what he'd got himself into. Or maybe he knew exactly what the problem was, and was determined to make me – an alleged foreign agent – the scapegoat for Anna's death, exculpating the Austrians from any blame by showing no tolerance to espionage on their territory.

When I ran out of explanations for what on earth might have landed me in this hellhole, I diverted myself from the attack by inventing a back story for my interrogator. I knew that different areas of the brain controlled physical and emotional responses and as the blows rained down I tried to park my mind in a region entirely separate from its pain receptors. Cold logic might not cut off the messages from my pounded nerve endings completely but it seemed to help a little. I pictured her earning a steely nickname from her peers at interrogation school: The Bitch, perhaps, or The Torturess. She had clearly been bullied as a child, probably for her diminutive stature, and might easily have been an orphan brought up in a loveless institution before being shipped off for a life in some penal establishment after one too many knife fights with her classmates. There she would have been recruited for one of the more unpleasant branches of the state's apparatus, rising from common snitch to highly effective inquisitor as her talent for brutality was recognised by her seniors. Kept firmly off the grid and under wraps, she would have been nurtured and promoted, held in reserve to be wheeled out when required to crack the toughest nuts among the enemies of the state.

What the hell all that had to do with me was anyone's guess.

My mental meanderings somehow helped me to survive her onslaught and when she finally threw the cudgel to the ground in disgust I found myself grinning, then maniacally laughing, at her inability to extract anything useful from me.

She was spent by her exertions and dropped to her knees in front of my chair.

'You may laugh, Mr Kemp, but we have only just begun. Tomorrow I will return with the blades.'

Whether it was because of the pain from my injuries or the prospect of another session with The Torturess I couldn't tell, but this time I knew I was in for a sleepless night.

NINE

The eye is an extraordinary organ. In normal light – either daylight or artificial – the pupils adjust to a comfortable size for taking in information from the world around us. When it gets dark, the pupils widen to allow as much light in as possible. Special cells at the back of the retina excel in peripheral vision and have extreme sensitivity to light photons and, while we'll never match the capabilities of cats, for example, our night vision serves us pretty well, even with a minimal amount of light to work with. When there is no light at all, however, we are rendered as blind as the unfortunate bat in the adage, only without that mammal's echo location equipment to make up for it.

After the woman had left me to ponder her parting words, two of the men from the Mercedes came back in and picked me up bodily. I was hustled out of the cell and down the corridor to another door, where I was thrown into a tiny room with just a metal bed frame and a blackened bucket. I only had a moment to take in the furnishings before the door was slammed shut behind me and I was left in total darkness.

Except that the darkness could not have been total.

Around forty minutes later, I was starting to make

out shapes as my vision fought to create a picture for my brain. I forced myself to move, in spite of the pain throbbing in every part of my body, and edged over to where I'd seen the bed. I found it when my temple made direct contact with one sharp corner and I let out an expletive as I felt a slow drip of blood creep down my cheek.

Then I realised that a sharp corner was exactly what I needed.

I hotched myself around so that my back was up against the bed and began to work the tape that bound my hands against the sharpened edge. Eventually I felt it give and I ripped it apart with a jerk of my wrists. Then my hand went to my temple, where I dabbed the new cut above my hairline and licked the tips of my fingers, confirming that what I had felt was indeed blood.

But I had more pressing concerns on my mind: escape. I toyed with the idea of waiting until I'd had some sleep, but I didn't want to risk an early reappearance from my torturer and, if her techniques so far were anything to go by, I wouldn't have been at all surprised if sleep deprivation were part of her modus operandi. The chill of her final words to me was far greater than the natural cold of this prison and I knew I had to do something now.

Exploring in the dark with my battered fingers, I found the cell door seemed to be made of wood, with huge hinges attaching it to the rough-hewn stone wall and a small opening cut into its centre, presumably with a sliding panel operated from the outside as a viewing window. On the opposite edge from the hinges, an old-fashioned iron latch remained intact, complete with a ring handle. I grabbed the handle and turned it rapidly back and forth, not expecting anything to happen. I was not disappointed: nothing did. At least, nothing mechanical with the door. But from outside in the corridor I heard a gruff voice – possibly disturbed from slumber – shouting something

unintelligible. I assumed it was the guard telling me to
desist so I rattled the handle again for confirmation and
called out.

'Hey – you there!'

Again a shout came.

I stepped back from the door and waited. Sure enough,
a few seconds later a panel in the door slid violently open
and a pair of angry eyes appeared in its stead. The sudden
light from outside made me wince but I held the stare
of the guard as he hurled a stream of incomprehensible
invective at me, then jabbed a finger through the opening
to point at the bed. His message was clear: he wanted me
to shut up and go to sleep.

The panel slammed closed and I was in darkness once
more. But in the few seconds and blinding light, I'd established one vital thing: now I had to work out a way to use
it to my advantage.

For the next two hours I toiled, hampered by the need to
stay quiet but also by the relentless darkness. My strength
was severely impeded by my injuries but determination
drove me on. I took hold of the loosest leg of the bed and
began wrenching it backward and forward, easing it away
from the frame by increments each time. I didn't know if
the bolt would give first or the rusting steel of the leg itself
but I didn't care. What I needed was the L-shaped, foot-
long piece of steel that eventually came away in my hand.

Next I wedged it into the crevice between the old iron
latch and the door, pulling it painstakingly from its moor-
ings. It took ten minutes to feel any movement at all, but
once it started to go, it came away surprisingly quickly
and eventually I stood in my black hole, a wrecked bed leg
in one hand and a heavy iron latch in the other, my hands
torn to buggery but with a huge grin on my face.

Now the fun could really begin.

I upturned the bucket and stood it in the direct centre of the cell. Then I put the bed frame on its end against the stone wall behind the door and climbed, the latch clamped between my teeth, to the ceiling, where a series of joists spanned the cell from side to side. This was the crucial detail I had spotted when the guard opened the viewing panel.

Awkwardly, and with every muscle in my body screaming out in agony, I jammed my elbows and knees between two of the joists so that I was suspended, face-down and supporting my own weight, from the ceiling. With some careful manoeuvring I was able to reach down with the latch and thump it against the door, making as much noise as I could and shouting indiscriminately.

'Hey, guard! In here – I need your help!'

I added a few random expletives, suspecting that he wouldn't understand anyway and it didn't actually matter what I was yelling. When I heard the panel slide back in the door I stopped instantly.

I could only imagine what was going through his mind. In a cell where, a couple of hours earlier, an imprisoned man had been staring back at him when he opened the slider, now there appeared to be an upturned bucket – and nothing else. From his viewpoint, there was no bed... and no prisoner. When your only job is to keep watch over an incarcerated jailbird, it must come as a sickening shock to discover that he has vanished into thin air right under your nose.

He took an age to work out what to do next and all the while my bruised muscles were crying out for relief. When he finally made the decision to come inside, the keys jangled in the lock for another age before he finally emerged from the doorway, directly underneath me and swivelling his bewildered head from side to side as he scanned the room.

I didn't wait for him to look up, even if he'd thought of it. In one fluid movement, I let go with my right hand, grabbed the latch from between my teeth, and dropped onto his head. His knees buckled and he crumpled to the ground while I landed astride him and kept my feet, bending my knees to cushion the drop. Before he had a chance to turn his head I brought the latch crashing down onto his skull and his body went limp.

I didn't know if I'd killed him with the blow but at that moment I honestly didn't care.

My first priority had to be making sure nobody else was around who might have heard the shouting and the crashes. Stuffing the iron latch inside my shirt, I turned and stuck my head out of the door, looking across to the empty desk before checking the corridor in both directions. Then I went back into the cell and, in the light now pouring in from outside, took the keys from his hand, which lay limp and outstretched across the floor. I backed out of the room, checked the corridor again, then closed and locked the big wooden door behind me. I stuffed the keys into my trouser pocket, hefted the latch in my hand and sized up my options.

There must have been an entrance to the building somewhere off to my right, because that was where I'd come from. I wasn't going to risk going in that direction: there were sure to be guards somewhere between me and the way out. The alternative – to head left, past the guard's desk and into the unknown – was hardly more palatable. I had no idea what to expect in either case, except that running into an opponent seemed certain on one route and only highly likely on the other. I've never been a gambling man but I was willing to take my chances on this one.

Ahead of me at the end of the corridor was another wooden door, as well bolstered with ironmongery as my cell had been. I was starting to think there was something almost medieval about the construction of the building and I could easily imagine the Spanish Inquisition going to work on the enemies of the Roman Catholic Church in a place just like it. I didn't stop to think too long about that and tried the door. To my surprise, it opened with a turn of the handle and I had to shut it again quickly for fear of finding more guards on the other side. I gingerly gave it another go, allowing the door to swing just a fraction towards me and squashing one eye up against the gap to see what was on the other side. The door opened on to a stone staircase going up, and it was empty.

Climbing higher in the building was not my preferred option, unless we were underground; I doubted that as I recalled the journey from the car to my original cell and couldn't place any steps down in my memory. But the thought of armed guards in the opposite direction prompted me to take the stairs anyway. Maybe I could find another way down somewhere else in the building. For now, I needed to get the lie of the land and try to make good my escape without being discovered.

At the top of the stairs, another corridor ran from left to right and I peered around the corner of the wall to investigate. This too seemed empty and my odds now were fifty-fifty. In my mind I flipped a coin, called 'Tails' and watched it land on Heads. With one last look over my shoulder, I set off to the left.

As I neared the wall at the end of the corridor I couldn't work out what was going on. There had been no doors as I crept silently along and now the walls seemed to be meeting in a dead end. Was it really a corridor to nowhere? I turned and looked back in the opposite direction, where a single door stood at the other end of the passage. I was just about to start heading back that way when I felt a draught of cold air from behind me. So there was an exit somewhere here.

I had stopped about ten feet short of the end wall, but now I went up to it to inspect it more closely I saw a small opening right in the corner on the left-hand side. It had been easy to miss as the only thing on the other side of it was a spiral stone staircase leading upwards.

Higher still or back to the far door?

There was something about the cold air that drew me on. Perhaps it was the tempting prospect of the outside world or simply that my sweat was now sticking my clothes painfully to my skin: whatever the reason, I wanted to get out of here fast and I figured the stairs were the quickest route to the open air.

I launched myself onto the first tread, not caring that my metal heel reinforcements echoed up the spiral in front of me. If I ran into someone coming down, I would have to take my chances. The air was getting cooler by the second, the draught stronger and fresher, and the sense of freedom put a new spring in my weary step. My run dwindled to a slow climb as the staircase seemed to carry on endlessly but I forced myself to go on, sniffing the air and hauling my aching body relentlessly upwards.

And then I was at the summit, bursting out through an opening onto a wide, flat roof and into a vast, starlit sky.

I stopped, gasping for breath and taking in the enormity of the heavens above me. The blackness of the night was punctured with a million tiny pinpricks of light and the whole giant backcloth fell away uninterrupted to the horizon, where the stars were cut off by a low wall at the edges of the roof. The strangeness of the sight took me completely by surprise and it took me a few moments to get my head together and my breath back. I seemed to be standing at the highest point in the area: nothing but the sky was visible to me from here. I wanted to know what this place was – how I came to be so elevated – so I checked behind me to listen for sounds on the staircase and, when I was satisfied that nobody was following me, I edged over to the nearest bit of wall and stuck my head over the side.

What I saw both dazzled and terrified me.

I was looking down on a colossal tract of blackness, cutting a swathe through the surrounding countryside and forming a huge, inky ribbon into which the starlight seemed unable to penetrate. I could make out trees on the far side and, off to my left, the towering walls fell away below me, giving onto a large courtyard that was only partially visible from where I was. More buildings rose on the far side of the open space but they were much lower and seemed to be modern. My standpoint was unquestionably a castle, and an old one at that.

What drew my attention most, however, was the view immediately below me. Strung along the near edge of the black ribbon was an array of cabins, lifted into the air on legs perhaps fifty feet tall, each one pumping out a harsh beam of light onto the ground beneath. As I watched, one of these beams swept the ribbon itself and I could see patches of white bordering the black. The light played across to the far side and I was staggered to see a spit of snowbound land reaching out into the blackness of what I now understood to be the River Danube. I knew that spit of land: I had lain on it, damp and frozen to the core, less than eighteen hours earlier. Before I was apprehended at gunpoint on it, I had marvelled at the exact location which I now occupied.

I had no idea how I had got there but I was standing atop the great rocky citadel of Devín Castle.

TEN

A strong wind was blowing, pushing a subzero iciness through my thin clothes. Somewhere along the line I'd been stripped of my anorak, and the wool sweater I'd brought from home was decidedly threadbare after years of service on the Dart. But the extremes of the weather offered nothing compared to the chill of knowing that I was beyond the Iron Curtain.

Somehow I had become the prisoner of a communist regime.

Along with the wind, a torrent of chaotic thoughts battered me and I realised I had to straighten things out in my mind before I could contemplate anything else. I hoped it might be a while before the guard in my cell regained consciousness – if he ever did – and I reckoned I had a little time to do some hard thinking. Even if he woke and started hammering on the door for his colleagues, it might take them some time to hear him and even longer to release him, given that I had the keys in my pocket. Equally, I didn't dare go back into the stairwell just in case they were already searching the place for me so I crouched down behind the highest point of the parapet that I could find, wrapped my arms around me for warmth, and began to consider my position.

From my research over the past few days in Vienna, I had been surprised to discover just how close the Austrian capital was to its nearest communist-ruled neighbour city. True, it required crossing the Curtain, which on a good day could cause considerable delays to the journey, but any crow unhindered by geopolitics and travelling at the speed of your average saloon car could fly in a straight line to Bratislava, in Czechoslovakia, in a bare hour. The hilltop fortress where I was currently cowering was just a handful of miles from the city centre. It was a tantalising thought that if I simply walked into Bratislava and surrendered myself to the authorities, I might just be passed back to the West.

Tantalising, perhaps, but also inconceivable. I had to work on the basis that the people holding me in Devín Castle *were* the authorities – or, at the very least, were operating with the consent of their Soviet paymasters. The idea that I would be allowed to wander calmly back to safety on the other side of the Iron Curtain was unthinkable, especially if The Tortures were to learn that I had handed myself in. In the absence of any other plan, I was forced to assess my immediate situation once more: after all, what I did next would be completely immaterial if I could not extricate myself from my present circumstances. One insurmountable obstacle at a time, I decided.

I turned and leaned over the parapet again, keeping my head low in case one of the searchlights happened to stray up to the top of the castle ramparts. I moved slightly to my right to get the best view over the confluence of the two rivers, where the heaviest fortifications were concentrated on the banks below me, and tried to count the watchtowers that surrounded the ancient lone turret overlooking the water. These stretched in a long line in both directions,

up the frozen Morava river to my right and away to
my left on the Danube itself. It was clear that the Soviets
were not keen on anyone getting out of the country by
boat: between the watchtowers, vast fields of barbed wire
covered the ground from the bottom of the castle walls to
the ice that marked the water's edge. Its cruel twists and
spurs were softened by a dusting of snow but there was no
mistaking their lethal intent. As the searchlights swept the
scene periodically I could make out a network of narrow
paths weaving through the wire, picking out a tortuous
route between the watchtowers. Even if I could somehow
get down to ground level and find my way through the
tangle of mesh, I would still be a sitting duck to the guards
in the towers with their blinding beams and, no doubt,
fully-loaded machine guns. And if, by some miracle of
fortune, I made it to the water, what then? The Danube
was wide and probably deep at this point in its progress
towards the Black Sea; the currents would be strong and
the water freezing. A man trying to swim that expanse
in such temperatures wouldn't last five minutes, even if
he could dodge the bullets that would inevitably be rain-
ing down on him. I remembered that this exact point was
the scene of the most numerous failed attempts to escape
communism, with the deaths racked up in their hundreds.
Any attempt to cross the Danube would be suicide: I would
become merely another statistic to add to the roll call.

I turned my attention to the Morava, much narrower
than its sister river and, as far as I could tell from the way
the snow was revealed in the lights, completely frozen
over. I had no way of telling how thick the ice would be
but at least there was a continuous surface leading to the
far side. Of course, that meant it was much more closely
watched than the Danube and the beams streamed back
and forth over the ice with an irregularity but also a frequency that suggested the guards really knew what they

were doing. Their pattern was random but effective, tra-
versing every inch of the river in the course of less than
five minutes and allowing any would-be defector no
chance of remaining undetected.

If the Danube was a rock, then the Morava was unquestionably a hard place.

It was all academic anyway: I was perched seven hundred feet above the ice, with no way of reaching it alive.

Over the next twenty minutes I completed a full circuit
of the castle roof, scouting the rocks below in the hope of
finding a route down. None looked appealing but a greying of the sky away over to the east forced my hand. If
dawn was on its way I would have to make the best use
of the darkness still available to me. I had no idea how
long it might take to scramble down this granite giant and
I needed to reach the ground before daylight if I were to
stand any chance of crossing the river without being seen.

I was halfway across the parapet when I realised what
a damned fool I was. Somewhere below me, in the belly
of the castle, lay an unconscious guard who might just
hold my ticket out of this place.

With the darkness still thick but time ticking against
me fast, I rolled off the wall and scuttled back to the staircase, descending as quickly as I dared. I sharpened my
ears for any sound of someone coming the other way but
I reached the bottom without confrontation and headed
back down the corridor the way I had come almost an
hour earlier. I was amazed and relieved to find no sign of
any other soldiers in this part of the building and could
only surmise that my incarceration had been deliberately
staged in a remote and depopulated part of the site. That
might have been because I was a secret to the main garrison of troops – and so much the better.

At the door of the cell I waited and listened again.
There was no noise either in the corridor ahead of me or

from inside the cell so I leaned my head close to the sliding panel and eased it open. Immediately I was aware of breathing too stertorous to be merely sleep so I took out the keys and unlocked the door.

Inside, the guard had not moved but in the cold light falling in from the corridor I found myself relieved and grateful that he was still alive: if I ever got the chance to look back on this escapade, inflicting a lethal blow on this unfortunate jobsworth would have haunted me for the rest of my life.

I was confident I would not rouse him from unconsciousness and got to work on stripping him.

Anyone who has ever tried to undress a fifteen-stone man in a state of inebriation – which, let's be honest, is probably anyone with a military background – will understand that the job proved a lot harder than might be imagined. The dead weight seems to far exceed the true mass of the corporeal lump, while the limbs and head make for awkward, unhelpful appendages when it comes to manoeuvring the body. Separating an arm from its jacket is like trying to unwrap an octopus; turning the entire lump over an almost Herculean task for one slighter person, hampered by injuries and fatigue. I wasn't helped by the fact that his frame was at least two sizes larger than mine – his green border guard uniform swamped me, even putting it on over my sweater – but better that way than the other, I mused as I hitched up the sleeves to free my hands.

Eventually I was fully kitted out, a Stan Laurel inside an Oliver Hardy uniform. I had noticed an overcoat near the table in the corridor outside and I figured the more I was wearing, the better disguised I would be. My main concern was how to cover my face but the guard even provided me with a useful answer to that: tucked into one pocket of the overcoat was a black woollen balaclava. I wasn't convinced it was standard issue but in this kind of climate at the furthest reaches of the Soviet empire, perhaps the rules weren't so strictly enforced. In any case, I didn't care: it worked perfectly for my purposes. I dragged it over my head, pulled the cap down on top of it and shucked up the collar of the overcoat to complete the disguise. I hoped that someone would have to get close to realise they weren't dealing with the real thing – and I didn't intend to allow anyone to get even slightly close.

What I couldn't find, and would have given a large number of Schillings to have, was a weapon of any kind. I wasn't sure whether border guards routinely carried them when they weren't actually on the border but I searched mine thoroughly, along with his possessions on and around the table, and came up with nothing. I consoled myself with the fact that if it came to a shootout in this hostile environment, it probably wouldn't make too much difference whether I had a gun or not. If I couldn't make it out unseen, I was dead meat.

I started to make my way down the corridor, away from the cell and the staircase that led to the roof. After a few paces I realised I didn't need to remain in the shadows – I was playing the role of a guard now, not my true identity as an escaped prisoner – so I stood up straighter and tried as best I could to fill out the oversized uniform I was wearing. I'd read somewhere that one of the reasons public schoolboys benefitted from their educational privilege was that it taught them to carry themselves differently from mere mortals and I tried to mimic that air of authority now: with luck, I wouldn't have to put my life on the line as I put the notion to the test, pulling my shoulders back and sticking out my chin with unwarranted confidence. I didn't want to tip my head too far back because the overhead bulbs would cast too much light on my face but I found a balance that left me almost swaggering while keeping my features relatively shaded.

As I turned the corner at the end of the corridor, my heart leaped into my mouth: ahead of me, in a room that opened out into a large common area, a group of half a dozen uniformed men sat smoking cigarettes and drinking from steel cups. Their chatter and laughter hadn't penetrated into the corridor but they were a surprisingly noisy bunch, their focus on a game of cards being played out on a big wooden table near a stone fireplace. Most of them had their backs to me and without breaking step I strode meaningfully past them, hoping to go unnoticed.

I thought I'd made it past when one of them half-turned from the game and waved a vague hand in my direction.

'*Chceš si hrát, Soudruhu?*'

I could see the hand held a packet of cigarettes but I had no clue what the man had said. He might have been asking me to sit down or have a smoke or ordering me to fetch more supplies from the stores for all I knew, but from the tone of his voice I guessed it was an invitation rather than an instruction. For a brief moment I considered attempting to vocalise an answer: the words '*no*', '*nein*' and '*nyet*' are similar in many languages but I had no idea if Czech was one of them. In fact, I didn't even know if the man had spoken Czech or Slovak or neat Russian. It would have been just my luck if whatever I uttered turned out to be some kind of egregious insult and I unwittingly started a riot. Instead, erring on the side of caution, I shook my head and extended a hand in a sign of what I hoped was a universally comprehended negative response.

To my relief he turned away, muttering to the man next to him, then the whole table burst out in an explosion of mirth as someone laid down a winning card, and I slipped past.

'*Idiot!*' I heard shouted behind me, and I didn't need a translator for that one. An angry voice responded so it sounded like they didn't need me for their riot and I wanted to get out before it turned into a full-scale fight. I quickened my pace, risking a glance over my shoulder, and headed for the door at the end of the passage.

The route from the walls of the keep to the main gate, out on the wooded hillside in the gloaming dawn, took me less than ten minutes to navigate, in spite of my bruises. Past the gatehouse I could see the lights of one or two houses twinkling in the valley beyond the perimeter, where early risers were up before the dawn, but the only other light came from the stars: the powerful searchlights on the rivers' edge were on the opposite side of the castle from me. I stumbled down the slope through the trees in almost total darkness, trying to keep as straight a line as I could and grateful that the snow hadn't penetrated the branches to hinder my progress. I emerged much closer to the gatehouse than I'd intended but the curve of the perimeter wall worked to my advantage and I was able to tuck myself against it as I neared the old gate, listening out for voices while remaining hidden from view.

A bank of raised earth fell away as the wall reached the gatehouse, dropping down to the road that ran through it. I sat down in the snow and eased slowly down the bank, tucking myself into a curved nook just beside the opening itself. I could hear no sound except the odd early bird chirping in its quest for the worm, so I gingerly put my head around the corner of the arch that marked the gate, ready to withdraw instantly if I caught sight of anyone.

There seemed to be nobody there so I edged around the corner, my back still firmly planted against the stones, and shuffled my way through the entrance. I could only surmise that the fortifications along the riverbank and the armoury up above me in the castle courtyard were considered enough protection for the occupying force, and that they had deemed it unnecessary to guard this gate as well.

Whatever their logic, it provided me with an opportunity. Ahead of me lay a straight stretch of road, the main service route to the castle as far as I could tell, with a couple of buildings over to the right. In the absence of any guards, I took the opportunity to flee into the trees on the left for shelter and began working my way down the hill towards the river – and the deadly no man's land that bordered it.

'There are four types of camouflage,' one of my old army instructors had announced to his eager batch of recruits. 'Concealment, disruption, disguise and mimicry.'

I didn't remember much else from his classroom as I was transfixed by his outsize belly jiggling up and down over his belt as he spoke, but I do recall being intrigued by his theory for blending in.

'Concealment involves hiding against a background of similar colour to whatever you're wearing,' he said. 'In nature, forest animals tend to be brown, snow creatures are more likely to be white. Some, like the octopus or the chameleon, have the facility to change their colour according to their location or mood.

'Disruption is when the outer covering is formed of broken or disrupted patterns to throw off the observer. A leopard's spots enable them to approach their prey unnoticed.

'Disguise, as you might imagine, allows for blending in to one's surroundings by changing one's appearance, while mimicry depends on taking on the actual characteristics of someone or something else in order to fool others around you. Some butterflies disguise themselves as leaves to avoid predators; others actually pretend to be those predators.'

As I sat in that classroom, watching the bouncing belly, I had never imagined the sergeant's words would come back to me years later on the frozen fringes of the communist bloc. Not for the first time, I was grateful for my military training. Some things just stick with you.

I descended the slope towards the fortified river bank, pondering whether my current camouflage fell under the heading of disguise or mimicry. I supposed if I'd had some Czech, or was wearing the correct boots, I might have been better able to pass myself off as a genuine frontier soldier: as it was, I was merely using the prison guard's uniform to blend in. However, as in the natural world, if anyone chose to look too closely I would surely be exposed as a fraud. I had to stay hidden for as long as possible and only resort to attempted mimicry if I had no other choice. On the other hand, the discovery that I could simply walk out of the castle under the noses of my captors without raising an eyebrow had emboldened me and I silently gave thanks to the guard I'd knocked unconscious for the temporary use of his uniform. Now I was about to put its camouflage qualities to the ultimate test by walking into the lion's den.

When I reached the road that encircled the riverside edge of the castle rock, I stood upright, straightened the peaked cap on my head and stepped confidently out of the trees and onto the icy tarmac.

Without any hesitancy, I turned to the left, into the teeth of the most heavily fortified stretch of riverbank, and strode purposefully towards the barbed wire. High above me I could see movement in the nearest watch-tower but it didn't seem to be concerned with me so I walked on, looking for traces of a path in the snow that I knew would be there to service and refresh the barbed wire every now and then. I hoped the snowfall wasn't so deep that I wouldn't be able to see it and I was relieved to make out narrow gaps in the wire that betrayed the route soldiers would take to retrieve the bodies of anyone mad enough to attempt to cross this wasteland.

Then I remembered that I was one of those mad people and I shuddered.

The searchlights played across the foreshore all the way around from the frozen Morava, where I was, to the larger expanse of the Danube, where a central channel remained ice-free and the water looked thick and black in contrast to the surrounding snow. So far the beams had not strayed in my direction, even though I stood clearly in the open, and I began to suspect that the concentration of the guards up on the towers might not be as committed as their superior officers would like. Yesterday's image of troops huddled around a brazier for warmth returned to my mind and I even dared to hope that they might be passing around a hip flask up there, dulling their senses still further and increasing my odds with every sip. I was probably fooling myself but I needed every last ounce of encouragement if I were to make a run for it across this lethal border.

Beyond the military posts I could make out the castle's isolated tower on its spur of rock, silhouetted against the night sky, which was now turning a distinct shade of grey. Time was running out: if I waited until dawn then I would increase the risk of being seen enormously. While it could be classed as misfortune to be picked out by a lucky spotlight in the gloom, for a dark-clothed figure to attempt to cross a white wilderness in daylight was nothing short of stupidity.

Keeping the searchlights in the periphery of my vision, I started out into the field of barbed wire. In front of me lay a fifty-yard stretch threaded with the fierce stuff, then an open patch of undisturbed white which I assumed was snow marking where the Morava streamed beneath a layer of ice. Beyond that was a line of trees – the far bank of the river and Austrian territory. I had no idea whether the barbed wire or the open snowfield would be my greatest enemy but it didn't matter: I needed to tackle them both.

For the first twenty yards I made good progress, weaving through lines of wire and using the supporting fence posts to vault it at a couple of strategic points. The quality of the installation was unconvincing and I found myself moving with relative ease, untroubled by the searchlights and following a route that opened up one new possibility after another. Then my coat snagged on a barb and I lost valuable time trying to extricate the material from the knot. I even attempted to rip a piece of material away from the rest of the coat but finally expediency forced me to wrench the damned thing off my back and abandon it on the wire, looking for all the world like a ragged escapee picked off by a sniper's bullet. I hoped that wasn't going to be the way I ended up.

I was colder but lighter and much more nimble through the fences now. I sustained several nasty grazes on my wrists and shins as I tramped the wire down with my hands and feet and I avoided crossing it wherever I could, preferring to go to the end of a section and use the struts to get over. As the concertina of wire had been unrolled, the soldiers had clearly chosen the lazy option and staked it at regular intervals: or maybe the climate in this region had required more stringent reinforcement of the defences against the inclement weather. The preponderance of upright struts certainly surprised me but I wasn't about to complain.

I was less than ten yards from the end of the field of wire when the searchlight hit me.

ELEVEN

The movement of the beam across the snow stopped abruptly and I was bathed in a glare of harsh light. It was hard to tell but I thought it was coming from the nearest watchtower. It was soon joined by another.

'*Stop!*'

There was no mistaking that word. The deep voice boomed across the night sky, followed by another, more reedy voice from the next tower along.

'*Co děláš?*'

For a moment I couldn't work out why they hadn't opened fire at this forlorn figure heading for the border through the frozen expanse of no-man's-land. Then it struck me that they would have seen the uniform and were probably bewildered that a colleague of theirs had ventured out into the barbed wire on such a cold night – especially without an overcoat. Maybe I could use it to my advantage.

'Snyd mos blege,' I half-called in the most unintelligible mumbling I could muster. At this distance I hoped it would be impossible for them to make out that I was talking gibberish. I accompanied my nonsense with a vague waving at the barbed wire around me, trying to indicate that perhaps I was undertaking some routine maintenance or plugging gaps in the defences. Quite why I should be doing that at this ungodly hour of the morning was a question I hoped I would never have to answer but it seemed to do the trick for now. I held my hand over my eyes to shield myself from the glare of the searchlight and they seemed to get the message: the beam moved away from me.

More indistinguishable shouts came from both towers and I guessed they were asking me to explain myself. I returned the shout with another meaningless collection of guttural consonants and threw a dismissive wave in their direction. Then I turned back towards the river and pretended to shake one of the struts, as if reassuring myself of its sturdiness. Mimicry or disguise? Whatever it was, I was camouflaging myself in plain sight and I prayed it would work.

Moving from one stake to another, I gradually worked my way to the far edge of the barbed wire, nearest the open snowfield, ignoring the occasional shouts that continued to come in my direction. I took comfort from the fact that the lights stayed off me and if they believed I was just some crazy soldier under instruction to check the fortifications then that was all to the good.

When I reached the bank of the river I stopped and stared out at the blanket of white, tinged blue under the starlight and marking the frontier between the West and this alien land behind the Iron Curtain. I had no idea where the border actually lay and at what point across this virgin field I would technically be on neutral territory but I doubted the soldiers in their watchtowers behind me would draw too fine a distinction if they opened up their machine guns in my direction.

Rattling the last bit of wire to keep up my pretence, I risked looking back towards the castle, trying to weigh up the best moment to make a break.

To my horror, not twenty yards behind me and following me through the prairie of barbed wire came a soldier.

His progress was hampered by the rifle slung over his shoulder and he also wore a long coat that hindered him as he trudged through the snow but he was taking a path that seemed easier than mine had been. I guessed he was a regular out here and knew the quickest and least injurious routes through the wire.

He was focused on his feet but after a moment he looked up in my direction and, when he saw me looking back at him, he raised one hand and shouted.

'*Hej, vojáku!*' He seemed more curious than angry, apparently wanting to talk. '*Co děláš?*'

If he got much closer I would be found out for sure. Leaving aside the problem of not being able to converse with him, once he got a better look at me and my ill-fitting uniform there was no way he would believe I was a genuine Czech guard. I reckoned I had another five yards at best before he rumbled me.

I didn't give him the chance.

Pushing my feet into the firm snow for traction, I launched myself around and ploughed towards the river.

The first cry was one of surprise: I suppose it startled him to imagine that a comrade should suddenly want to run away from him. The second shout was in anger; the third was blind fury. By now I was nearing the middle of the river, figuring that speed was my only friend. It was likely the ice was getting precariously thin by this point but if I kept moving quickly enough I hoped I might skate over any weaknesses underfoot.

I heard a shot ring out – I thought it came from the direction of the soldier rather than from one of the towers – and I ducked instinctively. The minimal available light and the fact that I was running towards trees, which would have made me almost invisible from his standpoint, were working to my advantage and I reckoned he would have to be incredibly fortunate to hit me at that distance and in those circumstances.

The searchlights changed all that.

A brightening of the snow around me alerted me to the fact that the watchtowers had got involved. As I ran, I glanced over my shoulder and saw that they had picked out my pursuer in their beam and he was gesticulating madly back at his colleagues to point the light in my direction instead. I estimated I was past the halfway point and therefore probably on Austrian territory but I knew that wasn't going to stop them. I would be as important to them as a fleeing defector and I had no doubt they would cut me down at any cost rather than allow me to reach the other bank. If I could stay clear of the light I might just have a chance but if they found me with their beam then I would be target practice for every soldier along the border for half a mile in each direction.

Another shot rang out but I was confident that it was purely opportunistic and I ran on without pausing. The snow beneath my feet became more treacherous with every step. I had felt it thin out within a few paces of running and guessed that I was already on a sheet of ice covering the Morava. Every impact of my boot on the surface felt risky and twice I slipped as the surface snow skidded away on the smooth ice beneath.

The third time it happened I stumbled and the searchlight found me.

My knees hit the snow with a heavy thump and I felt the ground beneath me sag ominously. At the same moment the circle of light illuminated my dark figure against the pristine white and half a second later the world erupted around me.

As a barrage of weaponry opened fire from the Czech bank I sensed, rather than saw, what happened. Letting off rounds indiscriminately in the direction of their fugitive, the soldiers bombarded the whole area where I was stranded on the ice. Bullets thudded into the snow nearby and I was sure I was facing my last moments on earth when the river decided it could stand the assault no longer. Weakened by my fall and now pounded by live ammunition, the ice all around me gave way.

I will never fully understand how one of those loose rounds didn't hit me. By some miracle I had evaded death by haphazard firing squad but the result scarcely left me any safer. I was plunged into the freezing depths of the Morava river, a hellscape above me and a chilling killer holding me in its icy grip. I'd managed to grab a lungful of cold air as I submerged but I had little hope of it doing me much good. If I swam in the direction of the Austrian riverbank there was no guarantee I'd be able to break through the ice again to breathe. If I resurfaced where I'd gone in, I'd be cut to pieces in seconds.

Squinting against the vicious cold, I looked up through the murky water at the hole in the ice, the searchlight still concentrating its beam on the jagged edges. It must have been my imagination but I could have sworn the hole was closing up and freezing over as I watched. Treading water a few feet below the surface, I became aware of something knocking against my chest and I thrust a hand inside my shirt pocket to discover the iron latch from the door of my prison cell, still where I'd stuffed it on my breakout from the castle.

I almost took it out and threw it away for fear of its considerable weight dragging me down. Then some instinct kicked in and I knew it could be my saviour rather than my doom. With the bitter chill of the water pressing in on my chest, I wriggled my body in what I hoped was the direction of the Austrian bank and kicked with my legs as hard as I could.

The blackness of the river almost matched that of the unlit cell I'd escaped from. I could easily have been swimming in completely the wrong direction, about to surface right under the noses of the very people I was trying to flee. All I could do was pray and keep swimming for as long as I could, getting as far away as I could from the searchlights. If I was right, I might be able to get pretty close to the far bank and crawl out onto the foreshore unseen after breaking through the ice with the iron latch. Even if the beam spotted me, I couldn't imagine the Czechs would risk an international incident by shooting someone who was plainly on Austrian ground.

I didn't know how deep the Morava was. The Danube, I guessed, probably cut quite a channel at this point in its long journey from the Black Forest to the Black Sea but it was possible that its tributary was much shallower, even where the two merged. The fact that it had iced over was a good sign, suggesting that it may not be too deep and the mercury might not have to fall too far to freeze it. When my flailing feet hit a gravel bank I knew I was near the edge.

I had only moments left before my lungs gave way. I rolled onto my back and began pummelling the ice above me with the latch, fighting to put some weight into it as the water slowed my every action. On the third strike I felt it give and I renewed my efforts until the latch splashed through the surface and I followed it up, gasping for air and wincing at the freezing wind that blew across my face.

I put my legs down below me and found that they touched the bottom with my knees still bent. Casting an anxious glance around to gauge my position, I caught sight of the searchlights over to my right and realised that I had swum further out into the Danube. They were still focused on the point where I'd gone into the river and unless they had a swift and radical change of plan, their beams wouldn't find me all the way over here. But I didn't

want to take any chances and kept my head low in the
water, bobbing through the hole I'd just created with my
makeshift weapon. The night air felt colder even than the
water and I stayed where I was for as long as I dared without wanting to risk hypothermia. I tried to guess if I could
make it all the way across the Danube alive – after all, my
Range Rover was stowed in the trees not far beyond that
shore – but I judged it to be at least three times as far as
the nearest shore and I was already shivering uncontrollably. When I could stand the chilling waters no longer I
used the latch to bang open a wider hole, then stood up at
full height and simply strolled to safety on the bank.

Taking refuge in a thin line of trees, I crept towards the
point where the Morava fed into the Danube and looked
back at the chaos on the far side of the Iron Curtain.

A line of trucks and armoured vehicles had assembled
on the foreshore at the foot of the Devín crag and in the
light of their headlamps I could see dozens of soldiers, like
little beetles, scampering around among the barbed wire
and watchtowers. At least three searchlights still hovered
over and around the hole in the ice, while two or three
more raked the snow on both sides of the Morava. One of
them even came close to the tree line where I was hiding
but stopped short of penetrating the branches. There was
plenty of shouting in what I presumed was Czech or Slovak but could just as easily have been Russian and there
was a general sense of pandemonium in the air. *Christ*, I
thought, *if they're willing to put this much resource into tracking down one escaped prisoner, they really must be paranoid.* Or
maybe I had underestimated my own significance to them
and I was a prize that was too good to abandon so easily.

I could feel my clothes freezing into a crisp, solid mass
around me and the wet chill was seeping into my bones,
so I watched for another five minutes then turned away.

As I left the trees and began crossing a ploughed field,

banging my hands against my arms to keep warm, I wondered what the hell I was going to do next. I was an hour away from Vienna, stranded in a location I didn't know, with no means of transport and precious little of the language to help me. I was also desperately tired. I hadn't eaten for almost twenty-four hours, my clothes were sodden and frozen, and I could still feel the tenderness of the bruises inflicted by The Torturess as I trudged wearily away from the Iron Curtain. The thought crossed my mind that, while I might not have to face the same kind of brutality she'd meted out the night before, I was still far from in the clear with the Austrian authorities. As far as they were concerned, I'd gone AWOL from their custody and no amount of explanation on my part about a mystery jailbreak by a sinister Soviet crew was likely to convince them that I hadn't simply absconded. I couldn't hand myself in here any more than I could have risked it in Bratislava.

My body hurt, my brain hurt and I had no strength left. When I came across a barn at the edge of a field, stacked with wrapped bales of straw, I seized the opportunity. I ripped open one of the bales, pulled out huge handfuls of straw, and bedded down in a corner. I was asleep in seconds.

The sound of an animal nearby woke me. I listened keenly but didn't hear it again. I didn't want to run into the farmer whose barn I'd borrowed, so I threw off the straw that had been keeping me warm and edged to the large opening that served as a door.

My surroundings looked better in the light of day. When I'd crawled into the barn for refuge, the world outside had been one giant ball of blackness – literally and metaphorically. The darkness of the night had cast a bleak pall over my thoughts and the gloom had extended into my dreams. Even now, although I felt bodily refreshed, my head was still caught up in a whirlwind of emotions

and fear. At least the countryside looked more appealing
on this side of the Iron Curtain. Snow still covered everything as far as I could see but I could hear birds singing
and sheep braying in the distance.

I wondered what time it was and how long I'd slept.
I couldn't recall exactly when or how but at some point
in one of the two prison cells where I'd been a guest the
past couple of nights, I had evidently been relieved of my
Grand Seiko and the pettiness of it got under my skin.
The sun was hiding behind a layer of pale grey cloud so
I couldn't gauge the time from that, but I guessed I must
have slept for several hours, judging by the feeling of recu-
peration in my bones. I contemplated scouting around for
a farmhouse and begging for something to eat but I realised that the uniform I was wearing would be instantly
recognisable to the natives in these parts and the last thing
I wanted was to be mistaken for the enemy and rounded
up – or, worse, shot on sight. I decided I would do better
making my own way in the direction of Vienna; if I was
lucky I might be able to pinch a change of clothes or at
least an overcoat from some remote property, along with
a bite to eat. I've never considered myself a thief but my
needs were pressing and I didn't think I had much choice.

I wanted to get as far away from the border as I could
and I knew the river would eventually lead me back to the
Austrian capital. Using the Danube as my guide, I stayed
half a mile or so inland and began walking. The farmland
in this corner of the country was flat and crisscrossed with
a network of tracks that I presumed were only ever used
by the landowners. Behind me, the castle crag and the hills
behind it became less and less prominent, fading towards
the horizon and losing their menace the further I walked.

A couple of miles from the barn where I'd slept I had a
stroke of luck. I came across a pair of single-storey houses,
painted white, facing each other across a rough track and

each surrounded by a hedge. I approached them carefully, watching for signs of life, but the first one I reached
looked abandoned. Its front door swung open and I poked
my head inside to see if there was anything worth salvag-
ing. The room was bare to its floorboards.

Across the road, its neighbour was almost empty
but this time not abandoned. After peering furtively in
through windows and making sure there was nobody at
home, I used the iron latch I was still carrying to break a
small pane in the back door and reached inside to turn the
key that rested in the lock. Security was evidently not a
major concern around here.

I didn't stay long: I had no intention of burgling the
place. I found a stick of Austrian sausage in the fridge,
attacking it hungrily before stuffing the remainder in
a cloth bag I found hanging on the back of the kitchen
door. A quick search of a chest of drawers in one bedroom
revealed a thick – and, importantly, dry – sweater, while
the inside of the front door offered me a heavy overcoat
and hand-knitted scarf. I wondered if the scarf in particular had a personal attachment for its owner but decided I
couldn't afford to be sentimental. I emptied the pockets
of the guard's uniform, feeling far less guilty about pur-
loining his wallet than I had about the sausage, and trans-
ferred everything into the overcoat, adding a few coins I'd
found in the kitchen: I didn't imagine the guard's Czech
currency would be much use to me in Austria. Then I
stuffed the uniform jacket at the back of a wardrobe,
where it would doubtless cause considerable confusion
when it was discovered at some point in the future.

I was letting myself out of the back door when I heard
a vehicle engine approaching.

I dodged past the hedge that surrounded the building,
making sure I was out of sight of the driver, and waited to
see what would happen. With the fields stretching out flat

to all points of the compass, I didn't want to risk making a run for it: I would almost certainly have been seen if the homeowner happened to turn in the right direction and it would have been the work of minutes to chase me down in their vehicle and apprehend me. The idea of theft being added to my charge sheet with the *Stadtpolizei* did not appeal.

The driver came to a halt and climbed out of the cab. Then he went into the house, leaving the engine running. The vehicle was a farm truck of the kind that must have been ubiquitous in this neighbourhood – equipped for all kinds of weather and geared for the terrain. I thought about jumping in and driving it away but figured that would be too big a chance. Registration plates are easily traceable and one phone call to the police would have half of Lower Austria on my trail. Instead, I watched as the owner emerged again, evidently having missed the broken window pane in his back door, and climbed back into the truck. With an overenthusiastic revving of the engine, he swung the vehicle onto the track and tore off in the direction from which he'd arrived.

Warmer, with some food inside me and better dressed for the conditions, I set off on foot after the truck. I was aware of the risks of travelling by road but the odds of being found accidentally by a police officer seemed remote and I stood a much better chance of stumbling across civilisation this way than by continuing my journey cross-country. Twenty minutes later, as small flakes of snow started to fall from the leaden sky, I hit a main road and tossed a mental coin as to whether to go left or right. I must have called it correctly because ten minutes after that, I was standing at a bus stop waiting for a lift to take me back to Vienna.

PART TWO

The Enemy

TWELVE

'Herr Kemp – how delightful to see you again. Are you feeling better?'

I looked curiously at Roland as I collected my room key. 'Why do you ask?'

'I – I thought you must have been unwell. I haven't seen you since we discussed my hat yesterday morning and I presumed you were resting in your room. Clearly I was wrong.'

It struck me that Roland's misconception might be something I could use to my advantage: it certainly wouldn't do any harm for him to believe I had spent the past day and a half holed up in the Viennese suburbs if anyone came noseying around asking awkward questions.

'No, no – you are right. I wasn't feeling too good yesterday.' I rubbed my stomach dramatically. 'Must have been overdoing it on the schnitzel. But I'm feeling much better today, thank you.'

'Indeed. Well enough to go out into the city again.'

For a hotel desk clerk, he made a damned good detective.

I smiled indulgently at him and took the proffered key. He held it a little longer than he should have done and I realised there was unfinished business to be addressed.

'I'm terribly sorry but I'm afraid I put your hat down somewhere while I was out and I seem to have left it behind. I know I promised to return it to you but I will of course replace it. If you'd like to buy yourself a new one and let me know how much to reimburse you – ?'

'That will not be necessary, Herr Kemp.'

'Oh no, I insist. You did me a great favour by lending it to me and I would hate to see you out of pocket on my account.'

He bowed slightly and inclined his head. 'You are very kind.'

'Not at all. The least I can do.' I smiled again and started to move towards the hotel lifts.

'Perhaps I could leave a note in your pigeon hole?' he said.

I looked back and saw him indicating the rows of wooden slots behind the reception desk where notes and mail could be left for residents alongside their room keys.

'In case I don't see you again.'

I spent the rest of the afternoon getting myself straightened out in my hotel room. I had a couple of chunky sandwiches sent up by room service, along with a bottle of local Riesling, and sat in the bath for more than an hour letting the heat sink into my aching bones and the alcohol warm my spirits.

The bruises on my arms, legs and ribcage were ripening to a rich purple and I knew there would be several more days of tenderness to endure. After drying myself off and wrapping myself in the cosy bathrobe supplied courtesy of the hotel, I sat at the desk staring hard at the heavy cell-door latch I'd brought with me all the way from behind the Iron Curtain. It had served me well on at least three occasions, I reflected, and I was reluctant to part with it but I couldn't see myself negotiating my way through an airport customs search with what amounted to an offensive weapon.

The thought of airports brought me firmly back to the present and I realised I was caught in an impossible quandary. There was no way I would be able to leave the country, with my name and face no doubt distributed to all potential points of exit, unless I fancied a spot of Von Trapp hiking across the Alps. My experience of anything mountainous was limited – while I could get by on a pair of skis I had never tried climbing – and I had no desire to deepen my acquaintance with such hair-raising pursuits in the depths of winter and with an unknown enemy at my heels. On top of my mysterious Czech kidnappers, I had also to contend with the Austrian authorities, for whom I was a fugitive from the law, an escaped prisoner and a wanted man. My pleas that I knew nothing of my true purpose in their country had already fallen on deaf ears once and the memory of Napoleon's smug face as he warned of a long spell behind bars gave me no confidence that it would work any better the second time around. There was, of course, the option of walking into the British Embassy in Vienna and stating my case truthfully but I had serious doubts about that. For one thing, I had made myself a slur on the good name of British tourism in Austria; for another, I couldn't imagine the ambassadorial diplomats would be all that bothered about protecting the interests of a man who'd been busted from a Viennese cell after being arrested on suspicion of murder. I feared that their obligations to a British national would not include harbouring a violent criminal, no matter how hard I argued my innocence.

As I thought about it, I realised I was again behind the curve: every minute I sat here in this tourist hotel I was leaving myself open to being found and incarcerated once more. Or worse. It wasn't just the Austrians who might come looking, but The Torturess herself; she'd already nabbed me once from behind foreign bars so I couldn't imagine that a hotel would be much of a barrier to her, and now she had the added spur of being slighted by my escape. The only question was how long it might take her to find out precisely where I was. Something turned over in my stomach at the thought that she might, even now, be walking into the lobby two floors below with a grimace on her face and a loaded gun in her pocket. In fact, the more I considered it, the more surprising it seemed that she hadn't already tracked me down. As for the *Stadtpolizei*, Roland had helped me slip out before but could he be relied upon to protect me again if they came calling? Somehow I didn't think his loyalty to the hotel's clientele would extend that far, especially since he was currently one fedora down on the deal.

I packed my suitcase as quickly as I could, wincing in discomfort as I pressed down to close it, and let myself quietly out of my room. I needed to find another place to stay but I also needed to leave here without officially checking out – and that was a problem since they held my passport in their safe. I wondered if Roland would be game enough to let me have it but rejected that idea on the grounds that it would raise even more suspicions, not least in Roland's mind, and I wanted to keep him on side if I possibly could.

There was another option which, the more I thought about it, took on the appearance of the only one available to me: I would have to leave my passport where it was in the hotel safe. If I could exit the building unseen through the back alley then the assumption would be that I was still recuperating in my room from whatever intestinal penalty the rogue schnitzel had induced.

Surely nobody would think I had fled without my passport?

I used the stairs to reach the ground floor then hovered in the rear lobby, listening for sounds in the kitchen, which led off the passageway I needed to use to get to the back entrance. When I heard a lull in activity I made a dash for the door, escaping into the evening air as a voice emerged into the corridor behind me. I didn't think it was directed at me but I didn't hang about heading for the gate onto the road. As I had done forty-eight hours earlier, I turned right, keeping my head down and moving fast away from the hotel and into the warren of back streets that made up this district of Vienna.

I walked for half an hour, trying to cover the ground methodically and constantly on the lookout for lodgings that might not be so particular about the need for a passport. I guessed that would mean somewhere considerably less agreeable than my previous resting place but I was in no position to be picky. The best I could hope for was to find a boarding house or hostel where I might be able to blag my way in without the need for my papers. It felt like a long shot but I had little choice but to try.

The first two places I ruled out even before passing the front desk because their proprietors – or whoever was in charge of reception – spoke no English. I needed something more practical, even if I couldn't have the benefit of another Roland. The third I almost missed, its tiny door tucked up a side alley off a pedestrian street deep in the heart of the district. It had a wooden name plate tacked to the wall beside the door, announcing it as the Pension Fräulein Maria, and it looked like just the kind of place I needed: anonymous, out-of-the-way and unlikely. I stepped into the tiny lobby, where a dark carpet led away to a wooden staircase, the whole ensemble interrupted only by a small table that served as a reception desk.

Behind it sat a young woman with the warmest smile I'd seen in my time in Austria.

'*Wie geht's?*'

I plumbed the shallows of my German. '*Sprechen Sie Englisch?*'

She nodded keenly. 'Yes, I have some *Englisch* – little. I write to…' She searched for the phrase she wanted. 'Friend with pen, yes?'

'Pen pal.'

'Yes, pen pal. Henrietta. She live London. You know her?'

I offered up a silent word of thanks for Henrietta in London, whoever she may be, and hoped her letters to this girl had passed on a level of language mastery decent enough to be able to hold a conversation.

'I'm afraid I don't, no. But London is a big place.'

She giggled self-deprecatingly. 'Of course. The question was a silly one.'

'No, not at all. It's possible I might have met her. You know what they say: it's a small world.' A look of incomprehension passed across her face and I suspected I'd reached the limits of her idiomatic English. 'Anyway, do you have a room available?'

She brightened again. 'Room? Yes – we have room. One people or two?'

'Just me,' I said, and wondered if I detected a twinkle in her eye.

'How many long?'

It was my turn to look confused, until her meaning dawned on me. 'Oh, how long for – how many nights?'

'Yes.'

I didn't know. I had yet to work out what my next move should be but I wanted somewhere quiet to do my thinking and I reckoned I should ask for three nights initially, with the possibility of extending further in the event of more thinking time being necessary. I condensed that thought process into as simple a phrase as I could.

'Three. Maybe more later.'

'Is OK. Three, maybe more. I show you.'

She waved at my suitcase on the floor beside me and I picked it up, ready to follow her.

'Don't you want me to pay first?'

She laughed again, the giggle infectious. 'Oh – yes, please.'

She told me the rate, which sounded paltry, even allowing for the conversion from Austrian Schillings, and I handed over a fistful of notes to cover at least a week. She looked down at the wad and back at me. 'Is too much.'

'Keep it,' I said. 'You can give it back to me if I don't use it up.'

I wasn't convinced she understood me completely but she seemed to get the gist. In any case she pocketed the money – no drawer in the table, I noticed – invited me to sign the reception register, and turned for the stairs. She hadn't asked for my passport and I hadn't volunteered it.

My room was a pale imitation of the comparatively grand salon I'd enjoyed in my previous establishment. It was barely large enough to accommodate the single bed that hugged one wall and the wardrobe and table that stood on the other side. Its sole advantage, at least from my perspective, was that it overlooked the front of the building from the first floor, giving me uninterrupted views of any comings and goings from behind a rather grubby-looking net curtain. With the lights out, I could sit on the bed and survey the street outside in comfort – or what passed for comfort in this hostel.

I soon came to the conclusion that watching the world pass by was hardly a productive use of my time so I took a sheet of paper and a pencil from the table and began to make a list. In the left-hand column I wrote down all the possibilities I could think of for how to get home. On the right, I listed all the reasons why I should stay in Vienna. By the end of the exercise, one column was considerably longer than the other.

I had already decided that if I were going to remain in Austria I would need to find a way of making myself available to the anonymous caller who had originally started me on this mission. I might not know what I was doing here but I had to see it through somehow, for Leotta's sake if not for my own sanity. And that meant I would have to check in at the other hotel regularly to see if someone had tried to reach me. I could also pay a visit to the Café Central, even though being visible in a high-profile location in the centre of the city was not my idea of remaining inconspicuous. While I would far rather stay hidden in the suburbs, the venue did seem to be a logical place to re-establish contact.

I skipped breakfast in the hostel's dingy dining room the next morning and headed for the front door, smiling grimly at the same young girl on the reception desk as I left.

'*Guten morgen, Herr Smith,*' she called after me, using the pseudonym I'd signed in with the previous evening. I waved a hand in hurried greeting and banged open the door.

A steady rain was falling and the snow beginning to melt away under its barrage as I snaked my way vaguely back towards the city centre. I took a deliberately circuitous route, even though there was no chance of my being followed, and I wondered if I had become obsessively suspicious in the course of the previous couple of days. Nobody would blame me if I had – I was sure of that – but it wasn't a trait I took kindly to in others and I didn't want to develop it in myself if I could avoid it. Maybe Vienna bred self-doubt: *The Third Man*, after all, exploited exactly that mood. In the long shadows of winter, every baroque pinnacle or Habsburg frontage seemed to recall the Dutch angles of Carol Reed's cinematography and the oppressive black-and-white footage that had hidden Orson Welles's villainous character in the dark ruins of the city. I brushed off the thought, convincing myself that Vienna was nothing less than the jewel of an empire that had left a remarkable legacy on this part of Europe. Besides, far from being monochrome and dull, all around me was a riot of colour in the fruit and vegetables of the market stalls, the flags draped from balconies and the post-festive afterglow of a living snow globe. This escapade wasn't going to finish in the sewers, I decided: I was going to come out on top.

When I reached the Café Central I decided against going in and sitting at a table. That would be just too provocative. Instead, I watched from the foyer of the Palais Niederösterreich opposite, concealing myself behind a newspaper I'd bought from a little shop nearby. All it needed was a homburg to make my transformation complete. After a fruitless half-hour I ventured across to the entrance and caught the eye of the same maître d' who'd been so obsequious on my previous visit. He didn't seem to remember me.

'My name is Kemp,' I said. 'Has anyone left any messages for me here?'

'One moment,' the man replied, and went over to a colleague at a desk in the centre of the ornate room. The pair conversed briefly, with the maître d' gesturing in my direction, but the other shook his head.

'I believe there have been no messages for anyone named Kemp,' said the maître d' on his return. 'Does sir have a forwarding address if that situation should change?'

I marvelled again at the facility of so many Austrians with the English language but declined his invitation to leave any contact details. It was risky enough that I'd given him my name.

I wandered back in the direction of the hostel, passing the university and Schottentor and picking up a bratwurst from a street vendor to stave off the rumblings in my stomach. I avoided the trams – they were too easy to get trapped on – but walked a mile or so along the familiar line of the track towards my original hotel. As I walked I made another decision: to hell with the subterfuge. I would stroll nonchalantly up to reception and ask Roland openly for any messages. There seemed to me to be two possible threats: The Torturess's gang could be inside, but I figured they wouldn't risk anything in the public lobby and, if they had turned up, would probably already be waiting in my room. The other risk was Roland himself, but if he were to be a secret informant of the police, I would be long gone before he had the chance to tip anyone off that I'd been there. I didn't suspect him – he seemed far too nice and innocent for that – but I concluded that I didn't care, whatever the outcome.

Roland wasn't there when I skipped up the few steps into the hotel.

'I'm Kemp – room 217. Are there any messages?'

The woman behind the desk looked drained and disoriented, her mind not fully on the job. 'Herr Kemp? Yes, I believe there was something left for you this morning.'

She turned to the row of pigeon holes and retrieved a small, sealed, white envelope from the one corresponding to my room. As she handed it over, she let out a despairing sigh of the sort one doesn't expect from one's hotel staff.

'Is everything all right?' I asked idly, my mind more on the envelope I'd stuffed into my pocket than on the emotional wellbeing of the clerk. It could, after all, hold the answer to my next steps.

She held my gaze for a second or two before a single

tear fell from the corner of one eye onto her cheek. 'No, Herr Kemp. Not really. Everything is not all right.'

'What on earth's the matter?'

'We have just heard some terrible news. The police are still here, talking to the manager.' She waved a hand behind her in the direction of the office door. I looked over, alarmed, and wanted to get away but I needed to hear the news.

'What's happened?'

She steadied her breathing and looked up at me again. 'We may need to close the hotel. A colleague of ours has been killed.'

'Killed? How?' I hardly dared to listen to her answer.

Another tear fell and a crack emerged in the woman's voice. 'My friend Roland. He went out for his lunch and never came back.'

I felt a nauseating lump rise in my throat as I remembered the last conversation I had had with Roland the previous evening before I slipped out of the hotel's back alley. I was about to ask the woman how he had died when she burst into tears and ran for the office.

As she crashed through the door behind her I caught a glimpse of the coat hooks inside. On the nearest one hung a brand new fedora.

I lay on my bed at the hostel and stared unseeingly at the ceiling. The nausea had subsided a little but I still felt wretched, unable to shake off the notion that by inveigling Roland into my subterfuge I had somehow laid him open to becoming a target. While I couldn't know for sure that he hadn't been the victim of a simple accident – knocked down by a lorry in the street outside, perhaps – the way his colleague had reacted and the presence of the police convinced me that his death had been anything but accidental. The question that kept resounding in the empty halls of my brain was simple enough: who had targeted him? But, like the oysters in *The Walrus and the Carpenter*, answer came there none.

I discounted the *Stadtpolizei* immediately. Regardless of any suspicions they may have had about Roland's involvement in my escape from their custody, murder was not part of their armoury. That left two options: either the people who had initially enlisted me in this deadly game wanted to tidy up their trail or The Torturess had indeed tracked me back to Vienna. If that were true, she – or members of her gang – could have kidnapped Roland as he went out on his lunch break and used foul means to extract from him my movements. It was certainly not beyond the far reaches of my imagination to suppose that their methods might have gone too far and Roland had succumbed to their brutality. I wished I'd discovered more about his death before fleeing the hotel but I couldn't risk sticking around there with the police in the building.

Of course, it was also possible that my puppetmasters and The Torturess were one and the same, but that notion scrambled my brain too much even to contemplate.

Whoever was responsible for Roland's murder – and I could come up with no less a word for it than that – I kept returning to the inevitable conclusion that his death was somehow wrapped up in my mysterious business. And that made me ultimately responsible. As I lay there in the darkening gloom I made a promise to myself and to Roland that I would seek out his killers and effect some kind of justice.

I just couldn't begin to think of how.

I sat up on the bed and stared out of the window at the street below, lights reflecting in the puddles of melting snow that streaked the tarmac. My mind wandered from Roland to Leotta, the other innocent caught up unwittingly in this whole nightmare, and I wondered if she had any idea of what was going on. If by some miracle we both got out of this alive I was going to make damn sure we made the most of it: I'd been lax in allowing our friendship to cool once she'd departed for medical school but the idea of her in danger had reminded me of the feelings I'd had for her during that summer together, and in the chill of the Viennese night I was suddenly overcome with a strong desire to feel them again. The odd dispassionate letter between us would no longer be sufficient.

The thought of a letter jolted me back to the present and I jumped up to search the pockets of my coat: with the shocking news about Roland I'd completely forgotten about the envelope I'd shoved there. I hoped it would be something more helpful than a bill for a new fedora. I ripped it open unceremoniously and pulled out a single folded sheet of white paper.

Delivery, the typed note was headed. *St Josef auf dem Kahlenberg, 2pm tomorrow.*

Perhaps I had a remote chance of avenging Roland's death after all.

THIRTEEN

With no package to deliver and two deaths on my conscience, I would be walking blindfold into a minefield at the drop-off the following afternoon. I spent a sleepless night mulling over how to approach the rendezvous and how I could wrangle the situation to extricate myself and Leotta from it. I didn't imagine for a moment that anyone would believe I had been kidnapped and whisked off behind the Iron Curtain only to undertake an unlikely escape and reappear at a meeting, albeit without their precious package. The very fact that they had left a message for me at my original hotel suggested they were completely unaware of the events of the past two days. It was quite possible that they wouldn't even know Anna Stern was dead and if it was me breaking the news to them then I was putting myself in considerable danger. If they decided that I was responsible for her death, who knew what their reaction might be? The truth, of course, was that I was responsible for it but only in the sense that I was trammelled up in something way beyond my comprehension and it was the fact of my presence that had led to her being killed rather than any direct action on my part.

One other consideration troubled me: it seemed entirely

reasonable to imagine that the delivery I was expected to make was to a group who might be just as cold-blooded and ruthless as The Torturess and her crew. I might be merely the messenger but I had a nasty feeling that wouldn't stop them from shooting me if it was expedient to do so.

I rose early and put on my warmest clothes. There had been a fresh fall of snow overnight and, judging by the frost on the outside of my window, the temperature was below zero. I had a busy morning ahead of me and didn't want to waste any time. I headed out into the dark suburbs and began searching for an open newsagent.

Three streets away I found what I was looking for. I bought a fresh clutch of maps, timetables and guidebooks in English, stuffing them into my inside coat pocket. It took longer to find a shop dealing in cameras, watches and optical equipment but I finally stumbled across one just when I was about to give up the hunt. I bought a cheap wristwatch and an expensive pair of binoculars, figuring that besides meeting my current requirements the field glasses would get plenty of use back home studying seabirds and dinghies – if I ever made it back home.

When I returned to the hostel the girl on the front desk had been replaced by a grumpy older man who didn't glance up from his newspaper as I hurried past to the stairs. Back in my room, I threw off my coat and dropped my purchases onto the table. I began scouring the guidebooks, searching first for St Josef, and quickly discovered it was the name of a Catholic church constructed high on a mountainside – the Kahlenberg – to the north of the city. The church had started life as a monastery inhabited by hermits and serving the village of Josefsdorf but was razed by invading Turks in 1683. Its replacement had fallen into disrepair before being revived in the early twentieth century. It seemed like an odd place for the delivery but maybe its remoteness from the city offered the advantage of secrecy.

The Kahlenberg itself had an interesting history, from its original name of Pig Mountain – after the wild boars that roamed in its medieval oak forests – to its acquisition and stewardship by a succession of emperors. There had even been an assault launched from the mountain on those damned Turks by a Polish king, who now found himself memorialised in a chapel inside the St Josef church. I hoped my forthcoming encounter on the snow-capped peak would prove to be substantially less violent.

I turned my attention to the timetables, working out how I could get myself up there. I wondered what had happened to the hired Range Rover I'd abandoned near the Danube and whether it had even been discovered yet but I vetoed the idea of hiring another, opting instead for the anonymity of public transport. The city's tram network would take me as far as Nussdorf, at the end of the D line, and I would be able to catch a bus from there to the summit and beyond, following a winding road which the map suggested might be pretty hairy in the depths of winter. I only hoped it was passable – I certainly didn't relish the prospect of a trek on foot to the heights of the Kahlenberg – but then I reminded myself that Alpine and Nordic countries were so much better at dealing with extremes of weather than back in Britain, where a lingering snowflake could shut down the entire rail system for a week.

I gave myself plenty of time for the journey, especially since I wanted to arrive early to scope out the territory. From what I could gauge from the maps, the top of the mountain stood slightly higher than the site of St Josef's and I decided I would try to go past the church and descend on it from above, buses permitting. Not only would it give me the benefit of an unexpected approach but I hoped it would also allow me to study the terrain before walking into the minefield.

The tram trundled through the city's northern districts, throngs of people in dark clothes going about their everyday business on the streets either side of the track. The carriages rattled and rumbled along their iron channels for miles, oblivious to the conditions, and I stared out through windows fogged by mist at the normality of the world outside. At one point the route took us along the enormous frontage of the Karl-Marx-Hof residential complex, stretching for more than a thousand yards along the Heiligenstädter Strasse, and I marvelled not only at the social engineering that had gone into such a vast municipal enterprise but also the readiness to embrace what could have seemed a contentious historical name. I didn't imagine Marxism was the most popular philosophy in this corner of the world, just a stone's throw from communism.

As the track swung away to the left we started up a slow but steady incline that would soon spell the end of the line. I dismounted at the terminus, where the trams looped around an imposing restaurant to head back in the opposite direction, and sought out the nearest bus stop. I didn't have to wait long for a connection to the route that would take me up the mountain.

Every winding turn that the bus took opened up the tantalising possibility of a new, more impressive vista the higher we rose, but even in their winter garb the trees were dense enough to obscure the full view. Every now and then I got a glimpse of what lay beyond the forest, down in the river valley, but the glimpses were frustratingly thin and I realised my sightseeing would have to wait.

The bus turned a final corner and eased into a large car park, which my guidebooks had told me served the church and a nearby hotel and restaurant, perched on the hillside with panoramic views. So much for the privacy of the mountain. Fortunately the bus stopped quickly, before we reached a bend that would have revealed the church, and

I was able to slip quietly into the trees unseen. I scrambled up a bank of scraggy roots and wet snow to gain height above the church and was surprised to find my route cut off by a wire mesh fence. Going left would have deposited me straight back out into the car park, so I went the other direction instead and took the long way round. At the edge nearest the mountain peak there was a damaged section of fence and I worked it loose enough to crawl through. Inside whatever compound the fence protected, I began working my way back down the slope to seek out a vantage point from which I could survey the rendezvous spot. As I topped a small mound of earth, I was amazed to find myself in the middle of what looked like an industrial construction site, oddly out of place up this mountain high above the city of Vienna. Giant lengths of metal tubing lay stretched out on the ground, with huge coils of steel cables wrapped among them. I dropped into a crouch for fear of running into any workmen on the site but it all seemed quiet. Ahead of me lay a sizeable field of concrete, to my layman's eyes the groundwork for a significant structure, and beyond it, one of the strangest buildings I had ever seen.

Rising at least seventy feet into the air stood a tower, perhaps twelve feet square and layered in alternating red and cream brick. At the top, what looked like a viewing platform spread wider than its base, giving the whole thing the look of a bizarre ice cream cone. After a moment it dawned on me: I had stumbled on the site of the giant radio mast which relayed VHF signals from Vienna to the rest of the world. I recalled from the guidebooks that the brick building had been constructed earlier as part of the old cog railway which ran up the Kahlenberg, and it had served as the control tower for the radio transmitter before falling into disuse. Now the old transmitter itself was being replaced and the concrete footings would soon provide the base for a new mast, expected to climb more than five hundred feet into the Austrian skies.

With construction seemingly well under way, and the transmitter still in daily use, I thought I'd better make myself scarce before someone happened upon me. I turned to the downward slope behind me and headed back into the trees. Over to my right I could make out the impression of a path that seemed to run from the brick observation tower down to the church. I avoided the track itself but followed its route through the trees, about twenty yards parallel to it.

Two hundred yards down the hillside, as the path fed down to the road beside the St Josefkirche, I stopped and took stock of my position.

From my vantage point above the church, peering out from the Vienna woods, the view was stunning. The scenery was whitewashed in snow and the mighty Danube revealed its bluest self as it wound through the landscape. With the rising mountain behind me and the expansive horizon stretching out to the east in front, it was easy to see why the Turks had favoured this approach on their mission to sack the city. Through my new binoculars I peered intently along the dark ribbon of river and wondered whether, on a clear day, the view extended as far as Czechoslovakia and the high crag of Devín Castle, currently lost in the distant clouds. It was a sight I was in no hurry to witness again.

Instead, I focused my attention on the church that stood between me and the view. St Josef's was a large, white-painted building, simple in its construction and topped by a square verdigris spire. I estimated it to be about three storeys in height, with a door firmly closed at its nearest western end. There seemed to be nobody about – there had been no other passengers alighting at the bus stop – and I checked my watch to see just how early I was for the designated meeting. Scampering across the mountainside had cost me time and I saw that it was a mere ten minutes until the appointed hour. I felt no urge to be punctual and I owed these bastards nothing so I settled in for a decent wait as I surveyed the situation and prepared to weigh up my imminent acquaintances.

As I leaned against the trunk of a wintering oak I thought back to the telephone conversations I had had with the anonymous caller back in Devon. In my mind I had cast him as a thickset, middle-aged man, possibly balding and undoubtedly short in stature. I realised my imagined portrait of him had probably been coloured by the reality of the Napoleon of the Viennese *Stadtpolizei*, whose interrogation had been revealed as distinctly amateur in comparison with my subsequent treatment at the hands of The Torturess. I tried to remember the timbre of the man's voice on the phone, recalling only that there had been little discernible emotion as he switched smoothly between civility and cruelty. Was I about to meet him? And if so, would his physical appearance match the picture I had conjured up in my mind?

The time ticked past two o'clock. Nothing happened.

At ten past I began to wonder if I had misread the note and maybe got the wrong church: there must be plenty of St Josefs in and around Vienna. But no, I assured myself, the message had definitely referenced St Josef auf dem Kahlenberg and as far as I knew there wasn't even another church on the mountain, let alone another St Josef's. The only conclusion I could reach was that they were playing a similar game to mine and that spooked me. All the evidence suggested that, whoever they were, they were professionals at this game and I had no inflated sense of my own abilities: I knew that if it came to it, I would surely be outwitted by superior skills and overpowered by greater numbers. This was no solo operation.

Whoever had summoned me might also be watching the church from a distance, wanting me to make the first move and put myself into the line of sight. If so, then the woods were by far the most logical option and I was overcome with a sudden sense of unease that there might be somebody else lurking in the trees nearby. I hugged tighter to my oak and attempted a full visual sweep of the surrounding area. I could see no movement among the branches but then, I reasoned, if they really were professionals, why should I expect to see any movement? I was left with the discomforting notion that I was the quarry here, not the hunter.

And then I heard voices.

From the far side of the church, towards some buildings that I assumed were the hotel and restaurant overlooking the panorama, came the unmistakable sound of two men in conversation. Although I could not make out specific words, from the intonation I immediately gathered that the pair were speaking English. The voices were getting louder and I guessed the men were talking to one another as they approached the church. I was still struggling to make out actual words but something else set my antennae alight: alongside an upper-crust, Queen's English accent, carried on a resonant, booming tone, the second speaker's articulation had a quality I recognised. With drawn-out and flattened vowels and an intonation that was inclined to rise at the end of a phrase, I knew I was hearing the voice of an Australian.

When the pair rounded the corner of the church into my sightline, my jaw fell open. There, strolling cosily beside a man in the uniform of a British Army brigadier, came my old friend Kenny Hines.

FOURTEEN

Kenny Hines was a man I knew I could trust. It wasn't just our long history over two decades, spread across two continents, or the fact that we'd been through so much together the previous year, when the horrific business in the outback had proved unbelievably testing for all concerned. Those alone were things that would have bonded us in ways that could hardly be verbalised. But the tragedies that had befallen both of us, albeit in differing circumstances, had formed an even closer link: we were united in a certain kind of grief that only its victims can fully understand. Paste that on top of a connection forged in the artificially knitted confines of national service and you've got the basis for a lifelong friendship.

So what on earth was he doing in Austria, fronting for an outfit of killers?

And why was he in the company of a senior military officer?

The only explanation that sprang to mind, as I dodged back behind my tree to avoid being seen while I thought it through, was that the army had got to the villains before me. Somehow, word had got out about my rendezvous and the boys in uniform had turned up first. The host of questions that threw up were not going to be answered by my remaining in hiding but they crowded in on my overburdened brain nonetheless. How had they got wind of the drop? What did it have to do with the army anyway? And what had happened at St Josefkirche before I arrived on the mountain? There was no sign of any confrontation and the voices of Kenny and his brigadier buddy seemed calm enough. But then there was the overarching question mark over Kenny's presence in the middle of a frozen Europe at all: that could only mean they knew of my involvement in the project and had drafted him in for his personal expertise. It was too much of a coincidence to suppose there could be any other reason for his being here.

The two men stopped near the door of the church and continued in what appeared to be casual conversation, the brigadier checking his watch from time to time. I worked things all ways around in my head for another five minutes but got no closer to reaching any satisfactory conclusions. The one constant I kept returning to was that Kenny Hines was a man I knew I could trust.

On that basis, I stepped out of the trees and shouted a greeting.

'Kenny, you old bastard!'

The pair interrupted their chatter immediately and stared at me. Even at this distance I could see that I had caught Kenny by surprise. I don't know what he expected – for me to stroll nonchalantly around the corner from the bus stop with a package in my hand, perhaps – but it certainly wasn't this. I blundered down the last few feet of the slope and reached the road as he crossed from the church, arms outstretched for one of his bear hugs. The relief of feeling his warmth, both physical and emotional, made me catch my breath and I let him keep hold of me for longer than usual. After the last couple of days, contact with a friendly face meant more to me than I'd realised and I relished the moment.

When he finally let me free of the hug he took hold of both my arms in his hands and stood smiling inanely at me.

'It's good to see you,' I said simply.

'You too, mate. You too.'

'But what are you doing here?'

Kenny didn't have a chance to answer before the brigadier caught up with us, a hand out towards me.

'Mr Kemp, I presume?' The accent was every bit as cut-glass as I'd supposed.

I met his hand tentatively. 'Not as memorable as Dr Livingstone, I'm afraid, but it's the only name I've got.'

He chuckled and the whole of his sizeable frame shook inside the uniform, his epaulettes heavy with the showy insignia of his rank. If you'd asked me to draw a picture of the classic brigadier in the British Army, this man would have come close. He had a full, waxed moustache that stood proud from his upper lip, gingerish hair combed neatly to one side and a ruddy complexion which, together with the sandy thatch, implied Scottish origins. A pair of wire spectacles perched on his prominent nose and under his left arm he'd tucked his forage cap. The famous trenches cartoonist Bruce Bairnsfather could hardly have drawn a more caricatured figure.

'But you've got the advantage of me,' I added inquiringly, letting go of his firm handshake.

Kenny waved an introduction in both our directions. 'Bill, this is Brigadier Campbell-Medlock.'

The big man laughed again. 'I know – it's quite a mouthful, isn't it? Please, call me Angus.'

'If you insist,' I said. 'But with that Caledonian pedigree I'd have at least expected a gentle Borders brogue, if not the full Glaswegian.'

'Had it knocked out of me early on,' said the brigadier. 'Eton and Sandhurst.' He almost looked embarrassed. 'Now, I imagine you have questions.'

The café was positioned to make the most of the view. Separated from the adjoining hotel to allow for passing clientele as well as residents, it had evidently been designed by an architect with an eye for a panorama and the mountain had delivered on all counts. Below the terrace, which was encased in glass from floor to ceiling to maximise the opportunity, the hillside dropped away dramatically, giving an arresting perspective on Vienna and the surrounding region. Without the church and other buildings obscuring the foreground, as they had from my vantage point back in the trees, it was a vast white expanse, bifurcated by the dark river and with spires, towers and forests pushing through the blanket at various junctures in greys and greens.

Even in my pent-up emotional state I let out a whistle of admiration as Kenny and the brigadier invited me to sit at a table by the window.

'Impressive, isn't it?' said the brigadier.

'I'll say. If I were a resident I think I'd probably spend most of my time up here.' I turned away from the view for a moment and inspected the café. The place was empty apart from a soldier in sergeant's uniform who appeared to be standing guard at the door. 'Talking of residents, why isn't there anyone here?'

'Oh, don't worry about that, mate,' said Kenny. 'We've requisitioned the place for the afternoon. The locals can't do enough to help these army boys – isn't that right, Angus?'

The brigadier smiled tolerantly. 'It seems they have a rather inflated sense of our potential to prevent the other lot from invading.' He nodded vaguely towards the Czech border and I shivered inwardly. Having seen the alternative up close, I could quite understand why the Viennese might prefer having Nato forces on their doorstep, however much it might affect café trade.

I took the cup of coffee proffered by a timid waitress, then waited for her to depart into the kitchen before launching into my tirade.

'Right, I want to know every bloody thing that's going on here. I need explanations, names, reasons – anything you can tell me about why I'm here and what the hell this is all about.'

Kenny held up a calming hand, palm towards me in an attempt at placation. 'All right, mate, all right. I know it looks bloody funny from where you're standing but I promise you it'll all make sense soon enough.'

I wasn't ready to be mollified just yet and I told Kenny so. 'There are two people dead on account of this craziness and you're calmly telling me that it'll all make sense?' I turned to the brigadier, sitting beside Kenny on the opposite side of the small wooden table from me. His jovial attitude had slipped somewhat in the face of my raised voice. 'Start giving me some facts,' I shot at him.

'You're quite entitled to be angry, Mr Kemp,' he began.

'Angry? I'm more than angry – I'm bloody steaming.'

'Understood. I imagine I'd feel much the same in your shoes.'

'So start talking and make it fast. You can begin with Leotta Tomsson.'

The brigadier gave a sideways look at Kenny and hesitated.

'What?' I thundered. 'Tell me what's going on? Is she all right?'

Kenny stepped in. 'Leotta's fine, mate.'

'What, then? Look, just tell me what this is all about, will you?'

'It's... delicate, Mr Kemp.'

I exploded at the brigadier. 'I don't care how bloody delicate it is. You've got me wrapped up in something lethal that has already cost two lives and you don't seem to want to tell me what's happened to a girl I feel particularly strongly about. "Delicate" is not a word I'd apply to the current situation. Now spit it out, whatever it is.'

The brigadier finally gave up his story. By the time he'd finished, my coffee was cold and untouched on the table in front of me.

'The first thing I have to do is apologise – to you and to your friend Leotta. Kenny is right: she's perfectly fine, as far as we know.'

I was outraged. 'As far as you know?'

'Please let me finish, Mr Kemp. Leotta is in the United States at the moment, attending a medical symposium in Boston at which her presence was specially requested at the behest of Her Majesty's Government – although she didn't know it.'

'So she *has* gone to a conference?' The brigadier nodded. 'I thought she'd been kidnapped or something. The phone calls – '

He looked down at his cup of coffee. 'Ah yes. The phone calls. As I said, I need to apologise.'

I gaped at him. 'The phone calls were from you?'

'Well, not me personally; but they did originate in official circles, yes.'

Fury got the better of me and I stood up. 'You outright bastard. You set me up.'

'Please, Mr Kemp, sit down. There's a lot more to this story and I need you to hear it in a rational frame of mind.'

'To hell with rationality. I'll hear it any way I want and there's not a damn thing you can do about it.' All the same, I sat down.

'If I may continue?' he said. I bit my lip. 'I realise our enlistment tactics might seem a little... heavy-handed. We had to be sure you would comply, you see. A straight-forward request to do as we asked would undoubtedly have been met with a curt refusal on your part – and quite justifiably too.'

'Why? What is it you needed me to do?'

'The job you have done very capably, Mr Kemp.'

I was out of my depth. 'But I haven't done anything – apart from get two people killed.' The bitterness I felt was plain in my tone.

'On the contrary. You have performed your role to per-fection – one might say, even more effectively than we could have hoped.'

I was losing patience fast. 'For God's sake, man, stop talking in riddles and tell me how I fit into this fiasco.'

'I'm coming to that. But first, I need to give you a bit of context. How much do you know about the Cold War?'

I had no idea where this was going. 'Superpowers bat-tling it out for world supremacy, that kind of thing?'

He grimaced slightly at my oversimplification. 'Indeed. That kind of thing.'

'Well, I know it's all one giant game of chicken. Our lot point our weapons at their lot, they point theirs back, and it's basically a case of who blinks first. As far as I can tell, the rest of us caught in the middle have just struck lucky so far that nobody has blinked.'

Kenny shook his head. 'Not so surprising, mate. We saw what happened thirty years ago when someone blinked; they're still clearing up the mess now.'

'You mean Hiroshima and Nagasaki?'

The brigadier said, 'That's why they call them nuclear deterrents. What happened in Japan should be enough to put anyone off using them again.'

I was unconvinced. I'd heard all these arguments and

more from plenty of colleagues, both in the military and during my time mixing with some of the hard nuts in the British establishment, where the chums of Lord Hosmer and his ilk could afford to play with people's lives from the safety and comfort of their St James's clubs. I'd stuck it as long as I could but I'd had no second thoughts about walking away from the whole business after the Caribbean debacle turned sour.

'That's fine in theory but your average civilian doesn't care one way or the other – he just wants to stay alive, whether he's from Japan or Jarrow. And it only takes one psychopath with access to the nuclear button for all that to go straight out of the window. Look at Cuba.'

'QED,' said the brigadier triumphantly. 'It was precisely the threat of nuclear escalation that prompted Kennedy and Khrushchev to come to a secret agreement. All-out war averted.'

Kenny intervened on my behalf. 'Yeah, but Bill's point about psychopaths still stands. If Castro and Guevara had had their fingers on the button instead of the Russians, they'd have bombed America for sure.'

This was getting us nowhere. I'm as interested in the pros and cons of the nuclear debate as the next potential victim but we had more pressing matters to discuss. I stared at the brigadier and put as much steel into my voice as I could.

'Just get to the point, will you?'

'Ah yes. All right, let's take your analogy at face value: one giant game of chicken. Now, assuming nobody wants to be the first to blink, as you put it, what then ensues is a series of lesser games of chicken, played at a range of levels within the espionage hierarchy – and that's where you come in.'

'Espionage?' Apart from Napoleon's pointed reference to murdering spies, this was the first time my recent experiences had been put in such blunt terms and it shocked me.

'Of course, espionage. What did you think we were talking about?'

I sat back in my chair and blew out a long, slow breath. 'I don't suppose I thought of it as anything in particular. But espionage is all about secrets, subterfuge, lies. That's not my world.'

The brigadier laughed. 'You've been watching too much film noir. I suppose you think Vienna is all Orson Welles and subterranean sewers?'

I winced inwardly when I recalled exactly that sequence of thoughts as I'd done the tourist thing around the city over the past few days.

Kenny said, 'Besides, secrets, subterfuge, lies – isn't that what you used to investigate with your insurance fraudsters? Not to mention last year's outback shenanigans. I'm sorry to break the news to you, mate, but it's exactly your world.'

Put like that, I could see Kenny was right.

The brigadier picked up where he'd left off. 'So, we have an ongoing series of games being played out across the world between various different actors in various different scenarios. Some locations are more contentious than others, some governments play a more active role than others, but even if they pretend it's not going on and choose to ignore it, everyone knows it is really happening, under our noses, all the time. Now, you may say that's fine and just a bit more sabre-rattling of one sort or another. But what happens when the sabres rattle a bit too loudly for the bigwigs to ignore?'

'Like Cuba,' I said grimly, beginning to grasp his theme.

'Like Cuba,' he concurred. 'That arose because of a combination of factors: highly-strung characters – Castro and Che, as Kenny has already pointed out – and location.

It was just too close to the good old US of A for them to comfortably ignore. And that meant it rose to the surface of those murky waters of espionage and became a full-blown international emergency.'

In spite of myself I was intrigued. I didn't know about the highly-strung characters in this part of the world but I could see how the location of a Western capital only a handful of miles from the Iron Curtain might provoke some concerns at senior levels. 'You're telling me that you've been using me as a pawn in something similar to Cuba?'

The brigadier smiled and there was something slippery about it that made me think he could have enjoyed an alternative career in the diplomatic service. He could certainly deploy an unctuous manner when he needed to.

'Don't flatter yourself, Mr Kemp. We're not in the realms of the Cuban missile crisis here. Just a little local difficulty, as Macmillan once said.'

'And look what happened to him – forced from office before his time.'

'Oh, I'm not sure that a retirement as chancellor of Oxford University and chairman of the family publishing company is all that bad.'

I grunted. 'I suppose not.'

'Anyway, my point is that this particular sabre-rattling is strictly of the lower-level variety in the grand scheme of things. It's important enough to those involved but it won't be making headline news.'

That didn't make me feel any better. 'So two people have died, and I've been put through possibly the worst few days of my life, for "a little local difficulty"? You really are a callous bastard, aren't you?'

The brigadier had the cheek to look affronted. 'Now hold on a minute, Mr Kemp. I don't make the decisions; I simply act on them.'

'Just obeying orders?' I said heartlessly.

'Come on, mate – that's below the belt,' said Kenny.

I suspected he might be right but I didn't want to admit it. 'All right, tell me just what this "little local difficulty" involves. Then I'll decide exactly how callous you are.'

He sighed and leaned forward to rest his elbows on the edge of the table. 'Very well. If you recall, I was apologising for our heavy-handed enlistment technique but unfortunately it was felt that there was no alternative. Those doing the recruiting believed a gilt-edged invitation through the post would not have been well-received. On today's evidence, I'm inclined to agree with them.'

I could have picked him up on the unnecessary dig but I let it pass: I really wanted to hear his excuse of a story. 'Low-level sabre-rattling,' I prompted.

'Look, what I'm about to tell you is highly confidential. I should really be making you sign the Official Secrets Act but your Australian friend here has suggested that might not go down too well either, given the current circumstances. However, I'm prepared to take Mr Hines's word that you are completely trustworthy.'

'And you won't be telling me anything really important anyway,' I said.

He didn't answer that one so I knew it was true.

'Anna Stern was not just a courier.'

That much I had guessed. If the spy novels I'd read were anything to go by, it was rare – although not unheard of – for a low-grade messenger to be eliminated in the way that Anna had. Occasionally someone menial might get caught in the crossfire but Anna's death had looked too specific, even to my untrained eyes, to be an unfortunate by-product of the Cold War. She seemed to me to have been targeted and that meant only one thing: she was a significant player.

'Go on.'

'Anna Stern was rather highly placed in the West German intelligence services.'

'A spy?'

'Quite so.'

So Napoleon had been telling the truth about that. He might have been wide of the mark when it came to my involvement in her death, but I was starting to see how it looked from his perspective.

The brigadier shifted in his seat. 'I can't tell you exactly what she did or how she went about it but she was a rather important cog in the espionage machine of that country. A large number of German intelligence officers depended on her for their security and long-term safety. Which made it rather unfortunate that she was also a Soviet double agent.'

For the first time, Angus Campbell-Medlock had genuinely surprised me.

Things got stranger. Anna Stern, it transpired, had been recruited by the East Germans very early on in her career with the West German intelligence service, the BND. Evidently, the organisation's head at that point, General Wessel, had been less careful than he might about infiltration by the enemy, even though his entire job seemed to be to keep an eye on the Russians and their satellites. Anna had been far from the only Soviet spy to sneak into the BND's workforce over the past decade or more. And she would still have been feeding information back to her Russian paymasters if she hadn't undergone a crisis of conscience when her father died and handed herself in to her own bosses.

Unsure of what to do with a self-confessed traitor among their ranks, the BND hierarchy debated whether to toss her into prison and throw away the key or embrace her warmly and thank her for her service to the state. Fortunately for Anna, they settled on the latter, agreeing to her request for immunity and a new identity in return for her Moscow intelligence.

'So was Anna Stern her real name or her fake one?' I asked when the brigadier paused for breath.

'Anna Stern is who she became.'

I frowned. 'It strikes me that the BND didn't do a very good job of creating a new identity for her if the Soviets were able to find her and kill her.'

The brigadier hesitated and I wondered whether he was weighing up just how much of the story to tell me.

'It's not as straightforward as you think,' he said eventually. 'Anna Stern was bait.'

I was bewildered. 'What do you mean, bait?'

'I mean she was being used to lure a Soviet operative out of hiding – someone the West has wanted to find for a very long time.'

'And Anna agreed to give up her new identity for that?' I was feeling outraged all over again on Anna's behalf. I might only have met her briefly at the Café Central a few days earlier but the sight of her limp body being carted off by Austrian policemen on the banks of the Danube the following morning still lingered horrifically in my memory and I thought she deserved better than to be sacrificed on the altar of an outsized game of chicken. Especially since nobody else seemed to give a damn about her.

'One thing at a time, Mr Kemp. If we're going to get you to agree to go on with this mission there are certain things you need to know.'

I laughed derisively. 'You think I'm going to carry on with this fiasco? After everything you've put me through and the deaths that should be weighing heavy your conscience? You must be out of your mind.'

I stood up quickly and made as if to head for the door.

The brigadier looked over his shoulder towards the soldier standing guard. 'Sergeant!'

But instead of the sergeant squaring up to prevent me from leaving, he reached under a table next to him and pulled out a brown leather briefcase of the kind I'd seen plenty of my classmates use at school. I stopped my advance towards him and watched as he unclasped the flap, put a hand inside and pulled out a beige folder containing a sheaf of papers. He offered me the bundle, which I took in bemusement, and indicated for me to return to the table by the window.

As I sat down again I looked at the brigadier and my old friend Kenny Hines, staring at me intently across the table.

'Read that, Mr Kemp,' said the brigadier. 'Then we'll talk.'

FIFTEEN

My name is Anna Stern, but it is not my real name
and I am still getting used to it. I was born in Germany
during the war: my father was a Wehrmacht officer
who managed to evade censure after the surrender
and instead helped to set up a new intelligence agency
known as the Gehlen Organisation, after its leader
Major General Reinhard Gehlen. It would later become
part of the West German Bundesnachrichtendienst,
or BND. There were a good number of former Gestapo
and even SS officers who were recruited at that time,
although I was too young to understand how this happened or the implications of this for European security. I only learned of my father's previous history
much later, after his death.

I have been requested to make it clear that I am giving this testimony of my own free will and completely
voluntarily. My decision to give this statement – and
to confess my treason against the land of my ancestors – came from the recent discovery of my father's
actions and activities both during the war and sub-
sequently, and my growing sense that I have dishon-
oured my country and my father by my own actions in

serving what I now believe to be the enemy. No money has been exchanged for this information and I do not wish there to be any confusion about my motives: my loyalty cannot be bought, I act on my own beliefs and values, and in rehearsing this history, I am doing what I now believe to be right.

I have explained my position within the hierarchy of the BND and its Warsaw Pact counterparts in other documents and interviews, and I have not been asked to repeat it here. It is enough to say that I supplied frequent and regular information of a sensitive nature to the Stasi in East Germany via channels that I have revealed to my superiors in the BND. I fully accept responsibility for the consequences of that. I am grateful to the authorities that my revelations have been received with appreciation and that my desire to live an anonymous life without further involvement in the security services has been met with acquiescence. It is these circumstances that have brought me to the new identity of Anna Stern.

The primary purpose of this document is to explain and record my connection to, and involvement with, the Soviet-run operative known as The Vixen.

The identity of The Vixen has been a closely-guarded secret, even within Stasi circles, but I am able to confirm that her name is Arkadia Krenč. She has been instrumental in subverting democratic institutions across Central Europe for more than a decade, and her methods should be regarded as both brutal and blunt. She operates with few ethical constraints and entirely outside of the law of any recognised nation, although her achievements have been approved and welcomed at the highest levels within the Soviet Union. She has been rewarded not only with financial and material compensation, but also with the approbation of the state, including the Order of the October Revolution, which is awarded for services furthering communism.

I first encountered Krenč while I was working for the BND on the purchase of a Swiss communications firm which built telephone and fax encryption systems that were sold worldwide. The value of such an acquisition was obvious both to the BND and to its equivalent services in the East and my instructions were to feed details of the negotiations to a contact in Zurich, not far from the company's headquarters in Steinhausen. It was hoped that the means could be found to complicate the purchase by raising its price exorbitantly and, ultimately, infiltrate the business in such a way that its function and purpose would become impossibly compromised – although never letting that be known to the BND, which was intended to continue to own and run this new part of its empire without realising it was useless.

My contact in Zurich was Arkadia Krenč.

Our initial meeting was arranged to appear innocuous and accidental. It had, of course, been engineered to perfection by our superiors. When we collided in a department store while looking at ladies' gloves, each of us knew exactly who the other was and what would happen next. Over the course of the following few weeks, as negotiations with the firm and its notoriously difficult founder wound on slowly, Arkadia and I developed what appeared to the outside world to be an innocent and unexceptional friendship, meeting in coffee shops or for shopping trips, gradually leading up to inviting each other to our respective apartments for dinner. To all intents and purposes we were two unattached young ladies forming an affection because of similar interests and the emotional absence of a man in our lives.

Once we had escalated matters to the point of visiting one another at home, the handover of information was simple enough. The usual method was that I would memorise as much material as I could, then simply write it down in a notebook when I visited Arkadia's flat. If there were more technical details to pass on, such as a graph or a chart, I had plenty of opportunity to photograph them clandestinely at the offices of the company and deliver the undeveloped film to her at our next meeting. Never in the eight months that I was stationed in Zurich did we experience a moment of danger or difficulty in our disruption of the takeover process. Indeed, so successful was our operation that the purchase almost fell through, as it had once before, and the BND was forced to increase the offer price far beyond its original expectations – much to the fury of the regional director. Our role was to make sure the sale went ahead, but at the greatest possible inconvenience and expense to the agency, and our handlers were delighted with the results.

During the time we worked together on the Zurich operation, I learned information about Arkadia which I am certain is not known to the wider intelligence community. Despite the potentially discouraging fact of our fathers fighting on opposite sides in the war, we got on well. Indeed, I believe that she came to regard me as a friend, rather than merely an agency contact, and in the rarefied world of espionage, where nobody is to be truly relied upon, she found me not only trustworthy but also likable. I do not hesitate to say the same in return – in spite of many of the things I learned, which dismayed me on a personal level. It was because of this increasing connection that she unfolded to me much more of her personal history than one would normally expect from a fellow agent.

How much of it is true I cannot be certain, especially given the nature of the business with which we were entwined, but these are the details she gave me.

She claimed to have been born in Poland, a few years earlier than I, in a tiny village in the Łódź province notable chiefly for the bizarre circumstance of an English garden park that was established nearby in the eighteenth century. Her unremarkable upbringing was interrupted by the invasion of the Nazis in 1939 and the next few years appear to have been extremely difficult for the family, culminating in the death of Arkadia's mother due to malnutrition while the war was still under way. Her father having long since disappeared, believed dead, the orphaned girl was taken in by a sympathetic family and looked after until the end of hostilities. As soon as she was old enough to look out for herself, she left the area, with its horrendous memories, and fled to Czechoslovakia, where she hoped to make a better life than in the ruins of Poland. She proved a natural linguist, even with the complex and varied languages of the region, and began to flourish in her adopted country. It was during this time that she took on the Czech surname Krenč – her own too obviously betraying her roots – and reinvented herself. Her only concession to her Polish origins, in honour of her dead mother, was to take the forename Arkadia, which was the name of the village where she'd been born.

With her flair for linguistics, she was identified as a potential agent while studying at university in Prague. The intelligence community nurtured her and promoted her, training her in dark subjects such as guerilla warfare and urban terrorism alongside her more acceptable studies in German, English and Russian. By the time she qualified with a first-class degree, she was ready for front-line action in the service and highly equipped to move easily among more questionable circles along the borders of what had become known as the Iron Curtain. She confessed to me that she had killed a number of people during this period of her life – something she claimed not to regret as she was serving a higher cause – and it would not surprise me in the least if this portion of her narrative were entirely true. Arkadia proved to have a streak of viciousness in her character that belied her natural idealism and outward charm. I expressed surprise when she told me, however, as it seemed odd to me that she would have been relegated to such a mundane task as the Zurich operation if she were experienced in political liquidation. Her response was that she had made a serious error of judgement in her last posting and was being required to prove her consistency once more. She never explained that or mentioned it again in all the time I knew her. For my part, I considered her to fall into a different category from myself – willing to kill or injure an opponent in cold blood. I had been asked at an early point in my career if I would be prepared to follow such a path but I knew that inflicting violence outside of a conflict arena was beyond my capabilities: I might be able to fire a weapon in battle but I knew I could not torture a defenceless prisoner or kill indiscriminately as, for instance, a sniper might be required to do.

It seemed to me that Arkadia Krenč was something of an anomaly in the espionage world: a girl's face concealing an assassin's heart of ice.

The Zurich mission had proved so fruitful that Arkadia's commander was determined to exploit our partnership again as soon as possible. The intention was that we should both be stepped up to a higher level of security clearance within our organisations, with access to much more important secrets, and we could again establish a double operation across national borders without any suspicion. My own handler was more hesitant, perhaps because he was worried that I would be seen as the junior partner in such a joint enterprise and the credit might not therefore go to where he believed it was due – in other words, to him. He made it tricky for another operation to be set up expediently, and as the months went by the idea of our working together again seemed to have been abandoned. I returned to more routine espionage in various locations across central Europe, and I was unable to get news of Arkadia through official channels. Unofficially, of course, she didn't exist at all, so we lost touch for a while.

It was an apparently chance encounter on a street in Vienna that renewed our connection. I was stationed there as part of a West German delegation working on preparations for the Vienna International Centre, which was to be built over the next few years to provide permanent headquarters for various United Nations agencies. My role, of course, was a dual one: ostensibly I was keeping a watchful eye on how Western intelligence services might be insinuated into this UN complex from the beginning – even though the VIC was designated an extraterritorial area, exempt from Austrian law. My other purpose was to maintain a constant supply of secret information to the Soviet Union.

On subsequent reflection, it was the opportunity to re-establish our Zurich collaboration that made me wonder whether the encounter on the street had been by chance at all. It seems to me now quite likely that it was engineered, just as our original meeting had been. Whatever the genesis of our reconnection, it didn't take long for our respective handlers to set up a new channel through which my secrets would now be passed. The old-fashioned method of transferring information to an anonymous Soviet operative via dead letter boxes would be superseded by completely innocent live drops between two old friends.

So the second phase of our relationship began, picking up exactly where the first had ended. Arkadia seemed pleased to rebuild our friendship and I offered her the same careful warmth I had provided back in Zurich. Her knowledge of Vienna seemed thorough and well-researched, and I wondered how it had been acquired: she seemed to know shortcuts through back streets, or the right person to talk to for a black-market item, in a way that could not have been gleaned from reference books. When I asked her about it, she said she had been to the city many times, for many different reasons, and had developed a large number of useful contacts across Lower Austria.

It was during this period, when I was handing over intelligence and United Nations secrets to Arkadia Krenč, that two significant things occurred. The first was my discovery that Arkadia was conducting separate operations for the Soviets under a codename different from her adopted name: The Vixen. The second was the death of my father.

The revelation that she was The Vixen came by chance. I had known of the existence of this agent thanks to my direct superior in the BND, who had been involved in a mission to locate and eliminate her and had asked my advice as a woman about certain feminine matters which might, it was believed, help to identify her. However, I was not involved in the operation to terminate her, nor did I know her true identity at that point. It was some weeks after I ran into Arkadia in Vienna that she mysteriously disappeared without notice, coinciding with the unexpected arrival in the city of my boss. His evasiveness over his reasons for being there, coupled with the unexplained disappearance of my Soviet contact, sparked the thought in my mind that the two incidents might be related. After my boss had returned to Bonn and Arkadia turned up again a week later, I concluded that she might be the quarry he was hunting. I undertook various veiled attempts to verify this information in conversation with her and, although she never openly admitted her alternate identity, there were enough clues in her answers to convince me that she was indeed The Vixen.

This left me with a quandary: with such an important figure purporting to be my relatively low-level contact, should I reveal what I knew to my boss and claim her scalp for the West? In the process, I would be admitting my treason and potentially laying myself open to a lifetime in prison. The alternative was to let Arkadia know that I was on to her, and that the BND would not be far behind.

It was the great English writer EM Forster who encapsulated just such a conundrum when he said that if he had to choose between betraying his country and betraying his friend, he hoped he should have the guts to betray his country. I was preparing to follow the same ethical path by alerting Arkadia when my father died.

I had not seen him for some months before his passing, although we exchanged letters regularly. He had been ill for quite some time but the end came more quickly than either he or his doctors expected, and I was taken by surprise. However, the greater surprise came when I began to sort through his papers during a fortnight's compassionate leave I was granted by the service. He had never spoken to me about his wartime experiences, nor about the later period when he helped set up the Gehlen Organisation and its subsequent incarnation, the BND. He had, however, kept copious diaries for reasons I could not begin to fathom. Whether he wanted to preserve his story for posterity or he wanted me to find them and know the truth about his past, I cannot say, but reading them was painful. He was apparently consumed by guilt over his part in Hitler's regime, and the deaths for which he had been responsible weighed heavily on him for the rest of his life. In his subsequent work for the BND he dedicated himself to eradicating despotism wherever it occurred in the world, and his primary target was the Soviet Union. He recognised in the months following the war that Stalin and his compatriots in the Russian politburo had constructed as vindictive and heinous a tyranny as any that the Nazis had inflicted on their subjects and he recorded in detail the examples to which he was exposed in his role. Those two weeks, reading his diary entries, had a profound effect on me. By the end – and perhaps more out of love for my father than for my fatherland – he had turned me comprehensively against communism as exemplified by the Soviet Union and its allies.

Forster may have drawn the comparison between friend and country, and found country wanting, but as far as I know he never took into consideration the strength of a blood tie.

On my return to my duties after my father's funeral, I made an appointment to speak to my superior. I had already put my affairs in order in expectation of immediate arrest, but I delayed the meeting by a few days as I wanted to see Arkadia one last time.

I gave her, I believe, no hint of my intentions or my knowledge. My desire was simply to see my old friend once more before I surrendered myself to the greater good. I knew it meant surrendering Arkadia too, and I grieved both the loss of my friend and the reality of my betrayal, but I could hear my father's voice in my head assuring me that it was the correct path. Arkadia and I met for a brief hour in her apartment in Vienna and I made a point of keeping the conversation light and unrelated to our joint venture. At the end of our meeting, I pleaded another engagement as an excuse to depart, and I left her for the final time.

Within two hours, I submitted a report to my superior.

The series of interviews that followed have been fairly and objectively conducted and, as I said at the beginning of this testimony, I have endured no intimidation, coercion or compulsion in my recounting of these events. I understand that I have no legal or moral rights remaining to me, given what I have undertaken on behalf of an enemy of the state, but if mercy might be conjoined with justice, as Shakespeare suggested, then I hope I might be permitted to request that Arkadia Krenč is not eliminated, in the traditional meaning used by espionage agents, but is instead apprehended and delivered before a court of law.

It would, I believe, be an appropriate conclusion to the career of The Vixen.

SIXTEEN

Kenny and the brigadier were still staring at me when I closed the file.

'What do you make of that, then?' asked Kenny.

I shook my head in disbelief. 'So Anna Stern was a triple agent?'

The brigadier said, 'Bad apple turned good. And bloody good too – the information she was able to give us about how the Soviets are operating in this part of the world was dynamite. It'll shake things up in the espionage community for decades to come and I'm not sure the Russkies will ever be able to trust their East German spies again. Too many of them have been exposed or compromised. The word is that they're having to restructure from the ground up and that will take them years.'

I could see why he was so gleeful about the turn of events but it still left me sick to my stomach when I thought of Anna and – even more so as a civilian caught in the crossfire – young Roland Wolf at the hotel.

'This certainly fills in one or two blanks in my understanding,' I said. 'But there are still things I don't get.'

'Such as what?'

'I don't know – why that codename for Arkadia

Krenč?' It wasn't exactly crucial to the narrative but it was the first thing that popped into my head.

The brigadier leaned back in his chair and clasped his hands together behind his head. 'It's an opera connection.'

I shrugged. Opera was beyond my frame of reference.

'Have you heard of the Czech composer Janáček?'

'The name rings a bell.'

'Contemporary of Dvořák. You must know him – the *New World Symphony*?' He began humming a tune that was vaguely familiar to me. 'Anyway, Janáček wrote an opera called *The Cunning Little Vixen*. Apparently the resonance with Krenč and her Czech background was too appealing for the backroom boys to resist. In the absence of her real name, she was dubbed The Vixen. It's only because of Anna that we now know her true identity.'

'All very interesting,' I said, putting a tone of utter boredom into my voice. Something more important had occurred to me. I turned to look at Kenny. 'But why exactly are you here? What's all this got to do with you?'

Kenny broke into a broad grin, a flash of the old Aussie compadre I'd known since national service days more than twenty years earlier. We'd been through some hellish times together but we hadn't seen each other since I left the shores of his home country a year ago and I worried that there had been a subtle shift in our friendship because of what had happened over there. His big, friendly smile demolished that notion convincingly.

'Mate, that's a story for a beer.'

He waved a hand in the direction of the kitchen and I looked around to see the timid waitress appear at the door. I didn't know if she'd been listening in or watching out for a signal from Kenny but she seemed ready for action.

'Three beers over here, if you wouldn't mind.'

He waited until the drinks had arrived – big foaming steins of Austrian lager – before picking up his tale.

'You know I was all set to go on with the legal firm after you left Sydney.'

I nodded, recalling Kenny's volte-face on his earlier decision to wind up the firm he'd been running in a suburb of the city. The events of that new year had taken a toll on him emotionally as well as physically and he had every right to be indecisive, and he'd switched from abandoning the whole thing to keeping it going – not least for the sake of his two secretaries, Carly and Ruth.

'Well not long after you flew home, I got a visit from another old Pommie acquaintance. Do you remember Major Mackintosh?'

I certainly did. 'Mac' had been a popular and likable officer in our regiment who'd spent many a raucous night with Kenny and me, downing pints and putting the world to rights from the comfort of a four-ale bar.

'He was in Sydney?'

'Came to see me specially. He'd got ears on the ground in Australia and had heard about what happened with Hamilton and Irvine. It didn't make the front pages but you could read about it if you knew where to look. After the story broke, he'd done a bit of digging behind the headlines and discovered what had really gone on. When he turned up on my doorstep he told me it was apparent that I had just the kind of skill set he was looking for.'

'What does that mean?'

'Oh, you know, the ability to ferret around in people's backstory without being noticed, that kind of thing.'

'But why would an army officer want that from a lawyer in Sydney?'

'Ah, that's the thing. He didn't want it from a lawyer *in* Sydney. He wanted the lawyer *from* Sydney to come back to the old country and do a spot of that kind of work for him there.'

The implications of his tale began to dawn on me. 'Mac's a spy?'

'Not when we knew him, but he's been rather a busy boy in the last twenty years. I'm not sure how much I can tell you – ' he cast a sideways glance at the brigadier, who studiously declined to return it ' – but Major Mackintosh has some compelling links to the security services, let's put it that way. And he's no longer a major.'

I looked at the brigadier for confirmation. He smiled and leaned his head to one side. 'General Mackintosh is overseeing this particular bit of business from Whitehall. That's all you need to know.'

Kenny said, 'Anyway, Mac had already found another lawyer who was interested in taking over my practice and willing to pay a decent price, Carly and Ruth were going to be well looked after, and I found I was in need of a change of scenery. Sydney had grown just a little too claustrophobic for my liking.'

'So what – you've been recruited by MI6, have you?'

Kenny didn't need to answer my question: the look on his face was priceless.

I tried to piece together the jigsaw in my mind. Kenny, with nothing to hold him in Australia any more, had returned to England at the request of old man Mackintosh and was now serving at Her Majesty's pleasure as an agent for the British government, courtesy of his father's native birth and his own innate accomplishments. It all seemed a little far-fetched but then Kenny had never been one for standing still and letting the grass grow around him. Given half a chance and a petrol-powered lawnmower, he'd be off at the first opportunity carving a swashbuckling path through the undergrowth.

The brigadier interrupted my thoughts. 'Naturally, you'll have worked out by now that it was Mr Hines here who introduced your name during our preparations for this mission.'

That hadn't, in fact, occurred to me.

'Of course! That explains how I got drafted in. It was you.' I was surprised at how angry I suddenly felt towards my old friend. 'You bastard, Kenny. You've tricked me into something that's made me not only vulnerable but expendable. I've been locked up, beaten up and shot at since I've been in Vienna and I didn't even know why. All the time it was because of you.'

A serious look came over Kenny's face. 'Look, mate, I didn't want to put you in any danger but you were the only man for the job.'

My voice rose a few notches. 'I don't know what the bloody job is, for Christ's sake! You've used deception and blackmail to bring me to this city. Hell, you could be lying to my face right now for all I know. And for what? I don't even know the answer to that question.'

'Calm down, Mr Kemp,' the brigadier began, waving his red rag at my proverbial bull.

'Calm down?' I shouted. 'How can you expect me to be calm when you've just admitted to me that I'm an unwitting pawn in your sordid little games?'

Kenny had a go at placating me. 'Mate, it's precisely because you were unwitting that we were able to – '

He'd been about to say 'exploit', I could tell, but he stopped himself.

'What I mean is, I recommended you for this job because you're a completely blank page in these circles. You're an unknown player in the world of espionage and that gives you two vital things: anonymity and plausible deniability. Nobody knows who you are or has any reason to suspect you; and even if they did, you don't know anything anyway so you can't give away any secrets. Put that together with your natural instinct for survival – as you demonstrated amply in the outback – and you were the obvious choice. I couldn't tell you anything or even let you know that I was involved without compromising your position.'

I snorted in disgust. 'Compromise? I could hardly be more compromised now, could I?'

'You're quite right, Mr Kemp,' said the brigadier. 'And I can only repeat my apology. But it does rather point up my earlier observation that you have done your job very capably thus far, even if you didn't know what that job was.'

'I get it. I'm in this thing up to my eyeballs and there's no way back.' I shot a glance at Kenny. 'Thanks for that.'

'I know you'd do the same for me, mate,' he said, his eyes twinkling in that familiar way.

I looked back at the brigadier. 'You said "bait".'

'I'm sorry?'

'Earlier on, before I read Anna's statement, you said she was bait.'

'Ah yes. To lure a Soviet agent into the open.'

'I take it that agent was Arkadia Krenč.'

The brigadier took stock for a moment and adjusted the collar of his shirt before continuing. 'Krenč has been a thorn in the side of Western intelligence agencies in Europe for a number of years. We've known of her existence – hence the codename – but we've never been this close to drawing her into the open.'

'What's so important about her?'

'In the period between Anna Stern working with her in Zurich and her appearing here in Vienna, The Vixen was turned into a veritable killing machine by the Soviets. We've lost a considerable number of agents and operatives at her personal hand and a whole bunch more through her indirect involvement.'

'How many exactly?'

'Exactly?' He looked fidgety. 'We don't know.'

'You don't know?'

'Espionage is not a straightforward activity, Mr Kemp,' he said. 'Some agents are officially recognised by the government, others inevitably operate under the radar, for fairly obvious reasons. Sometimes it's hard to say exactly who – or even how many – are on the books at any one time. Let's just say that The Vixen's kill count is considerably higher than any of her colleagues behind the Iron Curtain and it would do the service an awful lot of good if she were to be removed from the game.'

'You and your bloody euphemisms. You mean you want her dead.'

'Very well. Yes, we want her dead.'

I picked up the beige folder from the table in front of me and shook it under his nose.

'But isn't that just what Anna Stern requested shouldn't happen? My God, this shabby little business has got her killed – the least you could do is honour her dying request that Arkadia Krenč should be taken alive.'

I slammed the folder back down on the table and sank my head into my hands. I wondered if Anna had realised how perilous her situation was when she met me in the Café Central on the Herrengasse. I recalled the terrified look in her eye, the twitchiness of her demeanour – and the SOS note she'd left me on her napkin in Morse code. Had that been a sign that she knew Krenč was onto her? Or was it something more profound: maybe that she'd had enough of the whole spying business and wanted out? If that were the case, she'd picked the wrong man to play the white knight.

'Did Anna know she was in danger?'

The brigadier indicated the file in front of me. 'You've read her testimony: she gave up her friend. And she was under no illusion about Krenč. Anna knew as well as anybody how lethal she was as an operative.'

'Krenč has been on Anna's tail for months now,' said Kenny. 'And Anna was well aware.'

'I don't understand. If Anna had already given the identity of The Vixen to West German intelligence, Arkadia Krenč cover was blown. There'd be nothing to gain from killing Anna.'

The brigadier shook his head as if indulging a child. It made my hackles rise.

'Your view of the world is far too simplistic, Mr Kemp. It might have been too late to stop Anna divulging what she knew but her death would send a strong signal to any other Soviet agents considering betrayal.'

The sickening feeling returned in my throat.

Now the brigadier leaned forward again and clasped his hands together on the table. 'There's something else.'

I eyed him suspiciously then switched my gaze to Kenny, who looked studiously out of the window at the panorama and took a long pull on his beer.

'It wasn't meant to happen this way but your involvement has put you in a rather unfortunate position,' the brigadier said calmly. He hesitated but I'd already guessed what was coming next. 'Our sources have had word that you have been placed on a target list by the Soviets.'

I sat in silence for a long moment. I wasn't sure if it was to let the information sink properly into my brain or to leave Campbell-Medlock feeling uncomfortable. When I spoke, I tried to keep my voice even.

'I thought I was just collecting a package?'

'That was the plan, Bill,' said Kenny in a low voice, looking at me for the first time in several minutes. 'I only put you forward because I knew you'd be able to do the courier job. I never meant for you to get involved like this.'

The brigadier leaned back again, his hands still clasped. 'But then, you were never meant to get busted from an Austrian police cell and dragged across the border into Czechoslovakia.'

'Oh, so I've only got myself to blame, is that it?'

'He's not saying that, Bill.'

'Sounds like it to me.'

'Listen, Mr Kemp, the point is that there is still a Soviet agent out there who's putting our agents in mortal danger every day that she remains at liberty. It's unfortunate, I know, but you are now included on her list of potential victims. And that's why we need you to stay in the game.'

I laughed in contempt and stood up, my legs knocking over the chair behind me.

'Stay in the game? You have got to be kidding.' I looked at Kenny, who seemed at least a little ashamed by the situation. I didn't want to tear him off another strip but he had put me in an impossible situation and I was furious with him. 'I don't want anything more to do with this filthy affair. It's already cost two people's lives – and one of them was a completely innocent civilian.'

It suddenly occurred to me that these people might have the answer to the question that had been haunting me ever since I saw that forlorn new hat hanging on its peg.

'By the way, just what did happen to Roland Wolf?'

'The boy at the hotel?' At least Campbell-Medlock knew who he was. 'Unfortunate business. It looks as if the Soviets thought they could get more information out of him than he actually knew. When it transpired that they couldn't, he became expendable.'

That bloody word.

I said, 'I'm going to have to live with that somehow. I don't suppose it'll trouble either of you – ' I saw Kenny wince at that ' – but I'm going to have Roland on my conscience for the rest of my life. At least Anna knew what she was caught up in, even if she didn't deserve to die for it. You and your bloody righteous causes: you're as bad as the Russians. To hell with the lot of you.'

Neither of them had moved while I delivered my outraged sermon and it struck me that there was no point in going on with my tirade. I wasn't surprised that I couldn't get through to the brigadier, a military careerist with emotions long since trained out of him, but Kenny's reaction disappointed me. We'd been through a catalogue of ups and downs together and I'd believed him far more capable of feelings than he now appeared to be. Maybe signing up to MI6 had been a turning point for him, a way of shutting down his inner turmoil after what had happened in Australia. It seemed a damned funny way of coming to terms with things if you asked me, but here he was.

I was halfway to the door, wondering if the sergeant would make any attempt to stop me, when Kenny spoke.

'Bill, there's something that might make you change your mind.'

SEVENTEEN

Nobody said a word as we trudged through the snow from the café towards St Josefkirche. I was sandwiched between the brigadier on my right and Kenny on my left, shooting glances between the two of them but getting nothing back as we followed the line of darkened sludge that we'd made going the other way an hour earlier.

At the door of the church, the brigadier went ahead and pushed it open before standing aside and indicating to me to go first.

The interior was gloomier than I'd expected, its white-washed walls grimy with years of browning dirt and its heavy baroque furnishings adding to the dark atmosphere. A window either side of the altar, plus another arched one high above it, provided the only natural light in the nave, presumably intended to focus the eye along the length of the building to the florid altarpiece rising imposingly between the two windows. The vaulted ceiling was painted in rich colours and halfway down the nave a huge wooden pulpit towered over the congregation, cramped together in the narrow pews that stood empty on this wintry weekday afternoon.

I stopped and turned back to look at Kenny and the brigadier. 'What am I looking at?'

Campbell-Medlock waved his arm at me again, this time pointing me towards a side chapel that I hadn't noticed on first inspection. I started to head towards it, then realised the other two weren't following so I stopped again and looked back.

Kenny nodded encouragingly. 'Go on, Bill.'

When I rounded the pillar that opened out onto the chapel, I caught my breath in disbelief. Alone in a pew, her red hair falling around shoulders that were draped in a yellow windcheater, sat Anna Stern.

She was facing away from me, her head bowed as if in prayer before the simple chapel altar, but there was no mistaking her. As I approached, she must have heard my footfall and she glanced around, catching sight of me and offering a weak smile.

'*Guten Tag, Herr Kemp,*' she said, her voice echoing faintly in the vaults of the ceiling.

'Anna? But... I don't understand.'

I moved closer, reaching out a hand to touch her shoulder, as if I couldn't believe she wasn't a ghost. The plastic of her raincoat felt solid enough and as the reality of her presence sank in, she stood up and leaned forward, offering me a cheek on which to place a continental kiss. I obliged, bewildered, then stepped back from her to take another look at the woman I had seen drowned on the banks of the Danube.

'You're not dead,' I said stupidly.

'So it would seem.'

A rush of emotions coursed through me, recalling the pain, the horrors and the despair of the past few days. At that moment I didn't know where to direct my fury and relief and I think Anna saw that it was in danger of overwhelming me.

'Sit down,' she said, taking my arm and guiding me to the pew she had just vacated. 'It's a lot to take in, I know.'

I sat dumbfounded and stared at her, squatting beside the pew and looking back at me with a kindly warmth on her face.

'I'm sorry you had to go through everything you've suffered but there really was a good reason for it. One day I might be able to explain it to you fully but for now I can only ask you to take my word for it.'

Finally some of the questions in my head reached my mouth. 'I thought you needed my help – that SOS you left me on your napkin.'

'I know,' she said. 'It needed to look genuine.'

'What did? Who was looking?'

'Our meeting was being watched. It had to appear that I was terrified for the subterfuge to work.'

'It worked on me,' I said bitterly, remembering the anxiety I had felt on her behalf as she dashed from the Café Central into the Vienna morning. 'But I suppose I was just another pawn to be used – for "the greater good".'

'I know it sounds callous and cold-blooded but it's true. There are things that are bigger than any of us that sometimes require us to act in ways we would not normally countenance. That's why martyrs die for their causes and boys sign up to go to war.'

'I'm not sure I believe any of that.'

A deeper voice cut through from the main church, its echo hanging in the reverberating air. 'Well perhaps you should.'

From behind the pillar stepped a tall, greying man in the uniform of a high-ranking British officer: I recognised him instantly as 'Mac' Mackintosh.

* * *

I hadn't realised just how cold the church had been until we adjourned to a private hotel snug at the bottom of the mountain, not far from where I'd got off the tram to catch the bus. Here, by the comfort of an Austrian fireside and with a bottle of something strong to elevate the warmth even further, our little party of spies settled in for our debriefing.

Anna sat closest to the fire, warming her hands from her armchair. I sat next to her on a more upright chair while Kenny and the brigadier shared a small settee on the other side of the blazing grate, each cradling a crystal glass of the colourless liqueur.

'*Marillenschnaps,*' Mac had said as he stood by the sideboard pouring out five glasses before distributing them to the company. 'Local apricot brandy. A bit fiery but it does the job.'

I took a glass from him and tipped it down my throat. I figured I needed both its heat and its kick and I handed the glass straight back to him for a refill.

'Steady on, old boy. We're not in the Rose and Crown now, you know. And you'll need your wits about you if we're going to make a plan.'

I hadn't seen him for years, and the last time I had he far outranked me, but now I was a civilian and I could speak to him however I wanted. I elected to go for insubordinate.

'Who's making a plan? Don't try and include me in your twisted game. I'll drink your apricot brandy but then I'm off. I want nothing more to do with any of it.'

The brigadier chimed in, an edge to his voice. 'You wouldn't last five minutes out there with Arkadia Krenč on your tail.'

'All right, Angus, that'll do,' said Mac. 'Let's not spook Bill any more than we have to.'

It was a bit late for that but I wasn't willing to let on just how spooked I was. I still had questions teeming through my mind and if I was now in the sights of a crazed Czech killer then I wanted some answers, and quickly.

'If you want my cooperation in any way at all, then you're going to have to start talking.'

Mac made as if to speak but I cut him short.

'And don't give me any of your bull about official secrets or clearance levels. I've already put my head above the parapet for you bastards and I think I deserve to know why. Especially if there's now a bounty on my head.'

'Not so much a bounty,' said the brigadier. 'Krenč would kill you for the sheer pleasure of it.'

'Shut up, Angus.' The senior officer's tone had sharpened considerably. Now he looked steadily at me. 'All right, Bill. You win. I'll tell you what you want to know. But you'd better be sure you want to hear it. Once you're in, you're in.'

I swirled the drink in my glass and stared deep into it before returning Mac's look. 'I think I'll be the judge of that.'

Mac weighed me up for a full thirty seconds before he spoke again. Out of the corner of my eye I saw Anna switch her gaze from the brigadier to the general, as if in silent acknowledgement of his seniority. I simply stared at Mac, recalling the jovial mucking-in that he had espoused so readily as a more junior officer, rubbing along with his subordinates in the pub while still maintaining his authority on the parade ground or in uniform. He'd struck a careful, well-constructed balance among all ranks between respected leader and relaxed fellow-drinker. I wondered what had led him into the espionage line and whether it had changed his approach to the troops. For all I knew, he'd been a spy back then and his easy charm with everyone around him had been a front for his covert activities. I suddenly felt very weary of all the duplicity.

'The body in the river was a stooge,' he said eventually.

'A stooge?'

'A decoy. A stand-in. A double.'

'Is that supposed to make me feel better? Someone still died.'

'Correction: someone had already died and we simply repurposed her body before disposing respectfully of her remains.'

'What's that supposed to mean?' I was already wound up and if Mac was going to start speaking double Dutch then it wouldn't take much for me to reach my limits.

The brigadier answered my question. 'It means, dear boy, that the body of a recently-departed young woman was discreetly borrowed from the nearest *Krankenhaus* and dressed up to look like Anna.'

His patronising tone was starting to get on my nerves so I directed my next question back to the general. 'Can you do that?'

Mac let out a small, barking laugh. 'No, of course not. But we're not exactly operating within the confines of the normal rules here.'

'So you're not averse to a spot of bodysnatching when it suits your purposes?'

'They put her back afterwards, mate,' said Kenny unconvincingly.

I found it hard to believe what I was being told. If Mac was telling the truth – and given what I now knew, that might be quite a big 'if' – then the intelligence service of at least one country had trampled all over the domestic laws of another, neutral, nation to achieve what could only be classed as nefarious ends. The fact that it involved a dead woman, whose friends and relations presumably knew nothing of the grandiose scheme, made it considerably worse in my eyes, and it had seemed pretty intolerable to me in the first place. But then, I reasoned, it was all of a piece with the rest of their apparently ethics-free enterprise.

'Perhaps,' began Anna, her tone sounding anxious and determined at the same time, 'it would help if I explained it.'

I wasn't sure I wanted to be duped by yet another professional spy but I hoped Anna's version of events might at least take into account the feelings of those concerned.

'Try me,' I said.

'The woman whose body was used had been killed in a road accident a couple of days earlier. Her body was in the hospital morgue awaiting a post-mortem examination to determine the exact cause of death but that wasn't scheduled to take place for another few days.'

'What was her name?' I asked, to nobody in particular.

The brigadier looked nonplussed. 'What?'

'This woman whose body you used so readily. What was her name?'

None of them answered and I knew that they couldn't – not even Anna.

'Go on,' I said after the pause had dragged uncomfortably.

She said, 'Look, Bill, I know you think we're all monsters and this whole affair is grotesque but I promise you I wouldn't have got involved if I didn't think it was of supreme importance.'

'Important to what?'

'The Cold War, Bill. I don't think you realise what's at stake here.'

'It seems to me the stakes are pretty high already. Roland is dead, you're all playing fast and loose with international law, and there's a homicidal maniac on the prowl with my name on the barrel of her gun. Or is there more?'

Mac turned around quickly from the sideboard where he was pouring himself another drink. His bark was ferocious. 'Yes, there's more, damn it! Arkadia Krenč isn't just a loose cannon; she has the potential to destabilise the entire continent of Europe. If she isn't brought to heel, either by her own side or by us, she could spark a tit-for-tat conflict that would make the Bay of Pigs look like a schoolboy scuffle. She's a lethal weapon with the safety catch off and if the Soviets point her at the wrong target she could set off a chain reaction that could lead directly to the big red buttons in both Washington and Moscow.'

'You're seriously telling me that this woman has the power to unleash World War Three?'

The brigadier let out an exasperated sigh and threw one hand in the air. 'Finally he gets it.'

'There's no telling what she's capable of,' said Mac, his voice a little calmer than before. 'And there's no knowing what her paymasters are lining her up to do next. Every job she's carried out in the last two years has ramped up the stakes another notch. Every assassination has been strategically selected to cause maximum disruption. The Vixen is brilliant – and utterly unconstrained.'

Anna reached across from her armchair and laid her hand on mine. 'Now do you see, Bill? This is so much bigger than you or me – or even Roland.'

I looked deep into her eyes, desperately wanting her to be lying to me again, but I could see she was in deadly earnest. Slowly I withdrew my hand from hers, took another draught of liquor and allowed a strange calm to settle on me. After all the fury and outrage, I felt oddly in control of myself and the situation.

'Tell me why you wanted to fake Anna's death.'

* * *

For a supposedly world-beating organisation such as MI6, the plan seemed pretty mundane to me.

After Anna had given up her secrets to the BND someone twigged that she might be useful in another way: luring Arkadia Krenč across the Iron Curtain, laying her open to capture – or, perhaps even better, to assassination. The prospect seemed too enormous for the West Germans to achieve on their own so they had eventually decided to include the British secret service in their deliberations, partly because Krenč had targeted so many Brits in her killing spree and partly because Anna spoke good English and could therefore communicate directly with everyone concerned, instead of through an interpreter who might not get the nuances quite right.

MI6 had been particularly keen to get involved in removing one of the thorniest thorns in its side and quickly took on the role of senior partner in the operation. But the first attempt at entrapment had gone horribly awry, leaving at least three agents dead – although miraculously Anna escaped with her life. It was at this point that General Mackintosh was wheeled in to put his imprimatur on the operation. Under his command, nothing could go wrong. Could it?

Mac's big idea was to give Arkadia Krenč the impression that Anna Stern was already dead. He reckoned, not unreasonably, that it would make things a whole lot safer for Anna, while Krenč's desire to establish the truth of her demise would be just as strong a pull to bring her across the Iron Curtain as the opportunity to kill Anna herself. The thought of assassinating The Vixen on her home territory had evidently been ruled out as too risky, with the potential to trigger a conflict that could all too easily spiral out of anyone's control. Thus the plan to stage Anna's drowning was hatched.

'That's where you fit in, Bill,' said Kenny, draining his latest glass of *Marillenschnaps*.

'Where exactly?'

The brigadier took up the story, sitting forward and getting more excitable as the tale unwound. 'We wanted to add some credibility to the performance – show off Anna as a courier operating in Vienna, under the nose of The Vixen. But we also wanted to provide her with some genuine protection in the shape of a well-trained, resourceful man who could give a good account of himself if it came to a physical confrontation. Of course, we also needed someone completely outside the service, who wouldn't be known to the opposition. It would have been too much of a giveaway to use somebody they might recognise, and that was one of the downsides of Anna's double-dealing: the Russians already knew most of our agents in Austria.'

'Sorry about that,' said Anna. 'That was before I understood…' Her voice trailed off, leaving the rest of us to finish her sentence in our heads.

I looked at Kenny. 'And that's when you suggested me.'

He stretched out an arm for the general to refill his glass. 'Nobody better for the job, mate.'

I thought for a bit, then asked Anna a question that had been niggling me since I'd escaped from Devín Castle. 'Just out of interest, what was the package I was supposed to collect?'

She smiled. 'You're looking at it.'

It all seemed a little ramshackle to me. First of all, the idea of using Anna Stern as bait to catch a murderous secret agent was a plot straight out of the spy novels and I doubted that The Vixen would be stupid enough to fall for it.

'You don't know Arkadia Krenč,' said the brigadier morosely. 'That's more than enough motivation to blind her to the risks.'

'Even if that's true, surely the revelation that Anna was dead – or at least purporting to be – would persuade Krenč to leave the verification to some lesser mortal. Why would she put herself in so much danger?'

Anna said, 'It was personal. We were banking on the fact that she would want to see me for herself.'

'And we were right,' said Mac. 'She did come over.'

That was news to me. 'Have you got her, then? Where are you keeping her?'

He shook his head. 'She did come over but not in the way we expected.'

'What are you talking about?'

Mac looked across at the brigadier. 'Angus?'

Campbell-Medlock put down his glass, stood up and straightened his back, which he turned to the fire, warming his hands behind it.

'Once Anna's body had been dredged from the Danube – in full sight of the Czech border guards at the castle on the opposite bank – we knew Krenč would be on the move. We'd got agents, troops, the Austrian police all on standby.'

'The police were in on it?' That made sense. I recalled Napoleon's revelation after my arrest that my homburg-wearing tail had been one of his men. Mac certainly appeared to have some leverage.

'Some of them. The ones who mattered. The officers who found the body weren't in the know, although one or two of their senior ranks had to be tipped off that you would be watching from the bank nearby.'

'You set me up to get arrested?' The outrage was rising all over again.

'I've apologised already for your treatment, haven't I?' He sounded affronted, which made me marvel at the irony.

Kenny stepped in. 'Look, mate, you were only supposed

to be held overnight while we dealt with Arkadia Krenč. That way, you were safely out of trouble and she could be taken out of circulation without anyone being any the wiser – you included.'

My voice dripped with sarcasm. 'You're telling me you only did it for my own good?'

'It doesn't matter why we did it,' said Mac, stepping into the centre of the room for maximum effect. 'The point is that it turned into one massive cock-up when Arkadia Krenč didn't do what we expected.'

'Wasn't it Wilde who said that to expect the unexpected showed a thoroughly modern intellect? Doesn't sound as if there were many modern intellects at work on this operation.'

The brigadier scowled but Mac took it on the chin. 'That's fair. We fouled it up.'

'So what did Krenč do?'

He stared at me in amazement. 'What do you mean, what did she do?'

I didn't think it was so surprising that I shouldn't know. I had, after all, been locked up in a Viennese cell at the time.

'I mean what did she do that was so unexpected?'

'She busted you out of jail – that's what she did.'

Now it was my turn to stare in amazement. Arkadia Krenč may have been The Vixen in the world of espionage. To me, apparently, she was The Torturess.

The recollection of my ordeal at the hands of this vindictive woman brought a realisation home to me: I needed to get out. I didn't care how important she was to the delicate balance of power in Europe or how many people had died at her hand. For my own sanity – not to mention my health, as well as that of Anna Stern – I had to extricate myself from this unsavoury mess.

'Well, you've dug your big hole; now you can lie in it for all I care.'

Mac took half a step closer to my chair and I wasn't sure if he was trying to intimidate me.

'You can't back out now, Bill. You're in too deep.'

'I can do exactly as I please,' I said angrily, and got to my feet. Mac still towered over me but I wasn't frightened of him. 'I'm a civilian, I don't follow your orders and if you try to make me, I'll scream duress so loudly they'll hear me in Whitehall. This is your mess – you clean it up.'

'That's exactly what we're trying to do. But we can't do it without you.'

'Bollocks,' I said. 'You just want to use me like you did before, and look where that put me: on the wrong side of the Iron Curtain, being beaten black and blue by a homicidal maniac. Find some other mug to be your pawn. I'm going back to Devon.'

I could tell from the crestfallen look in his eye that he knew he was defeated. There was nothing he could do to persuade me to stay. He stepped back the same half pace and allowed me to pass.

I had my hand on the doorknob when Anna spoke.

'What about me, Bill?'

There was something about the softness of her tone, the plaintiveness in her voice, that made me stop. She might have been as bad as the rest of them, snaring me in their lethal undertaking, but it struck me that she had even more invested in the enterprise than the others. She was, after all, the person at the top of Arkadia Krenč's hit list. Closely followed by me, if the brigadier was to be believed.

I turned and studied her, still sitting in the little armchair by the fire. With her hair hanging prettily around her shoulders and her face upturned expectantly towards me, she gave off the impression of a primary school teacher waiting to read a bedtime story to a tired child. The ice inside me, solidified into a hard-hearted stoniness over the past few days, felt the first glimmer of thawing. I saw in her something of the innocence of Sophie Carrington, the naïve young English bride whose adventure into the outback last year had not only endeared her to me considerably but also transformed her from a girl into a powerful, self-sufficient woman. Was I detecting traces of the innocent in Anna Stern or was she simply deceiving me like she had before? If it was the former, then perhaps I still owed her something for letting her down at the Café Central; if it was the latter, then more fool me, but I had to give her the benefit of the doubt.

'Damn you,' I threw at Mac and the brigadier, standing side by side in front of the fire. 'What's your plan?'

EIGHTEEN

Arkadia Krenč had gone off the radar and Mac didn't seem to know why.

'Maybe she was wrongfooted by your escape from the castle,' he said, pouring another decent dose of apricot brandy into my tumbler. I noticed that between us we'd managed to polish off almost the entire bottle.

'Or maybe she just wasn't fooled by your Anna decoy,' I replied.

'Doesn't make any difference. We've hit a dead end. We can't get her if we can't see her, and she won't make herself visible without a damn good reason.'

'Such as?'

He didn't answer but switched his gaze to Anna, who was staring intently into the fire.

'You want to try the same trick twice? You know what Einstein said about doing the same thing over and over and expecting different results?'

'Mmm. The definition of insanity. I know.'

'So what's changed? If anything, you're at more of a disadvantage now than you were a week ago because The Vixen knows you've tried to deceive her once already.'

Anna looked up from the flames. 'It doesn't alter the fact that she will still want me dead.'

Mac agreed. 'And that's what we've got to exploit. Krenč's obsession with Anna is the weak link in her armour. We just need to get her into a position where we can take advantage of it.'

I didn't think much more of the new plan than I had of the old and I wasn't afraid to tell my new spymasters so.

'This has already fallen apart once, with deadly consequences.'

The brigadier said, 'But Anna's still alive.'

I gritted my teeth. 'I was talking about Roland.'

His shoulders sank a little and he turned away.

'Now you want me and Anna to rerun the whole performance in the vague hope that Krenč won't be able to resist having another crack, making sure of the job?'

'That's about the size of it,' said Mac. 'The two of you will meet at the Café Central at the same time every morning until it flushes her out of hiding.'

'And then what? She won't risk trying anything in a location as public as the Herrengasse so my bet is she or her henchmen will put a tail on Anna until they can safely kidnap her – or kill her on the spot. The best you can do is have somebody watching and that'll be too little too late for a killer like Krenč. It's a rubbish plan and you know it.'

Anna stood up from her armchair and sounded decisive. 'It's all we've got, Bill, and I'm perfectly willing to give it a go.'

It was checkmate. As long as Anna was prepared to risk her life again, I couldn't walk away.

'I don't care what headaches it gives you with the local *polizei*, I want at least a dozen armed men within fifty yards of the Café Central whenever we're there. And they need to be different men each day in case the other lot are watching. I want a round-the-clock escort for Anna and separate safe houses for each of us when we aren't actually on the street. The more we can disrupt our routines the better.' I thought I might as well get the best I could out of a terrible situation so I added, 'And I want a dedicated chef installed at each of the safe houses.'

'You don't want much, do you?' grumbled the brigadier.

'That's not all,' I said. 'I need a weapon.'

Mac tried to object but I wouldn't stand for it. 'If you want me to play a sitting duck then the least you can do is arm me with a blunderbuss.'

'It'll take some sorting out. There'll be paperwork.'

I wasn't sure I believed him but in any case I didn't give a damn about his paperwork.

The next morning I was sitting at the same table in the Café Central where I'd first met Anna less than a week earlier. Through the windows I could see a heavier crowd than before and I guessed much of it was made up of the security detail I'd demanded as part of my terms for continuing this damn fool exercise. As I watched I spotted at least three men going back the way they'd come and I made a mental note to put a rocket up Mac's behind when he briefed the next batch of guardsmen for the following day. If I could tell this bunch of amateurs from the average passer-by then it was a rock-solid certainty that a secret agent would be able to as well.

Anna arrived two minutes before the appointed time and waved at me from the door as she took off her heavy coat. I remembered the last time she'd sat at this table, looking anxious and nervous in her bright yellow windcheater, and wondered how she was feeling this time around. She didn't look particularly edgy but I already knew she was a supreme dissembler and the previous occasion had definitely been a performance. I still wasn't sure exactly who for but she'd taken me in comprehensively.

'Good morning,' I said as she sat down opposite me, her back to the leaded glass. I wanted to keep an eye on what was going on outside and I figured if she did the same for the café interior then that would be no bad thing. 'I've taken the liberty of ordering you a coffee.'

'That was a mistake.'

'Why?'

'Because I'll just get a cup of plain black coffee, like last time. The Viennese do it rather differently.'

She hailed a waiter and dashed off a stream of fast German that I couldn't keep up with. I gathered she'd cancelled my previous order and replaced it with something much more grand but I didn't know what it was until it arrived. Five minutes later, the waiter delivered two tall glasses filled to overflowing. Separated into three distinct layers, the coffee was rich and black at the bottom, tinged golden with milk in the middle and topped off with a whirl of thick, white cream that stood a full inch above the lip of the glass and reminded me of nothing so much as the crest of an Alp.

'Schlagobers,' said Anna.

'I beg your pardon?'

'A Gupf of fluffy whipped cream. Speciality of the house.'

I nodded appreciatively. 'I hope it tastes as good as it looks.'

'It does.'

With nothing to do but pass an hour in each other's company and wait for word to reach Arkadia Krenč that Anna was still alive, we chatted aimlessly about everything from the weather – the Englishman's favourite topic of conversation – to Anna's facility with languages. This she had discovered at an early age and it had stood her in good stead throughout her career in the intelligence services. It struck me that her multilingual background closely matched that of Arkadia Krenč – like her, Anna had Russian and English, which she spoke with only a hint of an accent, alongside her native German – but we were careful not to talk about anything too contentious for fear of prying ears in the café. Instead we kept things light and informal. I told her of my boating exploits on the Dart, my fondness for whisky, my past life as an insurance investigator.

'Oh, that sounds interesting,' she said, a smile playing across her lips. She might have been teasing me.

'It had its moments. But I can't say I'm sorry to be out of it.'

'Why's that?'

'Too many nasty pieces of work trying to get one over on you all the time. But I imagine you can understand that.'

She let her gaze fall to the coffee glass on the table and I thought I saw the smile falter, the melancholy I'd noticed at our first meeting returning once more.

'One day I'd like to know more about that,' I said.

'One day I might tell you. But not here and not now.'

For three more days we met, drank coffee and shot the breeze, in the American colloquialism that conveys so much about that nation's laid-back attitude to life. We'd sit for an hour or so, chewing the cud and sizing each other up without ever talking about anything real. Then, with nothing of note having occurred, we'd part, acquire our respective friendly tails, and head back to our safe houses for another day of kicking uselessly about. At least the food was good.

It was on the fourth morning that something finally happened.

Our allotted hour had passed inconsequentially, as every meeting up to that point had, and we were separating on the stone steps, me turning left down Strauchgasse, Anna heading right to take Herrengasse back towards Schottentor. Before I had reached the corner I heard her shout behind me and I whirled around to see her being lifted from the ground between two huge men in black greatcoats and trilby hats. Her cry was cut short as one of the men clamped a giant hand over her mouth, and the pair began bundling her towards a Transit van that was parked facing away from me in Herrengasse.

The junction erupted with movement as Mac's men leaped into action. By the time I reached them, four men were already tackling the abductors, preventing them from getting Anna into the van, and another two were onto the driver in his cab. I grabbed Anna's arm as she broke loose from the grip of her kidnappers and together we dashed up Herrengasse, deeper into the Innere Stadt. Behind us I could hear the crunch of something heavy on skin and bone but I didn't look back. This mess was for Mac to clear up: what I wanted was to get Anna away to safety.

'Keep your head down and hold on to me,' I ordered as we burst out into Michaelerplatz, dominated by the Habsburgs' imperial home to our right. I was keen to get away from the tourist sites as quickly as possible and ducked into the network of smaller streets to our left at the earliest opportunity. We hurried arm in arm for several minutes, taking random turns whenever one presented itself, then suddenly we were in a busy square with hordes of people jostling for a look at the towering frontage of St Stephen's Cathedral, seemingly hemmed in by buildings on all sides but with its skyscraping spire rising above the bustle of the city.

'I know where we are,' I hissed at Anna, recalling the

cat-and-mouse game I'd played with the man in the homburg when I'd first arrived in Vienna. Behind the cathedral, I knew, lay a warren of streets that housed, among other things, the home of Mozart – now a popular museum and therefore not high on my list of potential destinations.

To my surprise, Anna laughed. 'Good for you. I've known where we were the whole time. This is my patch, remember?'

'Sorry – I'm a bloody fool.'

'Are you looking for somewhere in particular?' she said, an amused look on her face.

'Somewhere safe, of course. We need to hide until Krenč's goons have either been dealt with or scurried back into their dark little corners. Any ideas?'

'Certainly. But why didn't you say so before?'

I ignored that and let her lead the way. She turned up a thoroughfare directly opposite the entrance to the cathedral and began marching purposefully towards the far end of the street. There, she took us to the left, then right, bringing us out into a small square that was completely filled by a layered cake of a building topped with a coppered green dome.

'Peterskirche,' she pronounced as we rounded the south side to reach the entrance. 'It's mostly hidden by the buildings around the square so your average tourist doesn't come here. But it's quite impressive inside.'

She wasn't wrong. As we stepped through the door into the vaulted oval chamber that made up Peterskirche my jaw dropped open. From the red-and-white tiled floor to the tip of its extraordinary cupola, the baroque masterpiece was a vision of gold stucco, fine art and marbled religiosity. I found it hard to believe that such ornate extravagance could be so well concealed in the back streets of Vienna's inner city, overshadowed by the vastness of the cathedral and yet with a shimmering brilliance that outshone even St Stephen's grandeur. Opposite the entrance, the high altar rose majestically, surmounted with world-class art and framed by a family of huge pillars. On either side of the building, two further chapels competed for my attention with their paintings and sculptures, while in every nook between the three altars hung superb examples of baroque creativity. No more than half a dozen people were witness to this amazing sight, most of them crouched in dark wooden pews, their heads bowed.

The sound of the door closing behind us echoed ominously around the cavernous interior but nobody looked around. Anna slipped off to the left, hugging the cool marble wall as she made her way around the edge of the space in reverent silence. I followed, eyeing the sparse congregation for signs of anything untoward, but it was easy to tell that these were just ordinary folk going about their worshipping business, paying no mind to the spies in their midst.

When she reached the rail in front of the magnificent high altar, Anna looked back briefly then sat on it, swinging her legs over to the far side before ducking into a doorway at the back corner of the church. I checked behind me and, confident that nobody was watching, followed suit.

On the other side of the door was a surprisingly plain room – a vestry or robing chamber of some kind – lined with cupboards and velvet curtains. Anna selected a throne-like chair over to one side and planted herself nonchalantly in it.

'At this time of day we should be safe here for an hour or two. I don't believe there are any services planned until later this afternoon, and if someone does come in we can just claim that we are tourists who have got lost.'

I perched on a simpler wooden chair opposite Anna and we sat in silence for a while, our usual trivialities having been exhausted in our hour at the café. I checked my watch and wondered how Mac would be feeling right now. With Anna and me having disappeared apparently without a trace, a Transit van full of Soviet agents confronted on an open Viennese street, and a dozen of his men tidying up the mess, I guessed he might be more than a little stressed.

We had agreed the protocol if anything were to happen at one of our rendezvous: anyone still at liberty should reconvene at 3 p.m. in a location that changed every day. Depending on what had happened, a debriefing would take place and plans devised for any next steps that might be required – such as the rescuing of a hostage. Today's venue was a bierkeller on the eastern side of the Innere Stadt, about half an hour's walk from where we were currently hiding – possibly less if Anna's evident knowledge of the back streets included short-cuts.

'You seem to know your way about,' I said. 'I take it you've been here before.'

'It was my regular church when I first came to Vienna.'

I was surprised. 'You're a believer?'

She smiled and put her feet up on a cassock lying near the chair. 'I'm not sure I'd go that far. But a Catholic, yes. If you've been brought up a Catholic it's very hard to leave it behind, whatever your rational mind might tell you.'

'And what about your conscience? Does that allow you to practise your religion?'

The smile faded and she looked away from me. 'How I live my life is a matter between me and God,' she said primly.

I let the topic drop. She was right: it was none of my business.

'I don't know about you but I'm hungry,' she said a few minutes later.

'Do you think we'll find any food stashed in here?

Communion wafers, maybe? I can't imagine there'll be much else.'

She looked shocked but the smile was playing at the corners of her mouth again. 'That's sacrilege, Herr Kemp.'

'Only if you're a Catholic.'

'I saw a hot dog vendor in the street outside. I could easily slip out and pick up a couple of Frankfurter Würstels.'

I considered the idea for a moment. My immediate instinct was to keep us both off the street for as long as possible and damn the hunger pangs but there was a long way to go until three o'clock and the rumblings from our stomachs were not going to get any quieter. I wished I'd had some *Küchen* to go with my *Kaffee*.

'All right. But I'll go.'

'Why you?'

'Because it's you that Krenč is really after – I'm just a lucky extra.'

'If you're on her hit list she won't care what order she takes us in. Besides, I'm the one who knows where the hot dog vendor is. I'll only be a minute.'

Before I could object further, she had dodged across to a wooden door in the outside wall to let herself out.

'Ketchup on mine,' I called, and she threw a disgusted look over her shoulder.

I followed her to the door and opened it a crack to watch. If someone did see her and tried to abduct her a second time, there wasn't going to be much I could do on my own but I couldn't just sit and wait for her to return.

Anna skipped down the street to the left and I caught sight of the hot dog stand fifty yards ahead of her. My field of vision was severely restricted, partly by the narrow opening of the door but also by the curves of the church's exterior wall, and she disappeared from view momentarily, making my heart leap in my chest. A second later she came back into sight, dodging a car as she crossed to the far pavement. The delay as she waited to be served seemed interminable and I was sizing up every passer-by as a possible kidnapper before she finally reached the front of the queue, accepted two long rolls from the vendor and handed over a fistful of change. As she made her way back towards me, a blur of black swung around the corner of the street at speed.

In one of those slow-motion moments in which you can do nothing but watch in horror, I saw the car make contact with Anna's body and she was thrown hideously into the air.

By the time I reached her, sprawled and dazed on the tarmac in front of the Volvo, the driver was already looming over her. I couldn't tell from the way he'd hit her whether it had been deliberate or not but I wasn't going to take any chances. I grabbed his shoulder and hurled him backwards, away from Anna; I was ready with a clenched fist to follow up but as I span around to square up to him, I realised he was even more alarmed than I was. His face behind the thick-rimmed spectacles and bushy moustache was a picture of terror – at mowing down Anna or at my assault on him I couldn't tell – and I knew he was no threat.

When I turned my attention back to Anna, she was easing herself up onto one elbow in the road. I knelt beside her, trying to assess her injuries and stop her from doing any more damage by moving.

'I'm fine, Bill,' she said, pulling her legs under her and holding on to my arm in an effort to stand.

I was surprised at how much it mattered to me that she was all right. 'I'm not so sure. Take your time.'

She seemed determined to get to her feet but as I looked her up and down I was appalled to see a dark red stain splashed across her white shirt.

'You're bleeding,' I said urgently. 'We need to get you to a hospital.'

'What?' She looked down at herself, nonplussed. And then she began to laugh.

'What are you laughing at?' I thundered, my concern spilling over into testiness. 'You could have been killed. As it is you've sustained a nasty injury of some kind.'

'No I haven't, Bill.' She smeared a hand across her chest, dragging the stain with it. 'This is tomato ketchup.'

NINETEEN

'I've pulled the plug. Officially.'

I stared at Mac, dressed in his ill-suited civilian clothes of tweed jacket and knitted tie. The look of a Home Counties country squire didn't sit comfortably in the rowdy bierkeller we were currently occupying and neither did his booming, plummy voice.

'Why?'

He seemed surprised. 'Do you really have to ask after what happened this morning at the café?'

I looked at Anna; she looked back at me. I couldn't tell if it was exhilaration in her eyes or residual animation from our dash across town but neither emotion betrayed any sense of fear.

'I thought what happened was exactly what was intended to happen. You wanted to flush out Arkadia Krenč and there she was – or her henchmen, at least.'

'Precisely. That's the problem. She didn't show up herself and her gang of hoodlums aren't giving anything away. We can be pretty persuasive when it comes to extracting information but they're not going to crack.'

I shuddered as I recalled the extraction of information that I had undergone at the hands of The Vixen and hoped that our boys wouldn't resort to the same kind of tactics. Somehow I doubted that but I had to cling on to some notion that we were the guys in the white hats.

I said, 'You didn't seriously expect her to turn up in person for a kidnapping, did you?'

'Why not? She did for yours.'

He had me there.

Anna said, 'What does this mean, then? You're abandoning the operation to trap The Vixen?'

Mac put down the stein he was holding and nodded. 'That's about the size of it. I've put the two of you in too much danger already.' He looked at me. 'Anna signed up for it when she joined the service but you...'

'What about me? Are you worried I can't hold my own?'

'It's not that, Bill. It's just that you haven't got the training or the background – or, if I'm honest, the mentality – to keep putting yourself in the firing line. You kept telling us, back at the hotel, that you wanted nothing to do with the world of espionage. Well, you've got what you wanted. I'm giving you your ticket home. Your services are no longer required.'

I stewed on what Mac had said for all of two hours before making a decision. An agent had escorted me back to my safe house, where I was invited to pack for a flight home that would take place later that evening, but as I folded my clothes and put them in my bag my resolve hardened by the minute. One stark fact kept surfacing in my brain, and it was one that I couldn't simply ignore: Arkadia Krenč would not rest until I was dead. The same was probably true for Anna Stern too, and that was more than enough incentive to see this bloody business through to its conclusion, whatever that might turn out to be. I stopped gathering my things and went down to the kitchen to speak to the agent.

'Take me back to Mac.'

He looked confused.

'General Mackintosh,' I said. 'I want to see him. Now.'

'I'm not sure if that'll be possible,' said the man, a wiry figure with the look of a sprinter about him.

'I'm not asking for permission.'

He hesitated but must have seen the look of determination on my face. 'I'll see what I can do.'

'Good.'

While he waited to receive his coded instructions over an ageing radio set in the living room, I unpacked my clothes. I wasn't going anywhere just yet. I tried to work out whether it was Mac's impugning of my abilities that had rankled most or the simple truth that The Vixen wouldn't give up as easily as he had. Either way, I was not in the mood for walking away, despite what I'd insisted at the hotel. I was going to have a damned good go at persuading Anna to stick with it too, although if push came to shove I couldn't force her to put herself in danger again. That was a decision she'd have to make for herself and I'd have to come up with an alternative plan to accommodate it if and when the time came.

'All right, sir – the general says he'll see you.'

'Damn right he will,' I said, and marched out of the front door to the waiting car.

Mac was at the safe house where Anna had been staying, which killed two birds. One of the downstairs rooms had been converted into a makeshift office, lined with filing cabinets and bookshelves and with an old-fashioned, leather-topped desk in the centre. On the near side of it sat Anna on a plain wooden dining chair, but on the far side, leaning back in an upholstered office recliner, sat Mac. He was still wearing his ridiculous tie but the jacket had been removed and it looked like they'd been deep in a conversation when I strolled in. I could guess what it was about.

'Can anyone join in?' I asked, not waiting for an invitation to take the chair beside Anna.

'I thought you were heading for a plane home,' said Mac, sitting upright.

'Change of plan. I don't imagine you've entirely dropped the idea of getting The Vixen.'

'Not entirely, no.'

'Then I'm going to be involved.'

Mac let out a heavy sigh and turned away to look out of the window at the property's rear garden, where I could see at least two uniformed men standing guard. 'You're a fickle bastard, Kemp.'

I smiled. 'I aim to please.'

Mac turned back to us and stood up. 'But no can do, I'm afraid. It's taken all the resources I can muster to get you safely out of the country tonight without Krenč having another go at you. It has to be top secret, you understand, not least because you're extremely vulnerable here in Vienna but also because she mustn't know you've returned to England. We can't keep tabs on you full-time back there so it's best she doesn't find out where you are in the first place.'

His bluntness was a reminder of what I'd got myself into but it also reinforced my decision.

'Sorry, Mac, but you're stuck with me. If what you're telling me is correct then there's no point in my going home. It would be the work of a few days at best for Krenč to track me down and if you can't protect me then I'm a goner for sure. There's only one way out of this for me and that's to face it head-on. I'd prefer it if I had your support – not to mention your resources – but if I have to do it alone then that's what I'll do. She's found me once and she'll find me again. The only difference is that this time I'll be expecting her.'

Anna reached over and touched my arm with a gentle hand. 'You won't be on your own, Bill.'

'Thank you.'

'No,' said Mac. 'I can't authorise it. Any operation that involves a civilian is especially scrutinised at the highest levels and the risks are just too high. I'm sorry, Bill, but you have to leave this to the professionals.'

I stood and leaned on the edge of the desk, hoping to add weight to what I was about to say. 'I was afraid you might come up with something like that. Just me, then.'

To my surprise, Anna stood beside me. 'No, Bill. I meant what I said just now. You won't be on your own. If I have to resign in order to help you then that's what I'll do but I'm coming with you, wherever you want to go.'

Mac spluttered and sat down again. 'But you can't – you're a government agent. You can't resign.'

'Watch me,' she said, and turned for the door.

I glanced back at Mac, who was more flustered than I'd ever seen him, and began to follow Anna out of the room, a grin spreading across my face.

'Wait!' Mac called, and we both halted. 'We need to talk.'

I had a plan but I knew he wouldn't like it. I didn't really care about that: the one person I needed to convince was Anna Stern. If she was prepared to go along with it then I suspected Mac would have little choice but to supply the necessary back-up. I revealed my idea slowly, watching for Anna's reaction.

'I'm assuming Vienna has got a little ticklish,' I began. 'I don't suppose the Austrian authorities are taking too kindly to being made to look foolish by both the Western and the Soviet intelligence services and I imagine this morning's rumpus at the Café Central will have ruffled a few feathers in the diplomatic quarters.'

I paused to see if Mac wanted to offer an opinion on any of that but he stayed silent, watching like a hawk from his padded chair across the desk.

'All right then. We're agreed, I hope, that twice is more than enough to try luring Arkadia Krenč onto neutral territory for the purposes of a straightforward abduction. But the fact remains that Krenč still has her sights set on the two of us.' I looked at Anna and she gave a brief nod. 'My suggestion now is that we let her think we're running away.'

A mystified look passed across Anna's face. 'Sorry, Bill. I don't know what you mean.'

'Neither do I,' said Mac, speaking for the first time since Anna and I had returned to our little wooden chairs. 'Get to the point, man.'

'I'm coming to that,' I said testily. I'd had enough of being manipulated by these secret service types and things were going to run according to my rules now or not at all. 'Look, Arkadia Krenč is hot right now.'

Mac grunted. 'More like steaming.'

'So you don't want her traipsing around in a neutral country on this side of the Iron Curtain doing even more damage than usual, do you?'

He didn't reply but shrugged non-committally, which I took as a yes.

'It seems to me the logical thing to do would be to get her onto Nato territory if we possibly can. If you're going to take her alive and especially if you're going to – what's your word? – eliminate her, then you'd be far better off doing it somewhere friendly. I have to say I'm not a fan of removing her permanently from the game and we know where Anna here sits on that subject.'

'I've never liked the thought of anyone being killed, no matter who they are,' she said.

'Needs must,' said Mac grumpily.

'All right, let's not open up that discussion again. The point is you need to get her to France.'

Mac looked surprised. 'France? Why so far?'

'Think about it,' I urged. 'Austria's neutral so we're ruling that out. Ditto Switzerland. And if you go north or south, to West Germany or Italy, you might find yourself in a Nato country but you're still nuzzled up to a Soviet satellite on your border. There'd be too much support for Krenč just a stone's throw away. The safest bet is to tempt her into France: then you can do whatever you're going to do without the threat of an international incident – or even sparking World War Three.'

Mac lapsed into a thoughtful silence but Anna wanted to know more.

'You've really thought this through, haven't you? And there'll be the added advantage that the French intelligence services haven't been infiltrated by The Vixen, as far as we know, so that'll provide an extra layer of security to the operation. But how do you suppose we're going to persuade her to go to France? She's not just going to jump on a plane if we send her an invitation.'

'No, she's not. And getting her on a plane wouldn't be sensible anyway.'

'Why not?'

'Too much potential for collateral damage – isn't that the euphemism? Security at the airports, local police hanging around, huge crowds of innocent travellers and, of course, a dedicated killer confined in a little metal tube. No; we need to keep her on terra firma and preferably in our sights as much as we can.'

Mac sounded sceptical. 'And how do you propose to do that?'

'I've thought of that, too. We've tried using Anna as bait in Vienna twice now and on both occasions it's gone horribly wrong.'

'All right. No need to rub it in.'

'My point is that we need to do something different.'

Anna leaned forward eagerly. 'Like Einstein said.'

'Like Einstein said. So this time, instead of offering you up to The Vixen, I propose we both put ourselves in the firing line. And we do it on the move.'

'On the move?' said Mac.

'We drive. Across the Alps to Geneva then on into France. We could pose as holiday-makers on an expedition to find the best skiing or something.'

'And how does that help?'

'We make a big song and dance about it, making sure Arkadia Krenč knows exactly what we're up to, then we lead her gently by the nose until we get to a location where you and your boys can step in and grab her. All we have to do in the meantime is stay alive.'

Mac laughed out loud, his opinion of my plan abundantly clear. 'It's a suicide mission. Even if the roads are passable – which may well not be the case at this time of year – you wouldn't get more than fifty miles from Vienna before she cut you down.'

'I think you're wrong. I think with the combination of Anna's spycraft and the protection that the terrain offers – especially at this time of year, with the snow hindering any attempt at an attack – we've got a much better chance than you think. Besides, it's not your decision to make.'

'It is if I have to provide the resources to make it happen. Not to mention the covert surveillance and protection we'd have to give you. We'd need agents within reach around the clock.'

'So sort it.'

'It's not that easy, Bill. There are people who need to sign off on this kind of thing. I'm not a lone wolf, you know.'

I bit a little harder than I intended. 'Oh come on, Mac –

Angus told me you're the top of the tree in this organisation and if you can't authorise a few armed men to cover us for a few days then what's the point of you?'

I could see I'd stung him with that but I didn't care as long as it worked.

Before I got my answer, Anna stepped in. 'Listen, if we're going to make this thing look believable from a distance then we should do it in style. Never mind holiday-makers; we should pose as a honeymooning couple. That way we can maintain an even higher profile – the best suites, a luxury touring car, that kind of thing. They couldn't fail to spot our trail.'

I liked that idea a lot and looked at Mac, who was paling visibly. 'I'm sure the coffers could run to that, couldn't they? After all, consider the prize if it all goes to plan. You'd have brought down the West's biggest target all on your lonesome.'

'Well,' said Anna, 'not quite. We'd have had a bit of a part to play.'

Mac looked from me to Anna and back again, his brow furrowed and his brain whirring. When he finally spoke, his voice had a note of resignation but I thought I also detected some grudging admiration.

'You're a bloody one-man crusade, aren't you?'

PART THREE

Running Blind

TWENTY

Mac needed a couple of days to get things fixed and I figured I could allow him that. As long as Anna and I stayed out of sight until we left Vienna there was little to be gained by rushing the operation. I gave him a long list of my requirements, ranging from top-quality ski equipment to a means of radio communication that would not be vulnerable to outside ears. That last proved something of a headache, given the territory we were heading into, but Mac found a frequency and a set of devices that would carry a signal for up to twenty miles with a clear view and maybe three with mountains in the way. It wasn't ideal but it would have to do.

While Mac toiled in the background, Kenny and the brigadier were detailed to look after me and Anna. There was little point in lodging us in separate safe houses any more, and Mac seemed keen to maximise his budget by saving on one dedicated chef, so I moved into Anna's, where Mac's makeshift office was also housed. She spent the next two days introducing me to the dark arts of espionage as far as she was able to given the time constraint and my natural unwillingness to learn anything much about the underbelly of the intelligence service. I picked up one or two techniques that I hoped I wouldn't need, such as how to disarm an attacker at close quarters, but I drew the line at how to kill a man – or woman – silently. It was as much as Anna could do to persuade me to carry a Fairbairn-Sykes knife, designed by two British Army captains during the Second World War for the express purpose of striking at an opponent's vital organs.

'If I ever get that close to Arkadia Krenč again I suspect she'll have the edge on my skills,' I said as Anna demonstrated the strategic target points on a body.

'You never know,' she said. 'And wouldn't you rather be aware of this stuff than have no idea at all?'

'I'm not so sure about that. Sometimes it's better not to know.'

'You mean if the bomb were ever to be dropped you wouldn't want a three-minute warning?'

I shrugged. 'What would be the point? You'd just spend those three minutes despairing, wouldn't you?'

'But isn't there someone you would want to telephone? Someone special?'

I considered for a moment. Maybe I would want to say goodbye to one or two people – Leotta Tomsson or Sophie Carrington, perhaps – but I figured by the time I'd found their phone numbers and dialled, my three minutes would probably be up anyway.

'Let's hope it's academic,' I said.

On both evenings, Kenny and Angus joined us for dinner, excusing Mac with the explanation that there was still a pile of things to be done before Anna and I could hit the road. Oddly, the subject of Leotta and Sophie cropped up as we tucked into a hearty roast-beef meal on the second evening.

'I've got news for you,' the brigadier said, carving into a crisp potato.

I looked up. 'Oh yes? What's that?'

'Your friend from the Caribbean.'

'Leotta?'

'She's safely back in England, conferenced to the hilt and attending lectures with her fellow students once more.'

'Does she know – ?' I began.

He lifted a hand to stop me. 'Not a clue. Still believes she was specially selected for the symposium in America. From what I've heard, she made quite an impression there. I don't think it will have done her medical career any harm at all.'

'She's that kind of girl,' I said. Then I waved my butter knife in his direction. 'But don't let that fool you into thinking I've forgiven you for the way you used her to get to me. That was and always will be a bastard's trick.'

'You really liked her, didn't you?' said Anna, watching me from across the table.

'Doesn't matter whether I did or I didn't. There was no way anything could have come of it. Our lives are playing out on very different trajectories. She's training for a spectacular career making people well; I'm learning how to kill them.'

'And what's your excuse for letting Sophie go?' Kenny asked slyly.

I was beginning to wonder that myself. After we'd returned to England from our Australian expedition, Sophie had been keen to stay in touch, even to see each other regularly. I had demurred but now I was struggling to remember why: the distance between her catering business in London and my semi-retired messing about in boats around Dartmouth was one obvious factor, of course, but there was something else. It wasn't so much the age gap that mattered – plenty of people had made successful relationships out of much bigger disparities than ours – as the divergence between her outlook on life and mine. It was hard to pin down but her innate positivity, which had been such a boon during our outback nightmare, was a distinct mismatch with my own propensity to melancholy. I feared that, rather than her lifting me up to her levels of optimism, I might instead drag her down to mine. I couldn't bear the responsibility of that so I distanced myself gradually over the next few months. She came to visit later in the summer and, during a walk in one of the coves near the castle, I suggested it might be better for her if we agreed not to pursue anything romantic. She'd pretended that nothing had been further from her mind, even faking outrage that I should imply such a thing, but I didn't believe her. We'd exchanged Christmas cards and the odd telephone call but as far as I was concerned she was free to live her life.

I felt a pang for both her and Leotta as they came to haunt me in this curtained, secret house in Vienna. They were lost to me and there was nothing I could do about it.

Our supplies were ready the next morning and Anna and I were taken in a blacked-out van to a location somewhere on the outskirts of the city. I didn't even bother trying to work out the route we were taking or the direction we were heading: none of that mattered. All that concerned me now was that we should get on the road westward as soon as possible, leaving clues in our wake that would look plausible without being too obvious. I didn't think for a moment that Arkadia Krenč would be fooled by our charade but that didn't matter either. The only relevant factor was that she should be intrigued or motivated enough to follow us. I was banking on the fact that she wouldn't hand the job over to some minion – I'd escaped from captivity on her watch and Anna had given her up to the West so we were too important to her for that – so we only needed to put ourselves on her radar. If Anna and I could enjoy a little touring luxury in the process then that was all to the good. I suspected a cloud of fear and apprehension would follow us just as closely as The Vixen.

We climbed out of the van to find ourselves in a large warehouse, its doors firmly closed and its windows too high and small to be seen through. Mac, the brigadier and Kenny stood in a line, like a wedding party waiting to welcome us to a reception, then Mac led us around to the front of the van. There, flanked by half a dozen men in camouflage uniform and with skis strapped to its roof, stood a smart new Alfa Romeo Alfasud.

'Your charabanc,' said Mac, going to the driver's door and opening it proudly.

'James Bond has an Aston Martin,' I said tartly.

'James Bond is fictional,' he replied with equanimity. 'Now do you want it or not?'

I made a show of looking less than enamoured with our transport but inside I was cheering. This was exactly the kind of thing we needed: practical but with an air of luxury and in a bright orange colour that would attract just the right amount of attention as we crossed the Alps. If they didn't know the truth, nobody would imagine for a moment that we were anything other than what we would claim to be: a pair of comfortably-off newlyweds exploring the mountains on their first outing together as a married couple. Even the skis matched.

'We've set you up with a few bits and pieces to go along with the masquerade,' said Mac. 'You've obviously got some of your own things already but we thought you might need a few extras such as ski suits and heavy-duty footwear. They're all packed up in the boot.'

'Very thorough,' I said, nodding appreciatively. 'And the armoury?'

Mac hesitated. 'I really shouldn't be authorising this, you know.'

'Look, Mac, this whole operation is so far under the radar it's almost below sea level so there's no need to get jumpy about putting a few weapons in the hands of a couple of off-the-books agents, is there? You know my army record and you've had Anna rehabilitated to within an inch of her life so quit playing coy and hand over the guns.'

He grunted, cornered again. 'Reach into the centre of the crevice in the back and you'll find a lever that gives you access to a hidden panel.'

I leaned inside the car and followed Mac's instructions. On pulling the lever, the upholstered frontage of the rear seat came away in one piece revealing a secret compartment within the cushions themselves. Clipped into a back board with some heavy ironmongery was an AR-18 assault rifle, complete with telescopic sights and bayonet, and two pistols whose design I didn't recognise. They certainly bore no resemblance to any service weapon I'd ever used. The ArmaLite rifle made me uncomfortable: during my time serving in Ulster it had become the favoured choice of the IRA and was responsible for more British Army deaths in recent years than I cared to consider. On the other hand, there were sound practical reasons for its implementation by the terrorists, even if it had never been adopted by a national army anywhere on the planet. The handguns intrigued me, not least because they featured a sweeping muzzle that joined seamlessly with the trigger guard, quite unlike the long-snouted Brownings I was used to.

'What are these, then?' I asked Mac, bringing one out of the car with me and showing it to Anna.

'It's new,' he said simply, taking it from me and popping out the magazine to demonstrate its ease of use. 'You want James Bond's knick-knacks? Well, this is a Walther PP. Only it's a particular variant that's been developed for special forces so it isn't in general use. Hard to go wrong with it, especially at close quarters.'

He offered it back to me but I indicated for him to hand it to Anna, who took it eagerly and ran it through its checks with a facility that I found impressive and appalling in equal measure. I made a mental note to ask her to do the same with the other one and the rifle before we set off.

'Anything else?' asked Mac.

'Yes. What about our cover? If we're going to go jollying off into the hills then I'd like to know who's looking out for us. You said you weren't a lone wolf – so show us your pack.'

Mac indicated the troops waiting patiently on the other side of the vehicle. 'This is your escort – plus Angus and Kenny. Of course, apart from those two, I can't introduce you to any of them.'

'Of course,' I said, and nodded a greeting to the men which I hoped would signify comradeship and a united agenda. 'Now, where are we going?'

Mac waved a hand in the direction of the warehouse's main doors, away at the far end of the building. 'The most straightforward route to Geneva will be via Innsbruck and Zurich. Plenty of scope for sightseeing and skiing and the roads are likely to remain passable even if the weather closes in. But there's no rush. Kenny thought you might like to stop in Linz for lunch.'

I turned to Kenny, who was waiting patiently near the van. 'That's very considerate of you. I take it you won't be joining us?'

He smiled. 'Watching from a distance.'

'No,' said Anna forcefully, taking us all by surprise. 'Not Linz. Salzburg.'

'That'll make it a very late lunch,' said Kenny.

I shrugged, not really understanding the difference

between the two, but if Anna preferred Salzburg that was all right by me.

Mac said, 'All right, Salzburg it is. Kenny and Angus will be ahead of you as far as that, with two others behind, and your security detail will be refreshed from there to Innsbruck. Because you're not cutting through West Germany, with all those border complications, it'll take longer on the second part than it should but all the switchbacks and Alpine roads will add verisimilitude to the pretence that you're tourists wanting to explore Austria in all its winter wonder. Mind you, I imagine you'll be ready for a good night's sleep at Innsbruck.'

I looked at Anna, who returned my enquiring glance with a brief smile, a curt nod and two paces to the driver's door.

'Give me the keys,' she said.

We took the first hour out of Vienna on the *Westautobahn*, an industrial slab of concrete and tarmac that could have been anywhere in the world were it not for the steadily rising scenery outside the car. Not long after we passed Saint Pölten, the skies darkened dramatically, even though it was still only mid-morning, and large flakes of snow began to splotch on the windscreen. The wipers battled with them for a while, still too dry to run smoothly over the glass and dragging their heels with an irritating graunching sound, but finally the snowfall grew heavier and wetter and Anna leaned forward in her seat to peer through the gloom.

'Do you want to change over?' I asked after another twenty minutes of plodding through the grey landscape.

'I wouldn't mind a coffee,' she said, and swung off the road onto a slipway that had signs for a nearby settlement.

She found a roadside café not far from the junction and steered the car onto its forecourt, bringing it to a stop near the front door.

'I'm not sure the brigadier would approve of an unscheduled break,' I said after we'd settled down at a small table within sight of the car and ordered our coffee.

'That's not our problem,' she said, casting a glance around the sparsely-populated café as if she expected a horde of Russian spies to come dashing out of the shadows at any moment. For all I knew she might be right about that. 'The brigadier should be looking out for us, not the other way around.'

She looked tired, the rims of her eyes red and watery, and I realised the drive must have been tougher than it seemed from the passenger seat.

'It's the non-stop concentration,' she explained when I asked if she was all right. 'I don't mind any of it – the weather, the traffic, the road conditions – on their own but when you put them all together and add the component of watching for potential assassins the whole time, it's a little wearing on the senses.'

I chided myself for not having factored in our pursuers to the arduousness of the journey. For some reason I had imagined that Arkadia Krenč would wait until we were high in the Alps, in some remote mountain pass, before launching an assault; but of course it was just as possible that she might try something on the open highway and make it look like an accident. While I'd been merrily taking in the scenery and studying the maps to see where we were, Anna had taken the full brunt of acting as lookout as well as chauffeur.

'Don't worry about it,' she said, but her face told a different story. I would have to step up on future legs of the trip.

We finished our drinks and sat watching big flakes fall onto the Alfa for a few minutes before rousing ourselves and heading back to the car. I insisted on taking the next stage and urged Anna to rest her eyes but she was determined to stay vigilant, regardless of her tiredness. I'd twisted her arm to come on this expedition but now it felt as if she was nursemaiding me.

I guided the car back onto the *Autobahn* and we barrelled down it for another hour or so, roughly following the valley of the Danube we'd last seen in Vienna, until we finally crossed a wide stretch of river on a high bridge.

'I didn't think we went north of the Danube,' I said, looking over at the map that lay open on Anna's knees.

'We don't,' she said. 'This is a tributary. The Danube is a few kilometres in that direction.' She pointed across to the right, where a town perched on the banks of the river. 'We're now entering Upper Austria, if you'd like to know.'

Fifteen minutes later we were passing the exit for Linz, where Anna had declined to stop for lunch. When the subject first arose, back in the warehouse, I had assumed that she thought Salzburg might present a prettier option for a honeymooning couple but now I asked her about it again.

'It's one of those places that we Germans are a little sensitive about,' she said without taking her eyes off the road ahead of us.

'Why's that?'

'Oh, it's not the town's fault. It's just that a certain wartime leader was brought up here and regarded the place as his spiritual home. If things had gone differently, he intended to make it the major cultural centre of the Third Reich, surpassing Vienna – which he hated, incidentally.'

'Is that so? I had no idea.'

'That's why there's so much industry here. Before the war, he wanted to develop it economically so he injected lots of money into its factories and businesses. He even planned a *Führermuseum* here, for all the stolen art the Nazis looted across Europe.'

'I can understand why it might be a touchy subject,' I said, glancing northwards into the river valley.

We lapsed into an edgy silence, both keeping a wary eye on the traffic and the weather, and we drove steadily for another hour. We were into the afternoon now and the skies were beginning to clear a little. I was hopeful that there might even be some sunshine for us to enjoy as we stopped in the city of Mozart's birth for that late lunch. I'd noticed the height of the surrounding countryside rising gradually the further west we drove but as we neared Salzburg the scenery to our left suddenly disappeared, to be replaced by a wall of dense grey.

'What's that?' I asked Anna.

She consulted the map, still open on her knee. 'It's Mondsee, one of the lakes that are dotted across this part of the country. You just can't see it because of the mist.'

The road descended almost to the water's edge and we skirted the lake for a few miles, the clouds breaking occasionally to allow a glimpse across to the peaks beyond. Then we left it behind and drove the final leg into Salzburg itself.

As we approached the exit from the *Autobahn* I said, 'Give Kenny a nudge and get him to find us somewhere nice for our lunch, will you?'

We'd agreed to maintain radio silence for as long as possible, only resorting to contacting our escort in an emergency, but after the murky drive we'd just endured I reckoned lunch qualified.

Anna took out the handset and fired it up. 'Kenny, are you there – over?'

The static crackled back at us for a moment, then the brigadier's voice cut through. 'Negative, Farrah. We do not copy. Please remain dark. Out.'

'Those bloody codenames,' I snarled. 'I wish we'd

insisted on something else.' It was Kenny who'd suggested Farrah and Lee, after the famous actors Farrah Fawcett and Lee Majors who had married the previous summer. He had this notion that it tied in with our pretending to be newlyweds and I had put up nowhere near enough resistance. Apparently the brigadier and one or two others involved in the operation found it all highly amusing and the codenames stuck.

'We need to know where to go for lunch,' Anna said into the radio but only the static replied.

'Looks like we're on our own,' I said. 'Where do you fancy?'

We drove into the centre of the city and parked the car prominently in a busy street. From there we walked through slush to the river, a couple of streets away, and selected a restaurant that had a covered terrace overlooking the water, with a view of the quaint buildings on the far side, overshadowed by the imposing fortress of Hohensalzburg. Somewhere in that network of little thoroughfares, the maps revealed, stood the house where Mozart was born. Something for another occasion, I decided.

I'd been optimistic about the weather and for the next hour we enjoyed the view and the veal as the sun shone favourably on our little terrace.

'Mac was wrong – as I suspected,' I said after we'd shared a plate of strudel.

'Wrong about what?'

'He said we wouldn't get fifty miles from Vienna without The Vixen having a go at us. Well, we're three times that and there's been no sign of her.'

Anna took a sip from her coffee cup and squinted out into the sun. 'Just because you can't see her doesn't mean she isn't there.'

'Fair point. But we're doing a pretty good job of making ourselves conspicuous, I'd say, and she hasn't made herself known so far. I'd at least expected to be followed by someone other than Mac's bodyguards.'

'We have been.'

I stopped with my own cup halfway to my lips. 'What are you talking about?'

Anna continued to stare aimlessly at the view. 'A blue Opel Rekord and a beige BMW. I first noticed the Rekord after we stopped for coffee but I didn't see the BMW until the last hour or so.'

I was astonished. 'You didn't say anything.'

'What would be the point? It was important that you concentrate on driving in conditions like today's, and knowing we were being followed by two vehicles would only have added to the pressure on you. It was enough that I saw them.'

I wondered if the occupants of the two cars had followed us to the restaurant and began glancing around warily.

'Don't look so shifty,' said Anna, still not looking at me. 'You don't want them to know we've spotted them, do you?'

I was seriously concerned now. 'Are they here?'

'No,' she said, and burst out laughing. 'I'm only teasing you.'

'What? You mean we haven't been pursued by two cars?'

'Oh no – the cars are real enough. But they haven't followed us to the restaurant. I would imagine they're parked somewhere near the Alfa waiting for us to return. They won't do anything without strict instructions from The Vixen and so far I haven't seen her at all. It's a little odd, actually. Almost as if she's not really trying.'

I couldn't sensibly comment on that so I drained my coffee and stared out at the fortress for a while. 'Next time

I'd appreciate being included in the surveillance exercise, if you don't mind,' I said eventually.

'Don't feel bad about not noticing them. I'm the trained spy, remember?'

We paid the bill and strolled nonchalantly back to the car, although my feigned insouciance was significantly hampered by the knowledge that even now we might be in the sights of several trained assassins. I took hold of Anna's hand in an attempt to reinforce the impression of two people in love and, after an initial twitch from her, she looked at me, smiled and squeezed my hand. I couldn't be sure but I didn't think it felt entirely fake.

I'd suggested over lunch that Anna might like to take the wheel for the next stage of the journey to Innsbruck, where we were already booked into a hotel for the night. It struck me that her familiarity with mountain roads, especially after dusk, might equip her better to make the drive. She declined, however, arguing that she was best placed to act as rearguard, having already identified the two vehicles behind us. There was also the little matter of her job, which made her by far the more useful of the two of us to be available for action if we did come under fire.

I turned the car out of its parking place and onto the street, almost causing an accident as I steered to the wrong side of the road before remembering and swerving back to the right-hand side.

'Look out!' shouted Anna superfluously.

'Sorry,' I said and redoubled my concentration.

We crossed the river and headed south, leaving Salzburg on the aptly-named Alpenstrasse. It was starting to get dark and the traffic was becoming busier – presumably we were hitting what passed for rush hour in this Austrian metropolis – but we still had several hours ahead of us to Innsbruck and I was beginning to doubt the wisdom of aiming so far in one day.

'The later it gets, the more I think we should stop some-where for the night,' I said after we'd turned off the main north-south road at Bischofshofen to head west. It irri-tated me that we couldn't take the direct route from Salz-burg to Innsbruck but it would have meant cutting across the furthest south-eastern tip of West Germany, with two border crossings; while Mac had at least managed to retrieve my passport from the hotel, the lethal cargo we were carrying made it too much of a risk. We'd have to face something similar when we reached Switzerland but we'd cross that bridge when we came to it. Instead we had resigned ourselves to going the long way round, staying in Austria and venturing onto smaller roads as we climbed into the mountains. Even with Anna as on-board lookout, I was growing increasingly uncomfortable.

'It'll upset Kenny and Angus,' she said.

'Damn them! If they aren't prepared even to talk to us on the radio then they'll have to make sure they've got their wits about them for when we make an unscripted stop. Incidentally, have you seen anything of them on this journey?'

Out of the corner of my eye I saw her shake her head.

'I hope that's because they're doing a better job of stay-ing out of sight than our Czech friends,' I said.

The road was becoming distinctly more Alpine the fur-ther we travelled. Although the mountains were mostly hidden in the evening gloom, their imposing presence could be felt all around us and I began to realise why the natives in these parts had such a rich history of fables and fairytales about creatures who supposedly dwelt among the peaks. The twists and turns kept our speed heavily restricted and I was overcautious in my approach to the winding route. On one side of the car the white slopes rose dramatically into the darkness while on the other side, forests of snowy trees ran away into deep ravines.

Occasionally we would follow the path of a river valley that cut through the mountains and at those times the edge of the road gave way to a troubling blackness, the only separation between us and a sheer drop being a flimsy metal barrier reflecting the light of the headlamps.

For mile after mile we stayed in convoy with a lorry in front and a sleek silver Porsche 911 behind. With no opportunity to overtake, we were stuck taking the trip at the truck's speed but that didn't bother me at all. I was far happier trundling through Upper Austria at a snail's pace, with traffic acting as a security escort, than if we'd had a clear, open road ahead of us, with its inevitable opportunities for ambush. We passed through villages and small towns, their chalet homes and guesthouses shining like beacons in the oppressive night, and I wondered again if we should find somewhere to stop. The thought of a warm bed and one of those apricot brandies as a nightcap was more than a little appealing. We'd be sacrificing the safety of the city for a *Gasthaus* in the middle of nowhere but, in the absence of any evidence that Krenč and her cronies had even stayed on our tail since leaving Salzburg, it was sorely tempting. Immediately, though, Anna's comment about The Vixen not really trying floated up in my mind and I had the uneasy feeling that we might be missing some obvious part of the puzzle.

Then, unexpectedly, the lorry turned off and we found ourselves on a wide plain, the road stretching relatively straight before us for at least a mile, if the headlights in the distance were anything to go by.

We also found ourselves under attack.

TWENTY-ONE

Within seconds of the lorry taking a right turn off the main road, the Porsche began gaining fast. I could see its distinctive bubble-eyed lights approaching in the rear-view mirror and initially I thought he was going to swing across to the other lane and overtake us: it would have been a tight manoeuvre but I figured there was just about enough room before the oncoming traffic reached us, even if it meant I had to slam on the anchors to allow him to pass.

Instead of overtaking, the 911 kept on coming at us.

'What the bloody hell – ?' I began, but Anna had spotted me looking in the mirror and turned around in her seat before I could finish my sentence.

'Hit the gas – now!' she ordered, and I floored the accelerator just as the front of the Porsche kissed our rear bumper. The Alfa's aerodynamics and sharp handling saw us surge away from it and I put as much distance between us as I could while the road was still straight. That wouldn't last for long, however, and I wondered what would happen when my inexperience of Alpine driving was tested by the bends that I was convinced would be coming up. I guessed the driver of the sports car behind us would have no such limitations – and definitely superior horse power under his bonnet – and I feared we would soon be in their sights again.

'You'll have to navigate for me,' I said urgently. 'We don't have time to swap over for you to drive so you're going to have to guide me around these bloody mountain roads.'

Without speaking, Anna shuffled through the maps and atlases that were strewn around her feet. I guessed she was looking for a large-scale map of Upper Austria, which I knew we were carrying, to be able to give me as much detail as possible about the road ahead. She grabbed one and unfolded it on her knee, then took a torch out of the glove compartment and pointed it at the open sheet.

'Where are we?' she asked, a slight tremor in her voice.

'I don't know. That last village was called Fibberbraun or something. I didn't see the sign properly as we came past.'

I could see her studying the map closely and wondered how far she'd have to go, tracing the line of the road from where we'd turned off into the mountains at Bischofshofen. We'd been driving for an hour and a half but much of that had been at the pace of the slow lorry so I hadn't much clue about how far we'd actually travelled. After a moment she let out a triumphant cry.

'Got it! Fieberbrunn.'

'Sounds about right,' I said.

'Well, that's great news. The road is pretty straight from here for the next few miles until we get to a town called Saint Johann. As long as you don't mind breaking the speed limit, we should be able to keep ahead of them.'

'I don't mind that at all,' I said, relief beginning to flood through me. I kept my foot firmly on the accelerator pedal and watched as the speedometer continued to climb, touching more than a hundred kilometres an hour as we glided around some gentle curves in the road. I was totally reliant on Anna's map-reading for reassurance that we weren't going to encounter any sharp bends but I'd lost sight of the Porsche and guessed I'd put a good half-mile between us already. Then a thought struck me and I eased off the gas.

'Do you think we should try to escape them? I mean, isn't this what we're here for, to lure The Vixen into a trap?'

'You're forgetting two very important things, Bill.'

'Which are?'

'Firstly, we're trying to lure her out of the country and we're barely into the Tyrol. We still have half of Austria and all of Switzerland to go before we reach France.'

I thought back to our briefing with Mac and realised she was right. The journey this far had been the easy bit. Now we faced winding roads, high mountains and the worst of the weather as we worked our way down to Innsbruck, then across the rest of the Tyrol and the Vorarlberg province at the western end of Austria to the Rhine, which created a natural border for the Swiss with their Austrian and Liechtenstein neighbours. We planned to skirt the principality to the north, hoping to cross into Switzerland on one of the smaller bridges over the river, where the guard posts might be less vigilant about a couple of spies and their entourage. From there it was a relatively easy run to Zurich then on to Geneva and the final crossing into France. At that point, Mac and his boys could take over – assuming Anna and I were still alive by then.

'What's the second thing?' I asked.

'We're on our own. I haven't seen anyone from our side since we left Vienna and the brigadier made it very clear that he didn't want us using the radio.'

'Sod that!' I said forcefully. 'If this doesn't qualify as an emergency, I don't know what does. Try them again.'

Anna grabbed the transceiver and snapped its switch. 'Farrah and Lee calling urgently – over,' she said, repeating the message three times before giving up. 'Nothing.'

'I thought they tested this stuff out in combat conditions?' I said.

'They do. But you can't legislate for the weather and if they're two or three mountains away then it's quite possible the signal wouldn't get through to them.'

'Are you sure you're on the right frequency?'

When she didn't reply I glanced at her and saw the look of disdain on her face.

'All right, so we've got no cavalry coming to the rescue, a vicious Porsche on our tail and another ninety minutes to Innsbruck. That doesn't sound like much fun to me.'

'We'll be all right if we can stay this far ahead of them.' She didn't sound convinced.

'That depends on whether they're on their own. From what everyone's told me, and from what I've seen firsthand of Arkadia Krenč's tactics, I don't imagine she'll be leaving anything to chance. I'd rather quit while we're ahead – out of sight of the Porsche – and find ourselves somewhere nice and cosy to wrap up for the night.'

'What about the car? They're sure to spot that if we stop at a roadside hotel.'

I thought hard. We were reaching the outskirts of a town, which I took to be Saint Johann, and I followed a sign for the town centre, ignoring the one indicating the route to Innsbruck.

'What are you doing, Bill?' Anna asked. 'Innsbruck is that way.'

'I've decided: we're not going to Innsbruck. Not tonight, anyway.'

'Are you sure that's wise? Kenny and Angus will be expecting us there.'

'I don't give a damn what Kenny and Angus are expecting. I want to throw off those bastards in the Porsche so we're taking a little diversion. If memory serves, we're not far from Kitzbühel here.'

Anna didn't need to consult the map for that one. 'About fifteen minutes to the south.'

'Perfect. With a bit of luck we'll lose our pursuers by leaving the main Innsbruck road and a winter resort will give us the ideal cover. I seem to recall it's where Ian Fleming learned to ski when he lived there before the war. Seems apt.'

'You boys and your spy books,' sighed Anna. 'Are you starting to understand that the real world of espionage is not very much like the novels?'

'I don't know about that,' I said, taking another turn to join a stream of traffic on a road that was marked in the direction of Kitzbühel.

Exactly fifteen minutes later we pulled up in front of a quaint Tyrolean inn just off the main road in the ski resort. I'd considered heading into the heart of the town, where all the *après-ski* action and high-class hotels would be, but instead decided on somewhere less obvious. I tucked the car in against its side wall, hoping to keep it hidden from a casually passing pursuer, and we went inside together to make sure it had a room before we unloaded the bags.

I let Anna do the talking and within minutes we were carrying our things up to a well-appointed, sizeable room at the top of the hotel. We'd stowed the pistols in our luggage but had to leave the rifle in its concealed compartment in the car: there was no way we could have smuggled it inside, no matter how much I would have relished having it within reach.

In the room I dropped my armfuls on the large double bed and walked over to the window, where I peered out through the half-closed curtains onto a wonderland of shimmering lights. The window turned out to be a French door so I flipped the latch and stepped out onto a sturdy wooden balcony, high above the street where people jostled happily among the bars.

'Close the door,' called Anna from inside, and I realised I was letting a blast of cold air in – and the pleasant heat of the hotel out.

'Nice room,' I said, turning back inside and closing the French door behind me.

Anna had already made herself comfortable on a huge settee that would be my berth for the night and was perusing a drinks menu that had been left helpfully on a coffee table.

'It should be,' she said. 'It's the honeymoon suite.'

I've never been a great one for the trappings of romance, preferring straight talking and honest feelings to the woolly game-playing and second-guessing of hearts and flowers or chocolates and champagne. On this occasion I was willing to make an exception: our whole expedition was a charade, after all. With one or other of our secret services footing the bill, we ordered a bottle of Dom Perignon from the hotel bar, along with some local delicacies to eat, and settled down side by side on the settee. Two glasses in, I ventured what might have been taken for an intimate question in other circumstances, but in the honeymoon suite of a pretty little Tyrolean *Gasthaus* counted as casual conversation.

'Thanks to the testimony that Angus showed me, Anna, I know quite a bit about your career in espionage, but what about your personal life? Is there a man lurking somewhere in the background?'

She looked at me coyly over the top of her glass and smiled, a hint of suggestiveness in her eyes.

'What a question, Mr Kemp. Would you mind if there was?'

I suddenly realised that I would. In the short time that I had known her, I'd grown surprisingly fond of this red-haired, multi-skilled spy with a facility for languages and a taste for exotic coffee. I could stand to know a little more about her private life.

'Maybe,' I said, equally coyly. 'Let's call it professional interest.'

'Let's call it what it is: nosiness.'

I laughed and took a long draught of my champagne but I noticed she didn't answer.

'I'll tell you what, Bill: you talk me through your love life and I might think about letting you in on mine.'

'That'll take all of three minutes,' I said, and proceeded to explain how I'd lost the love of my life in a tragic plane accident, married again too quickly and ill-advisedly, and had been all but celibate ever since. Leotta and Sophie she already knew about from our evening meals with the others back at the safe house. 'Your turn.'

'I think I need a little more of this,' she said, reaching for the bottle and brushing my arm with her wrist as she did so. I felt something I hadn't felt in a long time – not since Sophie and I had parted almost a year ago – and it jolted me. As she leaned back again with a full glass, her body was tilted significantly towards me and now she rested her head on my shoulder. 'I don't want to get too drunk, Bill.'

'Are you thinking we'll need clear heads in the morning?'

'No,' she said. 'I want to be able to remember making love to you.'

As we lay in the darkness, the sounds of the bars in the street below climbing gently to our eyrie, I felt Anna shiver a little and I pulled up the furry rug from the foot of the bed, where it had been pushed, to drape on top of the light sheet that was half-covering us. Her shoulder was tucked into the crook of my armpit and her head rested on my chest, where the fingers of her free hand toyed idly with a few hairs. I caressed the back of her head, running my fingers through the red tresses and trying to recall the last time I'd felt so relaxed. It had certainly been some time before arriving in Austria – even before the anonymous phone call telling me about Leotta's disappearance – but I couldn't place exactly when. I always felt a certain tranquillity on the boat so maybe that was it.

'*Pfennig* for them,' I said softly, bringing my thoughts back into the bed.

She lifted her head slightly. 'Excuse me? I don't think I know that idiom.'

'Oh, sorry. It's an old-fashioned expression: a penny for your thoughts.'

'I don't think my thoughts would be worth that much,' she said. 'I was just wondering what the next few days might bring.'

'Mountains, driving, cars, more mountains, gunfire – that kind of thing, I expect.'

'I was hoping for more in the way of cosy hotel rooms, expensive champagne and lots of delicious sex,' she said, plucking at my hairs playfully.

'Well, whatever they bring, we've certainly conformed to our backstory. Nobody could complain that we haven't tried to live out the roles we assigned ourselves.'

She laughed and hotched herself up on her elbow to look at me. Her fingers continued to fiddle with my chest hair.

'You must have known this was inevitable?' she said, a look of curiosity on her face.

It was my turn to laugh. 'Inevitable? You must be joking. This kind of thing is as likely to happen to me as... well, as racing across the Alps being chased by a madwoman. I don't get to go to bed with girls like you, Anna.'

'What on earth do you mean, "girls like me"?' She sat up properly now and clutched the sheet across her breasts, as if she were ashamed of what we'd just done.

'You know – spies,' I said quickly. 'I'm not exactly Double-O Seven.'

'Oh, that,' she said and let the sheet fall again. 'I thought you meant something quite different.'

I took her hand and drew her back down onto my torso, cradling her as I had before: I wanted the feeling to last as long as possible. I knew the dawn would bring a cold reality to our tryst and I didn't know if this closeness would ever be rekindled. If Arkadia Krenč had anything to do with it, we might struggle to make another nightfall at all.

'Do you think it'll matter if we don't sleep tonight?' she asked, and I felt a fresh thrill of anticipation.

'With what we've got to look forward to tomorrow, I don't think it'll make a jot of difference one way or the other. There'll be adrenalin coursing through our veins most of the time, I would imagine, and that'll be as enlivening as any good night's sleep.'

She fell silent for a long while and I wondered if she had, in fact, succumbed to slumber. Then she stirred again and moved across me, clasping her hands over my chest and resting her head on them. Her green eyes looked as wide awake as I'd ever seen them, although with that same familiar melancholy hiding deep within.

'Tell me what she did to you.'

'Who?'

'Arkadia Krenč, of course.'

I turned my head towards the window, where the lights of the town seeped in at the edges, casting a luminous glow across the room. 'Can't we have one night without thinking about her?'

'No, Bill. I don't think we can. She is the person who unwittingly brought us together, whether we like it or not, and I'm starting to believe that we'll never be rid of her as long as she's alive.'

'You think killing her is going to be liberating in some way?' I was dismayed at her shift in attitude but then I reminded myself that she was, after all, in the game of espionage and this kind of conversation would be standard fare in her world. 'I'm sorry, Anna, but I can't think like you do. I know you'll have your justifications for eliminating The Vixen but, to me, a life is a life and you can't simply scrub it out because it happens to be inconvenient to you.'

Her tone remained even and unemotional. 'It's not a case of her being inconvenient, Bill. She's a dangerous enemy to me, to you, to the whole of the West. There's a reason they call it the Cold War, you know, and she and I are merely soldiers in that war.'

'And me now,' I said bitterly.

'Only temporarily. Once this job is over you can go back to your nice little existence in England and nobody will be any the wiser. I have to go on fighting this battle for the rest of my life.'

I sympathised but still couldn't bring myself around to her way of thinking.

The darkness thickened along with the silence. Eventually she said, 'Why do you hate espionage so much?'

'Does it really need any explanation? Look at us, look at The Vixen – look at it all. It's just one big bloody mess and ultimately nobody is any better off.'

'But you must see that this is how the world works?'

I thought back to my history lessons in school and the origins of Queen Elizabeth's state-sponsored spy networks across Europe. Anna was right: the world had been working this way for centuries. It didn't mean I had to like it.

'Maybe it's not the espionage itself so much as the people it attracts. It's dirty, venal and amoral, and from the little I've seen, so are its practitioners.'

She grimaced. 'Thanks very much.'

I held her gaze for a long moment before speaking again. 'Why don't you just walk away? Nobody's holding a gun to your head, are they?'

She rolled away from me and got up from the bed. Taking the fur rug, she wrapped it around her shoulders and moved over to the settee, where she picked up her half-full champagne glass before tucking her feet underneath her and curling herself into the cushions. It seemed that the closeness had already dissipated.

'You don't understand, Bill.'

'You're damn right I don't. I don't understand how a girl as wonderful as you could have got caught up in this terrible line of business in the first place. I don't understand why you can't just give it up and go and live a normal life like everyone else. And I don't really understand why you and I are now the prime targets of a Soviet assassin who's prepared to bring down the whole of western Europe in some crazed vendetta. In the final analysis, I'm just a rather dull Englishman who struck lucky by escaping and you're just an old friend who's antagonised her by turning her in. I don't know why she's taking it all so personally.'

Anna put her glass down again and shrank back into the settee. She looked forlorn and tired.

'What am I missing?' I went on. 'This kind of thing must happen all the time in espionage circles. Surely she's seen enough of it to know that this is simply another turn of the wheel. Next week it'll be someone on their side who gets the upper hand. That's why it's all such bunkum

in the end: nobody wins so what's the point in even playing the game?'

To my amazement, Anna suddenly jumped to her feet
and began railing at me. 'No, you don't understand, do
you? How could you? You're a sad old widower living out
a lonely existence in the depths of the English countryside. What could you possibly know about the duplicities
of the Cold War? You listened to what Kenny told you
and you think that's what this is all about. Well, Kenny
knows nothing. You've read my file – you know how
all this has been handed down to me by my father. This
isn't just some petty squabble between a couple of "old
friends", as you put it. This is history. This is my father, the
Nazi. This is everything I've ever believed in turned on its
head, everyone I've ever loved turned against me. How
could I possibly expect you to understand?'

She slumped back down in the chair and even in the
darkened room I could make out a tear rolling down her
cheek.

I was utterly bewildered. Yes, I knew about her father
and his less-than-heroic past, but what on earth was the
rest of her diatribe about?

'Anna, what the hell are you talking about? Everyone
you've ever loved? What does that mean?'

She sparked into life again. 'You were right, Bill – this
is not just some spy's reprisal. This is personal revenge,
pure and simple.'

'Revenge?' I queried. 'Revenge for what?'

'Don't tell me you haven't worked it out yet,' she said,
staring at me in disbelief. 'Arkadia Krenč and I were lov-
ers.'

TWENTY-TWO

We started early the next morning, hoping to make the most of the daylight and get as far away from the Porsche as possible. We could have no way of knowing which direction it had gone but if it failed to find us last night after reaching Innsbruck, the chances were it would have doubled back, retracing the route to the point where we'd lost it and then looking for alternatives. I wanted to be long gone from Kitzbühel when they turned up.

We found a different route out of town, taking a road further south than the one we'd originally planned to use, which had the added advantage of keeping us on the opposite side of the mountains from any returning Porsche. Our idea was to pick up the main westward road at the Inn river and follow its valley to the city whose bridge had christened it as far back as Roman times. There, regardless of the brigadier's discomfort about using the radio, we'd establish contact with him and Kenny for a rendezvous and a re-evaluation of the operation. Having come under attack far earlier than we'd expected, I wanted to know if they still thought France was the best option; hundreds of miles lay ahead of us and the combination of a single viable route and the white wilderness that surrounded us was making me nervous. It had been my idea in the first place but I realised that I'd had no proper understanding of just how claustrophobic the journey would prove to be. It felt to me now like we were Spartans at the straits of Thermopylae, funnelling into a narrow gorge with no way out but forwards, where an unknown enemy awaited with superior forces and the element of surprise. If that was true, then I also wanted a much better back-up plan from Mac.

And then there was the uncanny absence of The Vixen herself. Just what was she playing at?

The stretch to Innsbruck proved uneventful. Whether it was because we'd dodged the Porsche in the run from Kitzbühel or they were simply waiting for us at the other end, I couldn't tell. I was just grateful that there was no sign of any pursuers. There was also no sign of Kenny and Angus or anyone else from our side for that matter but that was no different from day one and, besides, I intended to see them face-to-face at Innsbruck.

Given that this was supposed to be among the most dramatic landscapes in Europe, the scenery was remarkably dull. On both sides of the carriageway, reaching to within about a hundred yards of the road, a thick fog shrouded the mountains, obscuring the views and keeping any sunshine at bay. The resulting grey matched my mood. Anna's revelation from the night before had not bothered me in the way she suspected it might – her romantic history was none of my business – but the addition of another twist to the already tangled knot of complexity that bedevilled this whole operation could only be unhelpful.

Anna drove the first stint of the day while I handled the telecommunications side of things. Fifteen minutes out from Innsbruck I started trying to reach Kenny.

'Can you hear me, Kenny? It's Bill.' I was damned if I was going to use their bloody silly codenames. Krenč knew who we were and, in all likelihood, where we were so it all seemed pretty pointless to me.

For five minutes I got nothing but static; then a cheery Australian voice came over the speaker.

'Bloody hell, mate – we thought we'd lost you. Where the blue blazes have you been?'

That did not bode well. If Kenny had lost track of us for the past twelve hours or more then we'd been completely at the mercy of The Vixen and her crowd and it was only our ingenuity and quick-thinking, taking the alternative route via Kitzbühel, that had kept us alive. Either that or she wanted things this way.

'You ought to know,' I said acidly. 'You're meant to be our escort.'

'Yeah, sorry about that. Angus and I handed over to the next pair after lunch yesterday and they got stuck behind a tractor somewhere after the turn-off outside Salzburg. By the time they got past, you'd vanished. They drove back and forth from Innsbruck to Bischofs-hofen three times during the night but couldn't track you down.'

I laughed but it was a bitter amusement: these men were supposed to be the best in the world, trained, armed and detailed to protect us. 'We decided to try some *après-ski*; took a slight detour to Kitzbühel.'

'Then you're a bloody idiot. How can we look out for you if we don't know where you are?'

'You may not have known where we were but Arkadia Krenč certainly did.'

I waited for his reaction, which came in a suitably satis-fying explosion of alarm. I told him the story of our clash with the Porsche, the unexpected diversion south and our quaint little Tyrolean hideaway. I left out the more intimate details of the night's activities but I guessed he would get the gist.

'So where are you now?' he asked, an urgency in his voice that gave me some reassurance.

'Just arriving at Innsbruck,' I said. 'You don't fancy a spot of breakfast, do you?'

The chalet Kenny directed us to was extremely well concealed, high in the slopes above the city and almost unreachable through the snow that had fallen overnight. The Alfasud's tyres churned up slush as we climbed and at one point I wasn't sure if we were actually going to make it but Anna's experienced driving and the fact that there was already one set of tracks helped considerably. I assumed the earlier tracks had been made by Kenny's vehicle, whatever that was, but wanted to be cautious as we approached the building, which looked like a disused farmhouse hidden among a clump of pines.

'Stop here,' I told Anna as we neared the entrance to the site. 'I want to check it out before we go sailing merrily in.'

Anna pulled over at the side of the narrow road and I got out, cursing the wet snow that immediately dampened the cuffs of my trousers. I tiptoed to the gate, which stood open, and peered through the branches of one of the trees that grew either side of it. The house was about twenty yards back, a long, low building constructed of a few courses of rendered bricks topped with timber and glass. A Land Rover stood not far from the front door, the tracks from the road following it neatly to its parking spot. A few footsteps mushed up the snow between the car and the door but other than that there was no indication of any activity.

I clicked the radio in my hand. 'Are you there, Kenny?'

'Right here, mate. Where are you?'

'Come to the front door and step outside.'

'What game are you playing, Bill?'

'No game. I just want to make sure we're at the right place.'

He let out an audible sigh and moments later his jolly pink face appeared at the front door of the chalet.

'Thank Christ for that,' I said to the radio, and stepped out into the gateway.

Kenny caught sight of me and beckoned me over. 'Come inside, mate. It's bloody freezing out here.'

I signalled to Anna to bring the car into the yard and two minutes later we were in the kitchen of the rundown chalet, Kenny plonking steaming mugs of coffee in front of us.

'Are you on your own here?' I asked him after taking a sip.

The answer came from the doorway behind me. 'I'm here as well.'

I turned to see the brigadier, dressed in a bright red padded jumpsuit, standing in the hallway. It was all I could do to stifle a laugh.

'Who have you come as – Franz Klammer?'

'Oh, very funny,' he said sarcastically. 'But I think you'll find it's best to be properly equipped in the mountains.'

Anna nudged me in the ribs with an elbow. 'He's right you know.' But I could see a twinkle in her eye.

Angus and Kenny sat down at the kitchen table with drinks, completing our little party of four. 'Mac sends his apologies – he's got bigger fish to fry in Whitehall.'

'I got the impression from the way everyone's been talking about World War Three that there were no bigger fish than Arkadia Krenč,' I said.

The brigadier nodded. 'That's true, but not everyone needs to be on the ground to carry out the mission. He's overseeing matters from the panelled foundries of the Foreign Office.'

'Wouldn't want him to put himself too far out.'

'You know how it is, Kemp: the elected representatives need to feel they have some input into decisions and that requires rank. Nothing less than a general will do to keep their egos happy.'

'I didn't think the elected representatives knew anything about operations like this,' I said.

'Oh, they don't. But if the likes of Mac don't put on a show for the committees they start to get suspicious pretty quick and then they start sticking their noses in where they really shouldn't be stuck. Causes endless trouble for everyone. No, it's far better for all concerned if the top brass throw them scraps of red meat every now and then; let them feel involved.'

'Even if they know nothing of the truth?'

'The truth? What on earth makes you think that's got anything do with what we're up to? In any case, truth is a moveable feast, depending on where you're standing and who's feeding you your information. Propaganda can be a very powerful force. Why do you think Goebbels put so much effort into it during the war? No, no – it's all a matter of perspective. I imagine if you were a farmer on the far banks of the Danube you'd have a rather different view of world affairs from your opposite number in Idaho.'

I looked him steadily in the eye and spoke evenly. I'd seen enough of Angus and his methods already to know that they were wildly out of kilter with the average man's day-to-day existence.

'You're wrong, you know. I'd say that both those farmers have a pretty much identical view of the world. All they want is to make a living, look after their families and get on well with the farmer next door. Everything else is manufactured by the ruling classes to keep the peasants under control. Nobody in Minsk or Maidenhead really cares about the geopolitical status quo or who's running the Politburo or the White House. As long as it doesn't directly affect them – and most of the time it doesn't – they couldn't give a damn.'

'They'll give a damn if Arkadia Krenč wreaks her havoc across Europe, like the Russians are planning. Her next target could be another spy or someone more public – a politician, perhaps. Assassinate any one of them in a Western nation and you'd instantly put the whole world order in jeopardy. Who knows what could happen then.'

'Nobody's going to press the nuclear button, if that's what you're worried about.'

'Really? Are you sure?'

'I think Cuba proved that.'

He gave a derisive snort. 'The Cuban missile crisis was years ago. The world has moved on since then. The Russians are still smarting from the Americans beating them to the Moon. Meanwhile, the arms race has intensified more than you could imagine. And it's not just the superpowers. China, India, Israel – they're all getting in on the nuclear act and more countries are going to follow. Did you know there are enough warheads on European soil to obliterate mankind from the face of the planet several times over?'

'And you think The Vixen is a walking trigger?'

'All I can say is that if you don't, then you're seriously underestimating her.'

Anna leaned forward and addressed the brigadier urgently. 'Don't you think it's time Bill knew?'

'Knew what?' I said, immediately wary.

Anna stared meaningfully at Campbell-Medlock, who glanced at Kenny before looking back at me.

'You haven't signed the Official Secrets Act – ' he began.

'Damn the Official Secrets Act,' I said angrily. 'Tell me what in God's name is going on.'

There was a moment of tense hesitation before he finally gave way.

'Oh, all right. But this information is confidential – at the highest levels.'

I thought about telling him that I wouldn't agree to keep it that way if I didn't like it but I knew he wouldn't reveal it if I said that and I really wanted to know.

'I need your word, Bill.'

'My word's not worth anything,' I said, carefully dodging the request.

Anna burst out, 'Oh, for God's sake, Angus – just tell him!'

The brigadier stared darkly into his coffee and lowered his voice, as if he was worried there might be a bugging device in the kitchen.

'Arkadia Krenč has to be removed from the game completely. We already know who her next target is going to be.'

'Really? Come on then – spill the beans.'

He hesitated for maximum effect. 'The British Prime Minister. And there'll be nothing we can do to stop her.'

I laughed in surprise. 'Are you serious? You're telling me the Russians are planning to assassinate Edward Heath?' The idea seemed as ludicrous to me as anything I'd yet heard from this bunch of misguided lunatics.

'They tried to get de Gaulle.'

'That wasn't the Russians – that was some French cranks with a grievance.'

Kenny spoke for the first time. 'Listen, Bill. Does it matter who it was? The point is, if someone wanted to assassinate a world leader and destabilise the whole bloody house of cards, it'd be all too easy for them. The secret services can't guarantee the safety of every statesman and politician twenty-four hours a day.'

I hadn't thought of it that way. In Kenny's version, the

quotidian dangers faced by high-profile politicians seemed suddenly very real – and very disturbing.

Campbell-Medlock picked up the theme. 'You can see how an incident like that could escalate swiftly into something catastrophic.'

I certainly could. I just didn't understand why they would do it.

'And that's why we've got to stop her before she gets the opportunity. Her obsession with the two of you is what's given us our best chance of taking her out.'

'So yet again I get to play the role of pawn in your power games,' I said. My disgust at the whole business returned forcibly once more.

Kenny said, 'I'm sorry, Bill, but in the end it doesn't matter how you feel about it. One way or another, The Vixen has to be eliminated.'

I shook my head in disbelief. 'I still can't imagine that the world's leaders would let it come to nuclear war.'

'Are you willing to stake your life on that?' asked the brigadier.

I thought for a long, miserable moment before replying. 'Well,' I said eventually, 'it rather looks as if I am.'

The new context for our mission made it no more palatable but there was no other plan that I could see. It was one thing putting my own life on the line over what I believed might or might not happen in the event of the assassination of the British Prime Minister; it would be quite another to play Russian roulette with the fate of the world.

Anna and I were heading for France.

Having been far too successful in shaking off the Porsche the previous day, our first task was to make ourselves as visible as possible in Innsbruck: we had to draw Arkadia Krenč out of whatever dark hole she was

currently hiding in. One immediate advantage was that
the early morning's dismal weather had cleared up considerably and the sun was now shining generously on
our enterprise. We began by driving our orange advertising hoarding into the centre of the city, finding the most
ostentatious restaurant we could and sitting out on its
open terrace for our lunch, soaking up the sunshine but
wrapped warmly against the still-freezing temperatures.
Half an hour into our grandstanding, Anna whispered to
me through smiling teeth.

'We've got our shadows back.'

I took care not to look at her but copied her approach,
smiling and speaking as if through a ventriloquist's
dummy.

'Where?'

She twisted around in her seat, pretending to look back
inside the restaurant to attract the attention of a waiter.
As she did so, she hissed, 'Opel and BMW, thirty metres
to the left.'

Our two escorts from Salzburg had returned. We
couldn't know for sure if they were connected to the
Porsche that had tried to ram us but it seemed inconceivable that there would be two discrete teams on our tail.
The Porsche could still be about, of course, but it seemed
more likely that they were taking it in shifts, as our own
side were doing. I wondered if the four men in the Rekord
and BMW had notified the Porsche pair yet that their
quarry had been located once more. If it had been me in
the car that had been fooled when we turned off to Kitzbühel, I'd definitely be carrying a grudge.

Anna turned back to look out at the snowy view. 'How
long do you think we should we wait?'

'Oh, I think we should finish our lunch in a leisurely
fashion, maybe take a stroll along the river before we go
waltzing off to Zurich. It's only a few hours so we can still

be there by late afternoon. And we are on our honey-moon, after all.'

As I'd hoped, our bodyguards were doing a much better job of staying hidden than the other side and I didn't catch sight of their big, black Mercedes until we were well outside Innsbruck on the road west. The Opel and the BMW were tucked in together in a long line of traffic, about ten or twelve cars back from us, and the Merc was another five or six behind them. I first spotted it in the off-side wing mirror as it overtook a bread van on a stretch of dual carriageway before swerving back to the inside lane, keeping a regulation distance from the enemy's cars. We made quite a little convoy as we each ignored the others' existence and trundled our way across the map of Austria.

The route of the Tirolerstrasse took us into increasingly Alpine terrain, with snow-capped peaks on all sides and castle architecture on various slopes that looked as if it had come straight out of Hollywood's most clichéd vampire films. I was glad we weren't straying too far off the beaten track as some of the roads high up in the hills looked utterly impenetrable.

I kept our speed steady and constant, not wanting to undermine the pretence of a pair of newlyweds enjoying the scenery of their transcontinental expedition but also allowing our pursuers – of both stripes – to stay in reasonable contact with us. We weren't looking to provoke a fight on this side of the mountains but equally it was important that we didn't lose Krenč's gang a second time, causing her to abandon the current mission and turn her attention instead to Chequers, or wherever she thought she might be able to reach the Prime Minister.

An hour into the drive, the enemy made their move.

'Have you seen the Opel coming up the outside?' Anna asked soon after we rounded a bend where the road opened out onto a straight stretch.

'I've seen it,' I said, and watched it creep up the line of traffic behind us. In front, the line continued to the point where the road swung around to the right and I wondered what the Opel driver's plan was. Would he try to force us off the road or simply edge his way in behind us, ready to strike when the conditions were right? I checked the territory across to my right, thinking there might be an ambush waiting for us up some turn-off, but the hillside sloped up evenly for half a mile and I could see no roads departing from the Tirolerstrasse on this side of the bend.

Oncoming traffic was sparse but not completely absent and the Opel had to pull in four cars back as a large articulated lorry blared its horn in the opposite direction. I could imagine the driver of the car he'd cut up swearing vociferously in guttural German and I allowed myself a smile.

As soon as the lorry had passed, followed by three or four cars that were trapped behind it, the Opel was on the move again and this time I saw the BMW pull out further back as well. I tried to see if the Mercedes was keeping up but I had to switch my focus back to the road ahead and in the brief glimpse I had I couldn't spot it. Now we had the Opel just one car behind us, the BMW a couple of vehicles away, and possibly our rearguard out of touch to provide any assistance. I could feel the sweat prickling the palms of my hands on the wheel.

'Anna, can you reach the guns?'

'You think they're going to attack?' she asked.

'I don't know but I'd like to be ready if they try.'

'Where are Angus and Kenny?'

'Looks like they might be stuck a few cars back. We might need to start defending ourselves without them.'

She clambered between the front seats and reached into the middle of the seats behind. I heard her pull the lever and the secret panel drop down, then the familiar sound of weaponry being manhandled.

'Just the pistols for now,' I said. 'Let's not bring the heavy artillery into view until we know for sure if we're going to need it.'

Moments later she was back in her seat, dropping the magazines of the Walthers into her lap and preparing them for action.

Up ahead, the next bend was approaching and I was watching keenly for possible escape routes. We veered around the corner and I could see the river down to our left. Half a mile in front of us stood the mouth of one of the many tunnels that peppered our route but at this distance I couldn't tell if it was one of the older ones, hewn through the rock with jagged faces on all sides, or a newer, concreted construction with bright lights and emergency telephones for stranded motorists. In the distance, on the far side of the tunnel, I could see a bridge crossing the river.

'Can you check the map for me?' I said, my thoughts racing.

'What am I looking for?'

'Tell me what happens at the other end of this tunnel we're approaching.'

Anna peered hard at the map while I kept an eye on the Opel.

'Just on the other side there's a turning off to the left.'

'Over the bridge?' I asked, pointing vaguely in the direction we were heading.

'That's it.'

'And where does that road go?'

Another pause as she studied the map. She grunted unenthusiastically. 'Hmm. It heads up into the mountains on one of those winding back-and-forth roads which climb the hillside on a zigzag.'

I knew exactly the kind of road she meant and I cursed.

'What are you thinking?' she asked.

'I was hoping it might give us a way out if our Opel and BMW friends were thinking of launching an attack but I doubt that kind of route is going to be passable after the snowfalls we've seen. Where does it go ultimately?'

'It actually doesn't look too bad. After a few miles it seems to rejoin the river bed then goes south to the Swiss border.'

'Damn! It sounds like that would have made a decent alternative to Liechtenstein.'

Ruling out the escape route, I checked the wing mirror again, only to find the driver of the Opel up close on my offside quarter and staring hard at my reflection as he overtook the car immediately behind us before pulling in uncomfortably close. Even in the snapshot I got of him, I could see that he was bald, with low, thick brows and a squat neck. Beside him, his partner was leaner but no less menacing.

And he was brandishing a gun.

'Hang on,' I shouted to Anna, then swung the wheel over to the left, lurching out onto the opposite carriageway. By the grace of whatever higher power was looking out for us, I squeezed past a two-seater sports car coming the other way, its driver's face a picture of outright terror. Ahead there was just enough space to hammer past the car we'd been stuck behind and veer back in front of it. The Opel didn't have room to try the same manoeuvre but I knew it was just a matter of time before he was behind us again.

'This could get tricky,' I said and cast a sideways glance at Anna. She looked thoroughly resolute, a pistol clenched in each hand and crossed close to her chest, switching her gaze from one wing mirror to the other in a bid to keep an eye on the Opel.

I peered around the side of the van in front of us and saw that the road was clear as it disappeared into the tunnel.

'Hold tight: I'm going to make a run for it.'

I crashed down a gear and floored the accelerator pedal, pushing right up next to the van's bumper before making my move so as to give as little notice as possible to the Opel. Then I wrenched the wheel around once more and threw the car across the road. We were breaking all kinds of traffic regulations as we plunged into darkness and I prayed that anything coming the other way would have put on its headlamps through the length of the tunnel. In the absence of any beams I trusted to fortune that we could stay on the wrong side of the road as I ramped up our speed. The Opel followed suit, safe in the knowledge that I would hit any oncoming traffic first, and gained on us fast; behind him, I saw the BMW do the same.

'Come on, come on,' I yelled at the car.

Anna turned around where she sat and steadied her forearm against the shoulder of the seat, aiming the pistol behind us and readying herself to fire.

The first couple of hundred yards of the tunnel were open on the left-hand side, towards the river, with regular concrete supports dividing the view every few yards. Beyond them, a sheer drop fell away to the river valley. The Opel must have noticed that too because it was suddenly making contact with us from behind, trying to nudge us left and through the open side. There was a terrifying metallic crunch as our bumper was ripped away and I saw it go spinning off through one of the gaps and tumbling away down the mountainside. I tightened my grip on the steering wheel: if the car were to go the same way, we were dead for certain.

'Don't shoot!' I ordered Anna, worried that the bucking of the car from the shoving we were receiving would send any bullets off in a wayward direction, putting other drivers at risk of being caught in the crossfire.

She sounded outraged. 'Am I supposed to just let them force us off the road?'

'It's too much of a risk,' I said, holding the car steady as the Opel backed off for another ramming attempt. 'You'd better strap yourself in.'

She faced the front again and reached over her shoulder for the seat belt. I pulled mine across my body and she plugged it into the other end.

'What are you going to do?' she asked, peering back at the Opel which was enlarging in my mirror again.

By way of an answer I stabbed my foot onto the brake pedal and we both jerked forwards.

I was watching the Opel driver closely and I saw a flicker of panic cross his face as he tried to make an instant call on how to react. Then he made contact with us again, much faster than he'd expected, and lost control of the car. Its front end twisted sharply to the left then to the right as he tried to wrest it back under his grip. The van in the inside lane had already braked heavily, leaving a gap in front of it, and the Opel careered across to the rock wall, smashing into it at high speed and buckling like cardboard under the impact. As it burst into flames, the wreckage leaped into the air, hitting the roof of the tunnel before crashing back down in a fireball and flying out through the pillars into mid-air.

The last I saw of it, the burning Opel was describing a smooth, fiery arc down into the valley.

'Verdammt, Bill!' said Anna, her voice a combination of shock and respect.

A wave of nausea swept over me. I said lamely, 'I had to do something or they'd have killed us.'

I studied the mirror again and saw that there were still headlights following us through the tunnel. I pulled back onto the right-hand side in plenty of time to allow a fresh stream of cars to pass going the other way. I wondered if the crash had left debris strewn across the carriageway and whether the tunnel would have to be closed for a clean-up, but that wasn't going to trouble us.

The problem was that it wouldn't trouble the BMW either: it was bearing down on us as we continued to power through the rest of the tunnel.

And there was another worry. If the traffic had been forced to stop behind the crash scene, then Kenny and Angus would be no use to us now. Our only hope was that they might be able to signal for reinforcements, who could take over chaperoning duties at the earliest opportunity. Until then, it was just us and the BMW – and any other Krenč associates who might be lying in wait.

That prospect did not fill me with hope and I made another snap decision. As we thundered out of the tunnel into blinding sunlight, I threw the car off the main road onto the bridge over the river. Even though the winding route across the mountains would be impenetrable, the switch would at least wrongfoot Arkadia Krenč and make her lethal mission far trickier.

If we were going to die, I wanted to do it on my terms.

TWENTY-THREE

The water was flowing fast under the bridge as we crossed and hit a much narrower road than we'd been using up to now. I glanced back over my left shoulder and caught a glimpse of the BMW as it emerged from the tunnel. I switched to the rear-view mirror and saw its driver make the last-minute adjustment to follow us onto the bridge. I'd half hoped we might make it around the first bend and out of sight before they spotted us but that notion was just too bullish. Now it was them and us and whatever other forces they could muster up as we headed into no man's land.

Within a mile of leaving the main road we'd doubled back on ourselves four times, climbing the steep slope with every turn and keeping our speed as high as I dared in the conditions. By rights, on this track, we needed tyre chains and a sub-twenty miles per hour pace but the people who made those rules didn't have Soviet agents on their tail trying to kill them. I aimed for an even thirty-five, except for the corners, which I still took at a reckless lick. The little stone markers showing the edge of the road would have done nothing to hold us back if the traction had given at the wrong moment and there was a constant danger that we'd plummet down into the river valley from increasingly great heights.

Only once did I feel the car sliding away from me, on a left-hand bend near the summit of the first mountain. It was enough to make me reconsider our speed, adjusting it slightly to allow for the ice that seemed to cover the surface beneath the recent dusting of snow. But it was a fine balance between staying ahead of our pursuers and risking our lives on the slippery tarmac.

Fortunately, the BMW's driver seemed to be having even more trouble dealing with the snow than I was. Maybe the Alfa's front-wheel drive gave us an advantage, although the back end of the car was dangerously unstable on the bends, but whatever the reason, we seemed to be putting more distance between us and them.

After descending a little on the other side of the peak then climbing the next one, all the while zigzagging our way to greater altitudes, I decided I could ease off the gas a bit. Anna must have felt a little more relaxed too because she climbed back over the seats and stashed the pistols out of sight again. In the clear blue of the morning, we could see back to the slope behind us, where the BMW was making just as heavy going of the downward hairpins as it had of the upward ones. As long as the surface snow didn't get too deep, we might just manage to stay far enough ahead of them to reach the river valley and the open road towards Switzerland once more. If we did that, we could put even greater distance between us – allowing for the fact that we didn't want them to lose touch with us completely. I would, however, feel much happier at least half a mile in front of them.

It was on the descent into the valley that I overcooked things.

Rounding what appeared to be one of the final bends before regaining the valley road, I misjudged the nearside rockface and nudged it with the front wing. The resulting lurch to the left threatened to spill us over the cliff edge and it was only with some seriously physical manhandling of the steering wheel that I prevented the tyres from going over. The car came to a shuddering halt and the engine stalled.

'What the hell, Bill?'

I slammed the heel of my palm against the wheel and swore vehemently.

Anna's tone changed immediately, becoming more conciliatory and concerned. 'It's OK – we're miles ahead of them. We've still got plenty of time to reach the main road.'

I wasn't so sure. 'I think I may have done some damage.'

'I'm sure you have but it really doesn't matter, does it? We aren't looking to protect our no-claims bonus.'

I pointed through the windscreen at the first wisps of steam that were starting to emerge from under the bonnet. 'I didn't mean the bodywork.'

I let off the handbrake and allowed the car to roll a few yards, steering her away from the edge to give me space to get out of my door. When I did, and went around to inspect the wing, I breathed out through my teeth. A jagged hole had been punched through the metal and there was coolant fluid dripping steadily into the snow. The wing itself was so disfigured that I could see at a glance the bonnet would struggle to open.

I wasn't even going to bother trying.

'Right – slight change of plan,' I said, getting back into the car. 'I've no idea how far this thing will get us but we're going to keep driving until it stops. Meanwhile, you're going to stay on that radio until we get a response from Kenny – or anyone else, come to that. When we do, we get them to come and rescue us.'

'Isn't that just putting them in danger too?'

'Can't be helped. Once the car conks out, we're sitting ducks and our only hope will be if they can deliver us a new one.'

Anna wound down her window and leaned out to look at the damage. 'Couldn't we fix it?'

I'd read somewhere about leaks being fixable by cracking a raw egg into the radiator and hoping that it would solidify around the hole, plugging it at least temporarily. There were two drawbacks to that idea: the first was that nobody really seemed to know if it would work. The second, more prosaic, was that we didn't have an egg.

'Not a chance,' I said, and wrenched the car into gear. 'We'll take it a little steadier, try and keep the heat down, but once the coolant is gone, it's gone. After that, it's just a matter of how long the engine will stand running on empty. My guess would be ten minutes or so – if we're lucky.'

'And how far before the coolant runs out?'

I shook my head. 'No idea. Could be a mile, could be twenty.'

We reached the valley floor without further incident, although I was taking things much more gently. There was still no sign of the BMW in the rear-view mirror and I figured they were probably being even more cautious than we were. That was fine: they would see us turning south onto the main road from their position on the mountain and would no doubt be able to catch us up fairly quickly once they hit the valley floor again.

But another thought had occurred to me and I interrupted Anna from her attempts to establish communication on the radio to gauge her reaction.

'You know how everyone is convinced Arkadia Krenč will want to complete the job of finishing us off in person?'

'No question of it,' she said matter-of-factly. 'Why?'

'I'm just wondering why the Opel was trying to force us off the road in that tunnel. Assuming her team are under instructions to take us alive, so that she can kill us herself, why would the Opel want to drive us off a cliff?'

She fell silent as she pondered that one.

'Unless…' I began.

'Unless what?'

'Unless she was in that Opel herself. Completing the job.' I'd caught sight of the driver and front-seat passenger in my mirrors as they bore down on us on the approach to the tunnel but I couldn't have told you if there'd been anyone else in the car.

Anna paused before replying. 'But if that were the case, then – ' She stopped as the implication dawned on her.

'Precisely. If Arkadia was in the Opel, then she's burned to a crisp in some mangled wreckage at the bottom of a mountain.'

Neither of us spoke for several minutes while the car grumbled on at its gentle pace, the border inching closer. The prospect of reaching Switzerland unchallenged – and especially of the hunt being abandoned because its leader had been eliminated from the chase – seemed just too optimistic to contemplate. Finally, I found a reason to burst the bubble of hope.

'That can't be right,' I said, looking in my mirror for the fifteenth time that minute. 'If The Vixen was dead, the BMW wouldn't still be following us.'

Anna turned around in her seat and stared out of the back window.

'Damn.'

If it hadn't been for the steam that was now beginning to pour from the engine, I would have said we were doing rather well. We'd managed to draw Krenč and her gang almost to the Swiss border; we'd survived one attempt on our lives in the tunnel; and we had traversed a couple of mountains that I'd believed were impassable.

There was no way our luck would hold indefinitely.

Anna had been trying to reach Kenny on the radio almost continuously since I'd driven into the rockface but so far there had been no response. I wondered what was stopping them from picking up our signal but quickly realised that if they had lost us in the tunnel then they wouldn't know we'd turned off south and were now planning a different route to Geneva. That could easily have put them out of range of the radio, especially with all these high peaks blocking the signal.

The road signs told us we were mere minutes from the border when I spotted the BMW, which seemed to be making the most of the clearer roads and gaining on us fast.

'What are we going to do?' Anna asked, facing forwards again. I could feel her eyes boring into the side of my face and I wished I had an answer for her.

'We don't have a lot of options,' I said, stating the obvious. 'I'm going to put my foot down until we reach the frontier and we'll just have to hope that the border guards let us through before the other lot catch us up.'

'And then what?'

It was a bloody good question and another one that I couldn't answer.

The BMW was still half a mile behind us as we pulled in at the checkpoint. As I'd hoped, it was far less officious out here in the middle of nowhere than if we'd tried to cross near a city further north and Anna's easy facility with both the language and the customs in these parts enabled us to pass smoothly. I mentally thanked Mac for his organisation's expertise with passports, visas and the like. The only sticky moment had come when the guard questioned the damage to the car and the steam that was still seeping from the bonnet but Anna's response seemed to satisfy him and he waved us through.

'What did you tell him?' I said as we drove into a new country.

'I just said we were heading to the next town to get all that fixed right now.'

'Well, it looks as though he liked you a lot more than he likes them,' I said, nodding at the mirror.

Anna adjusted her position to look in her wing mirror, then swung around in the seat again for a better view out the back. Behind us, the driver and passenger of the BMW were both getting out of the car while a second guard was emerging from the hut that served as a border post. As we watched, one of the guards waved the two men away from the vehicle and stepped back, his weapon in his hand. Then we rounded a bend and lost sight of the frontier post.

'Do you think the guards saw that they were armed?' asked Anna, looking again at me.

'I don't know but that would be a good reason to take a dislike to them.'

'Where does that leave us now?'

I thought about it as we plodded on into Switzerland. Yet again, and defying all logic, we had succeeded in shaking off two more pursuing cars. Unless The Vixen had an unlimited supply of resources, it was quite likely that we had shaken her off too – and that wasn't the plan. We needed to remain on her radar and that meant allowing the BMW to catch up with us, assuming it ever made it across the border.

'I guess we just roll on along this road as far as the car will take us and see what happens next. I'd be happier if we could speak to someone on our side but that may be a luxury we won't be afforded.'

Anna was studying the map again. 'There are a few towns coming up between here and Davos. Couldn't we stop at a garage and get the radiator fixed?'

'Nice idea but it won't wash. For starters, we don't have the time to sit around while some mechanic rips the car apart. And secondly, I don't want her off the road and out of sight. The whole point of having this orange beast is that she can be seen and if she's tucked away in a workshop having her guts pulled out, they could easily drive through and get ahead of us without even knowing it.'

Anna seemed to concur with my diagnosis and she fell silent again, burying her head in the maps.

The car lasted another half-hour before spluttering feebly and losing power. Fortunately, we were making a gentle descent down one side of a valley, where the river continued to run through the mountains, and I dropped the car out of gear and allowed her to coast for more than a mile, looking around for inspiration. When the car finally teetered to a halt, I rolled her to a stop in front of a roadside bar, where she couldn't be missed by other vehicles passing by, and turned to Anna.

'This is where we leave her.'

She looked confused. 'And do what?'

I shrugged. 'Walk, I guess. With a bit of luck, that town down there will have somewhere we can hire a car. If not, we'll just have to buy one from somebody. Mac can stand the expense. Once we've got our hands on another vehicle, we'll need to let Krenč's crew know somehow what they'll be following from now on.'

We unpacked the car, taking only the essentials we thought we'd need in our backpacks, and set off towards the settlement half a mile down the hill.

We'd gone less than thirty yards when the BMW came screaming past my left shoulder, a passenger hanging out of the nearside window gesticulating frantically to the driver. It was clear that he'd seen the orange Alfa parked at the bar and was now trying to persuade his colleague to turn the car around.

I looked warily at Anna. 'Do you think they saw us?'

'I don't know – but we need them to, don't we?'

'Without a getaway vehicle? I'm not sure about that. I think I'd rather they didn't know where we were at this point.'

The question was rapidly becoming incidental. The enemy had found a turning spot a hundred yards ahead and were executing the manoeuvre even as we debated. I wanted to get us off the road before they returned and I manhandled Anna between two houses, where we hid as the BMW went sailing past in the opposite direction. I peered around the corner of the building and saw the car pull up in front of the Alfa. I could imagine what would happen next – breaking in, followed by a thorough search – and I hoped it would take them a few minutes. A few minutes that might help us enormously.

I pointed over Anna's shoulder where, a couple of hundred yards up the mountain, a ski lift ran up the flattened white snow.

'We're going up there.'

'Skiing? Are you mad?'

'Listen, this crazy chase has proved far too dangerous already. We could theoretically try and get to the town unseen and hire a car but even if we found one we'd only be putting more civilians at risk. This crowd have already shown they're not averse to fighting it out in public so we've got to take the battle off the streets and there's only one realistic choice. If we can get back to the car and pick up the skis, they're sure to guess where we've gone and follow us.'

She looked doubtful. 'How are your skiing skills, Bill? The terrain around here can be pretty challenging.'

Anna was only voicing what I already knew about my winter sports limitations but, having got us this far in our cross-country chase, I was determined not to be the weak link now.

'They'll do,' I said, but I didn't let on that I hadn't donned a pair of skis for more than a decade, and then only in gentle landscapes. Mountains, I knew, were a whole different kettle of fish.

I stuck my head out again just in time to see the two men going into the bar. One was taller and slighter than the other, who looked almost comically squat in his puffed-up winter jacket. Even under the layers of padding I could see telltale bulges under their armpits: it seemed they'd managed to pass through the frontier without a full-blown search of their car. Considering the last I'd seen was a border guard waving a gun at them, I found myself admiring their ability to talk themselves out of a tight corner.

There was no way of knowing if they were stopping for lunch or just wanted to ask some questions of the locals but we had to take the chance. I grabbed Anna's arm and pulled her with me, jogging back to the Alfa.

As we passed the BMW it occurred to me to try and nobble it in some way – maybe like the Land Rover had been nobbled in Australia the previous year – but nothing sprang to mind and we hadn't the right tools for that kind of job in any case. I also vetoed trying to steal it: hot-wiring cars had never been one of the talents I'd acquired as a young man and, although I guessed Anna might know exactly how to do it, I didn't want to risk being caught playing around under the dashboard when the goons emerged from the bar. Instead, we grabbed the skis from the roof of the Alfa and packed the weapons into a nondescript long bag that I slung over my shoulder, hoping it would pass for a spare set of ski poles. Then we skirted around the back of the building, stooping low under its windows.

We were hideously underprepared and provisioned for a trek onto the slopes but our options amounted to zero. It was just as we mounted the ski lift that a cry of recognition reached us from the direction of the BMW.

TWENTY-FOUR

'They could have killed us right then,' I said into a stiff, freezing wind as we climbed the lower slopes. 'The fact that they didn't suggests Krenč is not one of those two.'

'Agreed,' Anna replied, her voice muffled by a scarf and the outer edges of the hood of her thick ski jacket. 'But that's hardly good news, is it?'

'Why?'

'Because at the moment she's not the fish who's nibbling at the bait. We have to keep running until we know we've got her in pursuit.'

'True – but on the other hand it means they won't be killing us for sport until she turns up.'

'That's something, I suppose.'

We dismounted from the ski lift and peeled off from the line of holiday-makers who were heading for the comfort of a nearby café, ready to warm themselves with a hot drink before either taking the next step of their ascent or throwing themselves down the slope they'd just surmounted. I had decided we would do neither, taking a left turn away from the pack into an unmarked field of snow. One or two shouts of warning drifted over to us from the café, presumably more seasoned skiers – or perhaps instructors – advising us not to stray from the tourist path, but that was exactly what I wanted to do. I knew we were still within sight of Krenč's pair, who I'd watched getting on to the ski lift well behind us, and I was keen to take the earliest opportunity to draw them away from the masses. I was confident now that they were only tracking us and wouldn't launch an all-out assault but putting innocent people's lives on the line to prove my point would have been reckless and unconscionable. I wanted to get off the ski slopes and as far away from civilisation as we could, hopefully maintaining a clear distance between us and our pursuers: after all, I reasoned to Anna, while they might not actually kill us, they might take a certain twisted pleasure in disabling our progress by hobbling us physically until the puppetmaster arrived. I didn't fancy the prospect of lying helpless in the snow, crippled by a knee-capping or an iron bar to the femur, while Krenč strolled up from wherever she was currently masterminding the operation.

I let Anna take the lead in our negotiation of the mountains. She was far more proficient on skis than I was and I suspected she quickly gauged that my competence was likely to hinder our progress and made allowances accordingly. Every time she got more than ten yards or so ahead of me – which was annoyingly frequent – she stopped and waited for me to catch up. And each time she spotted the pair of hunters somewhere behind us, she would switch routes, dodging behind an outcrop or dipping into a small ravine to change our course and keep us out of their direct line of sight as much as possible. The aim was to be trackable without being conspicuous.

The weather worsened relentlessly. When we'd left the other skiers at the café, the sun was shining and the clouds overhead were fluffy and white. Now they had darkened to a thunderous grey and were thickening in great threatening masses over every peak in sight. As if in fellow feeling, my thighs were screaming in agony at the unfamiliar exercise to which I was subjecting them.

Three hours into our trek, as I caught up with Anna for the umpteenth time, she pointed higher still.

'I've been wondering which direction to take and I think we should head for Piz Buin. It's beyond this peak and a few hours' more climbing.'

I stopped and leaned my hands on my knees, trying to recover my breath.

'I'm no mountaineer, Anna.'

'You're no skier either but we've managed to get this far. You were the one who wanted to stay away from public areas and if we head down the mountain instead of up, we'll just end up in another town and back at square one.'

I could see she was right but I didn't relish the territory ahead of us.

'Come on, Bill, it's not like it's the Himalayas or anything. Regular tourists make this trek all the time.'

'In these conditions?' I couldn't believe this was the kind of place that the average ski school would take its students, especially the less accomplished ones like me.

She slid back down to where I was doubled over and placed a hand on my back. But if I was expecting any sympathy, I was sorely disabused of the notion. 'I know several Austrian children who could cover this ground faster than you.'

'Thanks,' I said bitterly, and pulled myself upright. 'But if we're going to go higher, shouldn't we rethink our kit? These skis are killing me on these upwards slopes.'

Anna thought for a moment, then appeared to reach a decision. 'You're right,' she said, and snapped off both her skis in a single fluent movement. 'It would probably be easier hiking.'

I followed suit and we abandoned the skis behind a rock that was poking through the snow. Our pursuers would be able to tell from our tracks that we were now proceeding on foot and I was interested to know if they would do the same – not that it made much difference to our plan. I looked back in the direction we'd come but could see no sign of them.

'Do you know where our stealthy companions are?'

'About half a mile back, behind that outcrop,' she said, pointing down the slope. 'They're not trying to conceal themselves but they also don't seem to be too bothered about catching up to us.'

I took that as a promising sign: they were indeed on a watching brief. If they weren't out to immobilise us, that was fine by me. I still couldn't begin to guess what Arkadia Krenč had in store for us or why she hadn't surfaced in person but a waiting game seemed much more palatable to me out here on this freezing mountain than the alternative of a face-to-face confrontation. Much less promising was the weather, which continued to close in by the minute. Hiking further into the peaks seemed like madness to me but Anna was adamant and we ploughed on as the first flurries of snow began to fall.

We didn't speak much. I was better able to keep up without the hindrance of two narrow planks strapped to my feet but the settling snow on top of freezing ice made the going treacherous and I was on constant alert for crevasses or loose sheets that might give way under us and carry us helplessly down the mountain. Dying that way would be even more ignominious than becoming the victim of a Soviet assassin.

After another two hours of climbing we topped a ridge and I stopped, open-mouthed. Even through the lowering skies and steady snow, the view was breathtaking. The entire 360-degree panorama was a circus ring of giant proportions, studded with jagged peaks on all sides and blanketed with a dense cloak of white, broken occasion-

ally by a sheer face of grim, grey rock where the geology
had left a vertical scar on the landscape. We were nearing
the highest point, which I guessed to be the summit of Piz
Buin itself, and I felt as if we were on top of the world. I
shivered, as much from the emotional impact as the cold –
although that was seeping into my bones with a chill that
I feared as much as the cliffs. It wasn't hard to imagine
how Edmund Hillary and Tenzing Norgay must have felt,
reaching the roof of the world on top of Everest a little
over two short decades or so earlier.

Anna brought me back to reality.

'We won't make it over the top,' she shouted into the
wind, pointing at the storm that appeared to be brewing
over Piz Buin. 'Let's take shelter on the southern side –
maybe we can find a mountain hut.'

'Up here?'

'Everywhere,' she said, and began heading over to our
left.

I had given up trying to keep tabs on our pursuers on
the basis that they could look after themselves without us
worrying about them. Having convinced myself that they
weren't an immediate threat, my focus now was on the
imminent blizzard. I trudged after Anna with little choice
but to trust her judgement, and pulled the hood of my ski
jacket tighter around my ears.

Halfway around the peak, Anna found what we were
looking for. Nestling in a snow drift, its rough stone walls
buffeted by the gale that was now blowing, a hut was
rapidly becoming submerged by the weather. Anna was
twenty yards ahead of me and didn't wait before pulling
the door open and going inside, slamming it behind her. I
buttoned my immediate instinct to take offence, reason-
ing that it would definitely make sense to keep the door
shut as much as possible, and when I reached it I realised
exactly why it had slammed: it was a tough job dragging

it open against the wind and once on the other side of it there was little hope of holding it open. The blast of icy air did the slamming job all by itself.

The hut was rudimentary but adequately fulfilled its function. With four stone walls and a floor of bare earth, it offered nothing in the way of provisions or appurtenances: it provided shelter from the weather, nothing more or less. For that purpose it worked perfectly well and we were able to make ourselves a little nest in one corner, where we settled down to sit out the storm. Besides the door, two small openings served as windows in the same facing wall, letting in what little light there now was from outside without causing too much of a draught. Overhead, a roof of wooden beams that looked almost like freshly-hacked tree trunks was lashed into place and I marvelled that such a simple construction could withstand the extremes that it was sure to face at this height and exposure.

We ate some of the food we'd brought with us and listened as the wind began to howl through the rafters, odd flurries of snow blowing in every now and then through the window holes.

'Do you think Abbott and Costello are still out there on the slopes?' I said after a while.

'I would imagine so, unless they've found another hut. They could have turned back, of course.'

I considered that and quickly ruled it out. There was no way on God's earth they would risk heading back to the safety of the nearest town – and potentially Arkadia Krenč herself – without knowing precisely where Anna and I were, probably to within a hundred yards. I imagined they would rather face the hostility of the mountain in a winter storm than the ire of The Vixen on the rampage.

'I think they're still up here somewhere. And I suppose that means we should post a lookout.'

Anna began to scramble to her feet.

'Where are you off to?'

'First shift as lookout,' she said without turning back, and planted herself at the nearest opening in the wall. Immediately a rush of snow blew straight into her face and she backed off, spluttering it out from her nose and mouth. The effect was so comical, given our present circumstances, that I burst out laughing.

'Thanks for that, Mr Chivalry,' she said acidly. 'May I suggest you try and get some sleep? I'll wake you in a couple of hours for your turn at the front line of the Cold War.'

Despite my usual propensity for easy sleep, I hadn't believed I would be able to drop off in the freezing temperatures and basic surroundings of the hut. I hadn't accounted for the sheer physical exhaustion of our Alpine trek. As I drifted off, my mind played treacherous tricks, first casting doubt on Anna's trustworthiness because of her background in espionage and then dropping the poisonous notion that I might be killed in my slumber, like some fond-witted King Duncan. The poison followed me into my nightmares and I slept fitfully, rolling from side to side and surfacing frequently to a wearying semi-consciousness.

I was woken properly by a rough shake of my shoulder and I opened my eyes to see Anna's face close to mine. I was relieved to feel reassured.

'Everything all right?' I said, rubbing one eye with a gloved hand.

'No,' she said, her tone low and grim. 'We've got company.'

I was awake fast now, leaping up and scrabbling for the sack of weapons as Anna went back to the window.

But the bag was empty.

I turned to look at Anna, the unsettling ruminations of my drowsiness returning to the forefront of my brain. Had she betrayed me to the enemy while I slept? Then I saw her miniature encampment by the window, where the rifle stood propped and ready for use and the two pistols lay side by side on top of a rucksack, within easy reach.

'Is it them?' I said, shaking off my uncertainty as Anna picked up the rifle, put it to her shoulder and poked the snout through the window.

'Twenty yards outside the hut. It's about as far as I can see in this weather.'

'What are they doing?'

She paused. 'That's the strange thing. They're doing nothing. They came around the corner a few minutes ago, stopped in front of the hut and are just standing there.'

'Do you think we're surrounded – that they've brought up reinforcements?'

'Doesn't look like it. And if they had, it wouldn't make any difference. They can't get in anywhere except the front door so we've got it covered.'

'Could they come through the roof?' I asked, looking nervously at the beams overhead.

'Not without some serious machinery.'

I picked up one of the Walthers and moved across to the second opening, peering carefully through its narrow slit into the storm raging outside. Just as Anna had described, the two men stood a short distance from the door, their mismatched frames standing out like silhouettes against the grey blizzard. As I watched, they both took off their backpacks and removed the rifles that were slung across their torsos, placing them gently in the snow beside them. Then they reached inside their ski suits and drew out a handgun each, which they put down beside the rifles.

'What the – ?' I began, but Anna shushed me.

'I think they're surrendering.'

'Surrendering?' I couldn't think of anything less likely. If this pair of comedians were part of Krenč's crew – and we had no reason to doubt that – then the thought of surrender would be as far from their minds as apple strudel. 'Why the hell would they do that?'

'Oh, I don't know, Bill – survival, perhaps? Do you have any idea how cold it will get overnight on this mountain? Without protection, death is a very serious possibility. And we're sitting in the only protection for miles around.'

Put like that, their actions made more sense.

The men raised their hands and took a couple of tentative steps towards the hut. I shot a glance at Anna, wondering what her reaction would be. Her eye remained fixed to the telescopic sight and she didn't move.

'*Stoy*!' she yelled through the opening, and the men halted, their arms aloft like broken marionettes.

She seemed to be battling with a decision. I made it for her.

'Open the door.'

'Bill – '

'What do you want to do – let them die out there in the storm?'

I went to the door and heaved against it, pushing back the layer of snow that had built up on the outside and fighting the gale that immediately blew in, accompanied by a cloud of icy flakes.

Anna launched into a tirade of what I took to be Russian and the smaller of the two men began to walk towards me. The other remained motionless, his arms still in the air.

'Bring him in and pat him down,' Anna shouted above the wind.

I backed away from the door, allowing the man to come inside, and waved him over to the unoccupied end of the hut. I performed a brief but thorough search of his person, checking out every pocket I could find and slapping my palms against his body to feel for any concealed weapons. Anna kept one eye on him, with a pistol in her left hand trained in his general direction, while the rifle stayed pointing at his colleague outside the hut. If either of them had tried anything, she would have cut them both down before they'd got three yards.

When I was satisfied that our prisoner wasn't armed I stepped away and indicated to him to sit down in a corner.

'Tie him up,' said Anna.

'Is that really necessary?'

'Unless you want to wake up dead,' she said tartly.

I dug around in my backpack for the length of rope I knew we'd brought with us, then made a decent fist of trussing him up with it, wrapping it first around his hands behind his back then taking the line down to his feet and encircling them with it. He made no attempt to resist, possibly because Anna kept up a constant stream of fast Russian to which he nodded every now and then. When he was immobile and no threat, she shouted out to his companion.

The second man stepped gingerly inside the hut, his hands high above his head and a nervous look on his face. Anna moved away from the window and handed the rifle to me.

'Unclip the sling and use it to tie his hands.'

I did as she asked without hesitating, the second man offering up his hands behind his back quite willingly.

'Now go and get their guns.'

I wasn't sure that was wise. After all our discussions about the nuclear arms race, I'd been left thinking the proliferation of weapons was one of the worst upshots of the Cold War: the more armaments there were in circulation, the more dangerous the world had become. I didn't want to replicate that scenario in miniature inside our little hut.

'All right,' Anna said after a moment's consideration. 'Just fetch a sling from one of their rifles and use it to tie his legs.'

That made more sense and I complied. Outside the hut, the weather had turned particularly foul and there was already a layer of snow covering the small stash of guns the Russians had brought with them up the mountain. I unclipped the sling from one of the rifles and wound it around my wrist, then picked up each weapon in turn and flung it out into the storm, hoping there was a nice cliff edge for them to drop off. If the blizzard kept up for very much longer they'd be safely buried in any case but the further they were from the hut, the easier I was going to rest.

After I'd bound the second man, Anna began another torrent in a foreign tongue. It wasn't so much a conversation as a lecture and although I didn't understand a word of it, her tone was perfectly clear and the pair's body language revealed that they too had got the message: they were to keep still and not move.

'We'll have to take shifts to keep watch,' I said as Anna and I resumed our positions at the opposite end of the hut. We each had a pistol trained on one of the Russians but it was clear we couldn't all stay awake through the night without seriously hampering our chances of getting off the mountain alive. 'You've done your first stint already so I'll take it from here.'

'Not so fast. I want to see what information we can get out of them first.'

The taller Russian, more surly than the other, was eyeing us closely and I half-wondered if he understood English. I watched him as we continued talking.

'What does it matter?' I said. 'We're stuck in here until the storm passes and they've got no means of communicating with The Vixen.' I thought I noticed a twitch in the Russian's cheek at the mention of her codename so I pushed it further. 'Besides, nothing these two clowns can tell us will change the fact that we're top of Arkadia Krenč's hit list.'

His shoulders gave a heave as if he'd laughed contemptuously.

I leaped to my feet, dropping my gun into Anna's lap, and rushed the man. I caught him off-guard – not that he could have defended himself anyway with his hands and feet tied so comprehensively – and grabbed him by the upper arm. I dragged him heavily into the middle of the floor and dumped him face-down in the dirt.

'What are you doing, Bill?' asked Anna, her lips creased in mild amusement. 'I thought you wanted to look after them?'

'He knows something,' I said, and wrenched his shoulder to half-turn him over. 'He understood what we were saying and he knows something about Krenč.'

'Then maybe we can persuade him to tell us,' she said, getting to her feet and waving a pistol in the general direction of his groin.

'No – not that. Let's try the diplomatic approach first.'

It was Anna's turn to laugh in disdain. 'Be my guest.'

I crouched down beside our captive and studied his face. His jaw was unshaven and swarthy, his skin chapped by the cold. Behind the icy blue eyes I saw nothing but hatred and I feared Anna's techniques might indeed be the only way to get him to talk. But my first-hand experience with The Vixen had proved that you didn't need to be a trained spy to be able to withstand torture or a skilled escapologist to abscond from an enemy prison. We might never get anything out of him.

'You know what I'm saying, don't you?'

A flicker of understanding – too instinctive for him to conceal – told me he did.

'Then talk. Unless you want my friend here to carry out her threats.'

I could almost see his brain whirring as he computed the options. Did he fancy his chances of cutting loose, maybe grabbing a weapon, and turning the tables on us? If so, it didn't take him long to re-evaluate the situation. Maybe he'd heard about Anna.

'You arrogant English,' he said, his voice heavily accented but his language fluent. 'Do you really think you are the main priority for The Vixen? Such self-importance. You have always been so, since the days of your empire, but the truth is you know nothing beyond avarice and destruction.'

He spat disgustedly on the floor and sneered at me once more.

I could have begun a philosophical discussion about the rights and wrongs of British imperialism as compared to the brutal expansion of the Soviet dominions over the preceding thirty years but now was not the time.

'All right,' I said. 'If we're not her main priority, then who is?' I thought I knew the answer to that one but I badly wanted to know what he believed Krenč was up to.

The man looked away, aware that he had said too much.

Behind me I heard a gut-wrenching sound and the man beneath me jerked vigorously, a look of pain twisted across his features. I span around to see Anna with one knee pressing hard on his shin, the pistol reversed in her hand just above the man's kneecap. I could guess what she'd done but I didn't want to think about it.

I turned back to his face and leaned in, suppressing the nausea.

'You'll have gathered that I'm much friendlier than she is. Do you want to answer my questions or should I leave her to it?'

He writhed into a position where he could stare directly at me; this time he spat in my face.

Out of shock as much as anything, I stood quickly and backed away to the far wall. Anna immediately replaced me, looming over him and grimacing dangerously at him.

'So you want it that way?' she said, and grabbed his collar to haul him to his feet. He stumbled crazily as she dragged him towards the door, his strapped legs unable to match the pace of her manhandling, but she threw the door open and shoved him outside with a hefty thump between the shoulder blades. I caught a glimpse of his bound feet flying through the air as he went headlong into the snow, then Anna shut the door behind her as she followed him out.

I picked up the pistol that was lying beside me on the floor and pointed it back at the stouter hostage. I could tell from the terror on his face that he was not about to try any funny business.

There was nothing to do now but wait.

TWENTY-FIVE

'Pack the bags – we're leaving.'

'What? We can't go out on the mountain in this weather.'

'I'm not going to argue with you, Anna. If you don't want to go, then you can stay here until the snow clears. But if our Russian friend is right and Krenč's reinforcements will be on their way as soon as it's reasonably possible, they won't treat you anything like as well as we've treated them.'

I was including Anna in that 'we' but I was far from convinced that her dealings with the man she'd taken outside were any less brutal than Arkadia Krenč's methods.

'We'll die if we head out there in the middle of the night.'

I stopped cramming equipment into my backpack and looked at her. 'We'll die if we stay here. And besides, we have a new mission.'

'What new mission?'

'We can talk as we go. We're wasting time.' I shot a glance at Shorty, still cowering against the opposite wall, and wondered if he was listening. 'What about him? Shouldn't we untie his feet, at least?'

'No. His comrades are sure to find him and being tied up will help mitigate his punishment for letting us get away.'

I tried not to contemplate what would happen to him once Krenč got hold of him but at least he was in a better state than his companion. I finished packing the rucksack and heaved it onto my shoulders with the flap still open. Anna caught up with me as I went out of the door into the howling wind.

'Is he dead?' I shouted to Anna, averting my gaze from the crumpled body not far from the hut door, a pool of red widening around him.

'Not dead, no. But I imagine he's regretting that he didn't talk sooner. Or faster.'

I stopped and offloaded my pack.

'What are you doing, Bill?'

'I'm sorry, Anna, but I can't leave him out here to freeze to death.'

Five minutes later, the unconscious Russian was slumped next to his colleague inside the hut and I was putting on my backpack again.

It was impossible to communicate as the blizzard raged around our ears and we fell into a silent trudge through the deepening snow and thick night. The new fall meant we were less likely to lose our footing on sheet ice but the conditions were still shocking. For twenty minutes we battled on, Anna following in my footsteps as we climbed towards the next ridge in what I hoped to God was the right direction for Davos.

It had taken Anna longer than I'd wanted to get the Russian to talk. Inside the hut, my prisoner and I stared wordlessly at each other over the barrel of my Walther while I listened for sounds from outside but all I could hear was the undulating whistles of a squalling winter. When Anna reappeared – ominously without her captive – she had a grim expression on her face.

'What did he tell you?'

'He was right: we're not The Vixen's top priority right now. She's having us tailed – and not only by these two idiots – but they are under instruction not to kill us.'

'As we suspected. But what is she doing? And where on earth is she?'

'That's where it gets interesting.'

I imagined my definition of interesting might differ considerably from Anna's.

'Arkadia Krenč is in Davos. It's a few miles west of here.'

'She's waiting for us there?'

'In a manner of speaking.'

This was all getting too cryptic for me. I suspected the world of espionage was playing tricks with Anna's ability to speak plainly in any circumstance. 'What's she up to?'

She sat down beside me and joined my staring match with Shorty. 'Have you heard of the European Management Symposium?'

It rang a vague bell. 'Isn't that a group of industrialists who meet up every year to put the world to rights?'

'Something like that. It was founded three years ago by a German engineer named Klaus Schwab. Depending on your point of view, it's either a forum devoted to global improvement for the benefit of all mankind or a lobbying exercise for corporations to get the world to run the way they want it.'

'So international companies have their own agenda. What's that got to do with Arkadia Krenč?'

'If you let me finish, I'll explain. So far the annual symposium in Davos has been mainly businessmen exchanging ideas and enjoying the après-ski. This year, for the first time, they've invited a number of political leaders to attend. One of them – although it appears that neither of our secret services is aware of the fact – is President Richard Nixon. He is due to arrive in Davos tomorrow and The Vixen is waiting for him.'

I let out a long, slow breath. For all his domestic troubles around the allegations of wrongdoings in the Watergate building, Nixon remained the most powerful man in the world – for now, at least.

'Bloody hell. That's a bit of a step up from Ted Heath, isn't it?'

'You can see the implications, can't you?'

I certainly could. If Krenč had the President of the United States in her sights, then Anna and I – and even Ted Heath, bless him – were very small fry indeed. More worryingly, if the intelligence services of two of America's closest allies were unaware that Tricky Dicky would be flying secretly into the Swiss ski resort the following day, then how on earth had Krenč managed to discover it? Her network of spies must reach to the highest levels of the CIA and the whole foundation of US espionage would be damaged irreparably, whether or not she accomplished her mission in Davos.

And now the answer to that question – and possibly the future of the free world – lay squarely with us.

So much for sabre-rattling.

At the top of the ridge we paused, gazing out at the interminable field of snow interrupted by the occasional craggy outcrop, shrouded in darkness and cloud. Then I noticed the first glimmer of hope I'd felt for many hours.

The snow had stopped falling.

'How long to Davos?' I said.

'Hard to say. If we keep up a decent pace we might make it by dawn. It's good that it's stopped snowing but if the wind keeps up – especially in our faces – that could slow us down.'

'Better get on with it then.'

My legs were exhausted, my eyes wretched from staring at the endless gloomy white ahead of me, and my brain was fogged into stupefaction. It was all I could do

to put one foot in front of other and force my body in
the direction of Davos. Every now and then Anna would
overtake me, putting on a spurt of speed, and I would up
my pace to stay in touch with her, taking as much as half
an hour to regain the gap between us and pass her once
more. I wasn't sure if she was doing it deliberately to keep
me energised but, whatever the reason, it worked.

Two-hour hiking stints were broken with a fifteen-
minute rest and chunks of Kendal mint cake, that mountaineer's friend which has kept many a lost soul alive in
dire straits. We barely spoke because there was little to
say and even less breath to say it with. It was enough that
we shared a resolute determination to reach Davos before
light – and the President of the United States – descended
on the Alpine town. I reckoned the sun, if it rose after such
a bleak night, would arrive somewhere around 8 a.m.,
giving us precious little time to raise the alarm before the
business of the symposium's day got under way. I had no
idea what we would do when we arrived: we didn't even
know where the event was being held and the chances of
two ragged hikers being believed as they came down off the
early-morning mountain with outrageous tales of assassins
and espionage were, to my mind, extremely slim. Our best
bet would be to try and raise Kenny and Angus on the radio
but they were expecting us to be travelling many miles to
the north and there was no guarantee that we would be
in communication range. Failing that, we'd have to track
down the British or West German delegation at the forum
and do our damnedest to persuade them of our bona fides.

Even if we made it to Davos in time we had our work
cut out.

* * *

The wind had dropped considerably and we'd made decent
progress through the night but we were still some dis-

tance short of the town when the first hints of dawn crept over the peaks behind us. The lightening sky at our backs somehow made the receding night in front of us seem even darker and I was grateful for that optical anomaly when I saw a crest over to our left picked out in silhouette by a glow that came from beyond it.

I reached out to tap Anna's arm and pointed at it.

'There are lights over there.'

She nodded briskly and immediately set off towards the glow. It was the first clue we'd had that the direction we'd been walking was anywhere near correct and it put a spring in both our steps. If we'd stopped to consider it, we'd have realised that the lights could just as easily have come from Klosters, further north, or one of the remote villages dotted along the mountain passes but there was something about it that convinced me we were approaching the head of a valley that would lead us down into Davos itself.

When we stumbled across a lodge at the summit of a ski lift, the edge of town now visible at the bottom of the run, I started to believe we might just make it in time.

I was heading for the door of the large wooden building when Anna barked an order at me.

'Bill – don't!'

'Why not? We need to get help and raise the alarm.'

'Think about it for a minute. Two armed skiers turn up at dawn with some story about a plot to kill Nixon – they'd think we'd gone mad. If I were in their shoes, I'd barricade the doors and call the police.'

When I looked at it that way, I could see that hammering on the lodge door was perhaps not the best plan.

'What do we do then?'

Anna indicated a small wooden shelter off to one side where a collection of skis had been jammed upright into the snow, like some miniature forest of sports equipment.

'They're very trusting, aren't they?'

'Who is there to steal them up here?' she said by way of an answer.

We hurried over to the shelter and selected two pairs of skis that we fastened over our boots; the fit wasn't ideal but they would have to do. I wasn't sure about attempting a high-speed downhill run in the crepuscular light but it seemed like our best option with the clock ticking relentlessly towards eight. Poles in hand, we shuffled across to the top of the run and launched ourselves down the mountain.

Half a mile into the descent, we came under fire.

I heard the shot and saw a plume of snow flare up in front of me at the same moment. The ricochet was still echoing through the valley when the second came. Ahead of me I saw Anna dive to the left into the pines that bordered the piste and I threw myself in the same direction. I hit the tree line just as a third bullet thumped into a trunk to my right and I sprawled headlong into a bank of soft snow, rolling over two or three times before coming to a halt. At first I thought I'd been lucky not to plough into one of the pines in the dense thicket but then I realised the greenery ran out close to where I was lying. I spat out some of the ice I'd inhaled in my fall and crawled over to where the trees ended. When I looked over the small ridge of snow, my head span: a cliff fell away hundreds of feet below me, the crags sticking out jaggedly in a death trap for anyone unfortunate enough to go over. I had escaped that fate by a matter of inches.

Anna was already back at the edge of the run, assessing the lie of the land.

'Can you tell where the shots came from?' I asked breathlessly as I heaved myself up next to her.

'I wasn't in time to see that last shot and there's been nothing since but if you pressed me I'd say the shooter was pretty close, slightly up the hill on the far side. Certainly no more than a hundred yards away.'

I peered through the gloom at the tree line opposite but could see nothing.

'If they were that close, any half-decent shot would have hit us, even in this light.'

'That's what worries me,' she said. 'I don't think they were trying to hit us. I think they were trying to drive us off the piste.'

'And over that cliff?'

'What cliff?' she said, spinning around in alarm.

'That one just behind us. It was only by the grace of God that I didn't go over the edge.'

She turned back around and squinted across the slope again. 'I don't think they can know about that. My bet is that they want us alive. That cliff wouldn't have served their purpose at all.'

I was mystified. 'Why would they still want us alive?'

In chilling response, a voice drifted out of the trees to our right.

'Oh, that's an easy one to answer, Mr Kemp.'

From behind a pine, an Uzi submachine gun in hand, stepped Arkadia Krenč.

My first thought was unexpected: if The Vixen was up here on a mountain with us, then perhaps Nixon was safe. My second was much more unwelcome as reality crashed in. Nixon was no safer than I was right now – it was just that Krenč had decided to deal with us first.

And that meant our time was up.

'How did you know where we were?' I said, trying to make my voice sound nonchalant.

She laughed. 'Your communications might have failed but mine are certainly in order. My men at the hut alerted me last night that conveniently you were heading for Davos.'

So Shorty had been able to understand us as we planned our operation. I berated myself for not disposing of the Russians' backpacks at the same time as I'd hurled their weapons into the storm. They must have stashed a high-powered radio in the hope that we might overlook the rucksacks – there had certainly been nothing on their persons when I'd searched them.

She went on, 'That was very helpful of you. You have saved me a major diversion from the main business of my day.'

'Oh, I understand it now,' said Anna. 'You never intended to come after us in Austria.' She sounded almost disappointed.

Another grunting sneer. 'You don't really believe you are so important to me? The only reason I am here now is because I was by chance in Davos today for the forum. I have a rather pressing appointment.' Euphemisms could work for both sides, it seemed. 'We were not supposed to meet until you reached Liechtenstein or Zurich.'

I kept my voice as casual as I could. 'I'm delighted we've made it so much easier for you – you're welcome, by the way. But you couldn't have known we'd be coming down this run in particular. There must be a thousand ways of crossing these mountains.'

'You might think so but in truth – especially if the weather is inclement – the geography forces you into one funnel that inevitably leads you here. I'm so relieved that you found it.'

So was I but I didn't want to admit that to her.

'Surely it would have achieved your objective if we'd perished on the mountain?'

She took a step closer, lifting her feet high to clear the snow that was piled up among the trees. The corner of her mouth curled into an ugly shape.

'But then I wouldn't have seen the look on your faces as you died. The only question now is which order to kill you. Should I eliminate Anna first to watch your horror at her death a second time, Mr Kemp? No – I think you should die first so that Anna and I can resolve our outstanding business before I kill her too.'

Anna's voice was raw and rasping. 'We have no outstanding business. You and I were finished years ago.'

Krenč smiled cruelly. 'You probably thought so when you gave my identity up to the Western intelligence services. But the truth is that you are burning inside at that decision. Whether or not you choose to deny it, you are still in love with me.'

Now Anna laughed, a guttural, animal sound that came from the depths of her being. 'I was never in love with you. We shared some common interests and expertise and we had some fun but you don't know the meaning of the word love.'

'Oh, and you do, I suppose? Do you imagine yourself in love with Kemp, here?' She waved the machine gun in my direction.

The longer we kept her talking, the better the chances of survival for the man who was probably, even now, being transported to the symposium in the town below us. I had given up hope of making it off the mountain alive the moment I saw Krenč with her Uzi but if we could delay her long enough for Nixon to get in to the forum and out again without an assassination attempt from The Vixen, at least we wouldn't have died in vain.

'I'm inclined to agree with Anna,' I said, easing myself to my knees and brushing off the snow from my ski suit. Out of the corner of my eye I saw Anna do the same. 'I don't think you have the first idea of what love is.'

She sneered again. 'I know what it is to love my country. That is the highest form of love. You westerners can never understand that.'

By now, Anna and I were both on our feet. I felt emboldened by Krenč's engaging with my banal conversation so readily. 'Is that why you're doing all this – because of some misguided sense of patriotism? Oh, you may talk about your adoration of the Motherland or your devotion to preserving its values and history but that's not love. That's just posturing.'

'As I said, you westerners do not understand.'

'So it's worth all the lives lost, is it? The continuation of your stupid non-war in which nobody really wins.' I'd had a go at Mac for his wilful perpetuation of hostilities; I might as well try the same line with Krenč. 'And what about those of us caught in the crossfire?'

'You?' she said dismissively.

'I was thinking of Roland Wolf.'

She looked confused but also disinterested. 'And who is Roland Wolf?'

I became vaguely aware of a thrumming sound in the distance, familiar but not quite recognisable. 'I wouldn't expect you to know. He was a hotel clerk in Vienna. He got caught in the crossfire.'

'Oh, the boy. That was unfortunate but necessary.'

'Unfortunate?' I baulked at her casual dismissal of his life, which seemed to mean as little to her as a lab rat's in some vast, hideous experiment.

'Yes, unfortunate. He should have told us where to find you.'

'He didn't bloody know,' I shouted, the stupidity of his death hitting me hard once more. 'He was just a hotel clerk.'

'I didn't know that at the time,' she said simply, as if that were explanation enough for his murder.

'How did you even find him?' I asked, shaking my head.

Krenč's voice sharpened and the frost in the air deepened. 'You really don't understand what you are dealing with, do you, Mr Kemp? That was the easiest thing in the world. Although it was especially kind of the Austrian police to write his name in a notebook for us.'

Napoleon! Not the sophisticated interrogator he imagined himself to be, then. In fact, a rank amateur. I hadn't just given Roland up to the *Stadtpolizei*: thanks to Napoleon, I'd signed his death warrant for The Vixen as well.

The noise was getting louder and I felt my stomach turn over as I registered what it was: the sound of helicopter blades whirring. Was this the American President unwittingly approaching his Rubicon?

The sound seemed to spur Krenč into action. 'Now, throw your guns onto the ski slope,' she said, indicating with her weapon.

Anna picked up the rifle and slung it out onto the flattened snow. Then we both lifted our pistols from our snow jackets, slowly so as not to spook Krenč, and tossed them after the rifle. In the process, Anna stumbled and fell to one knee, picking herself up again after a moment's hesitation.

'Now go and stand over there,' said Krenč, gesticulating in the direction of the cliff edge.

I didn't move. 'What are you going to do – throw us off?'

'I will happily shoot you where you stand, if that is your preference, Mr Kemp.'

It wasn't and I moved. At least if we were still talking then we were still alive.

I led the way through the narrow band of trees and emerged onto the five-foot strip of snow that separated the greenery from the precipice. Anna followed me out from the protection of the branches and we stood side by side with our backs to the edge, watching Krenč come to the nearest trunk and lean offhandedly against it, the Uzi cradled under her right armpit.

'Wait a minute,' I said, a thought striking me that

could perhaps keep the conversation going for a few more precious minutes, allowing the choppers to take Krenč's quarry somewhere far, far away. 'If you were so keen to murder us yourself, why did the driver of that Opel try to kill us in a tunnel?'

A grimace returned to Krenč's face and she shifted the weight of the gun in her hands. 'If only people would do as they are told. You and I, Anna – we were trained the correct way. Obey commands from your superiors, never question orders, do as you are told. But the young people today seem to believe they are entitled to think for themselves. I can only assume that he saw what he thought was an opportunity and attempted to take it. He will not make the same mistake a second time.'

He won't make any mistake a second time, I thought morosely.

Snow was beginning to fall again.

Over the tops of the trees I could see three helicopters in formation, circling across the valley a little way to the north and turning roughly in our direction. They seemed to be moving fast and I guessed the conference centre couldn't be far from where we currently stood.

'Ah,' said Krenč, pointing a finger vaguely towards the sound and cocking her head to one side. 'My appointment.'

If Krenč was true to her word – and I had no reason to doubt it in these circumstances – she would pick me first. Anna must have realised the same thing because she began speaking to Krenč in German. I thought I detected a hint of urgency in her tone but Krenč remained calm and unemotional.

'That's not very nice of you,' she said after Anna ran out of steam. 'I don't think Mr Kemp can understand what you're saying to me.'

'What was she saying to you?'

She stirred and pulled herself upright, balancing her

weight evenly between her feet. 'She was trying to remind me that we once had strong feelings for one another and that must surely count for something. I'm not sure if she was pleading for her own life or for both of you but I'm afraid she didn't mention you in her little speech.'

Anna looked sideways at me. 'Don't listen to her. She will twist anything to make it sound evil.'

I managed to crank out a thin smile. 'Don't worry, Anna. I'd much rather die believing you than a murderous monster with no conscience.'

Arkadia Krenč laughed, the cackle echoing hollowly off the mountains behind us. 'What you don't seem to realise, Mr Kemp, is that Anna and I are the same. Just because you may have shared a bed, it doesn't make her any more virtuous. I learned that for myself.'

'Shut up, Arkadia!' hissed Anna through gritted teeth, and I laid a restraining hand on her arm to check her involuntary movement towards the trees. I was relieved to see that Krenč had either missed the lunge or was ignoring it.

Anna turned to face me and pressed her body up against me. 'I'm sorry I got you into this, Bill.'

I shook my head. 'Nothing to be sorry about. It was my idea and my decision. I'm the one who should be apologising to you. If it hadn't been for me and this crazy trek across the Alps, you could still be safely dead.'

'How touching,' Krenč mocked, and I looked across in her direction. The choppers were close now and she turned away from us to glance up into the sky. As she did so, I felt Anna's hand brush mine. In her palm she held the cold steel blade of her Fairbairn-Sykes and I understood: when she'd stumbled in the snow, she had drawn the knife from its hiding place in her boot.

The Vixen was saying something but I wasn't listening. All I could hear above the helicopter blades was Anna's voice, loud in my ear but imperceptible to Krenč, giving me my brief instructions. As she counted down from three, I placed my weight onto my left foot and prepared to dive.

Then she yelled 'Go!' and the world exploded.

I went right; Anna sprawled to her left, simultaneously flinging the knife at Arkadia Krenč. I hit the soft snow and rolled fast towards the trees, which meant I missed what happened to the knife, but from the scream that went up behind me I guessed it had hit its mark. Krenč's Uzi went off, spitting bullets into the air and God knows where else, then she stumbled forwards out of the trees, the gun banging wildly against her thigh with her finger still glued to the trigger. Spurts of blood shot up from her leg and foot as bullets pumped into them, jetting scarlet into the pristine white of the snow, and then she was down, her body writhing and her head jerking uncontrollably. Protruding from her chest I could see the grim, sleek profile of the fighting knife.

The choppers were hovering almost directly overhead and I wondered whether their pilots could see the bright red that was leaking into the snow around Krenč's body or if it was just a coincidence that they veered sharply away and sped off into the mountains.

Then Anna was back, looming over Krenč and wrenching the Uzi from her twitching shoulder. She tossed it behind her and fell to one knee, close to her one-time lover. I had no idea what Anna said as she bent to Krenč's face but when she rose again I could see the Fairbairn-Sykes in her hand once more.

With a single, sickening motion, she drew the blade across Krenč's throat and rolled her body over the cliff.

'You didn't imagine I'd throw her off alive, did you?'

I shot Anna a look intended to convey horror at her

easy calmness. In all my dealings with shady types, I had never encountered the calculated coldness of Arkadia Krenč and I hadn't doubted for a moment that she was willing to die in the cause of her mission – and take as many with her as necessary, from either side.

What I hadn't expected was the same coldness from the woman I'd gone to bed with two nights earlier.

'I didn't imagine you'd throw her off at all,' I said, but I knew I was wasting my breath.

We didn't trouble to seek out the gunman who'd forced us off the piste. Anna reckoned – and I thought she was probably right – that whoever had fired at us would be long gone, especially if they had any idea what had happened to their boss. If she was still alive, the machine gun spray would have meant she was dealing with the irritating foreigners. If not, then they would be better off as far away from Switzerland as they could get.

'What about Nixon?' I asked, concerned that other Soviet spies might be roaming Davos with assassination on their minds.

'He's safe,' said Anna with certainty. 'For now.'

'How can you be so sure?'

She gave me an unimpressed look. 'I know how these people work. There won't be a back-up plan in place for this symposium. It would be too risky – too much danger of exposure if more than one operative went after him. The Vixen was a one-shot mission.'

It pained me but I had to trust her.

We'd lost three of our four skis but it didn't matter: we were in no hurry now. Keeping to the edge of the run, we trudged slowly down the mountain, watching the day break over the valley and the lights go out one by one in Davos. I couldn't imagine feeling any bleaker than I did now but the biting wind chilled every part of me. I tried to console myself with the thought that we had probably averted an international disaster – maybe even World War Three – but it was small comfort. Images of Roland in his fedora plagued my mind and the ice closed in around my heart as I stared at the figure ahead of me in the snow, apparently unmoved by the roll call of death.

After twenty minutes of silent descent, I shouted to Anna.

'It's no good.'

She stopped and turned to look back at me, her cheeks red from the cold but a fire in her eyes that seemed in stark contrast to the deadness I felt behind mine.

'What's no good?'

'This. You and me. I can't live with it.'

I could tell she knew exactly what I meant.

'Bill, you don't have to. But this is my life and my way of fighting for my future. I understand if that is unacceptable to you.'

'It's not about whether it's acceptable or not. It's about me being able to live with my conscience. If we stay together then I don't think I can.'

Her gaze dropped and she looked more subdued. 'Then perhaps we should part here. You go on to Davos and make contact with Kenny or Mac or whoever you can. I shall take this opportunity to disappear.'

'Disappear?'

'From this operation, yes. I am no longer needed but I am also no longer in danger. That at least has passed.'

'But you're going back to your old life.'

She stepped close to me now and stared deep into my eyes. Then she leaned forward, placed a gentle kiss on my mouth, and turned away into the trees. I stood and watched her fade into the pines until she was consumed by the darkness.

I couldn't remember ever feeling so lonely.

EPILOGUE

The brigadier slid a whisky tumbler across the desktop but I was in no mood for drinking – with him or anyone else. Besides, it was barely eleven o'clock in the morning.

'Look, Bill, I know this has been taxing for you,' said Mac from his huge winged chair on the far side.

I bit my lip. He really had no idea.

'But everything's worked out beautifully. Your Leotta is safely back at medical school, Anna Stern has vanished like a puff of smoke into the West German spy network – which is probably best for all concerned – and our American friends are particularly grateful for your intervention in Davos. You saved them quite a bit of embarrassment there. You'll end up with a medal, likely as not. Although you'll have to keep quiet about it.'

I considered giving him a broadside about the needless deaths of Roland Wolf, the men in the Opel who'd bought it in the tunnel, the countless Soviet agents removed by our side – or theirs – because of Anna's double-dealing. I decided against it: nothing I said would make a jot of difference.

'You can keep your medal,' I said simply.

'Don't be like that, mate,' said Kenny from his seat beside me. 'You've got to admit it was one hell of an adventure.'

I looked curiously at him, wondering how this friend I had known for so many years could be so blasé about the secret and deadly organisation he'd wound up in. I couldn't imagine the Kenny from our army days being so laid-back about the whole bloody business of espionage.

'I can do without that kind of adventure, thank you very much. I'm feeling in the mood for something rather more mundane right now.'

'Well, that's a shame,' said the brigadier, pouring himself a slug from the decanter he was clutching. He held my gaze as he slowly took a sip, waiting for me to bite.

I resisted.

'Because we were thinking of offering you a job.'

I'd had no idea why I had been summoned to the Foreign Office, sneaking in by a side entrance just behind the stage door of the Whitehall Theatre by Admiralty Arch. All I knew was that Mac wanted to see me. It had been a surprise to find Kenny and the brigadier in tow but I figured it might just be a final debrief. I'd already undergone my main one at the hands of some sinister officers from MI6 at a safe house deep in the Wiltshire countryside but there was always the chance they wanted one last go at me. The offer of employment had never entered my head.

'You have to be joking,' I said, staring around the desk from one to another.

Mac shook his head. 'No joke, Bill. You've proved you're more than capable of handling yourself in the toughest of situations, against the most barbaric of enemies. It seems to me you're exactly the kind of field officer we could use. My only question is why it took so long for us to think of it.'

He looked pointedly at the brigadier, who turned his attention swiftly to his drink.

'Did you put them up to this?' I asked Kenny.

'Nothing to do with me, mate. Angus came up with it all by himself. Although I can certainly see the benefits.'

'For you, maybe. But definitely not for me. I've had enough of the delusions of espionage to last a lifetime.'

Mac leaned forward and clasped his hands together on the polished mahogany. 'Don't rush into a decision, Bill. Give it some thought.'

'I've given it all the thought I need,' I said, and left.

Emerging from the building into Admiralty Place, I turned left to avoid the noisy havoc of Trafalgar Square. Somewhere in St James's Park I needed to find a kiosk selling bird food. I had a sudden urge to feed the ducks.

MICHAEL DAVIES

Michael stopped being a newspaper editor to start writing fiction. He is now an award-winning playwright, scriptwriter, author and journalist. His work has appeared on stage, screen, radio, the printed page and online. As well as writing the book and lyrics for *Tess – The Musical*, Michael completed for publication the posthumous release of Desmond Bagley's 'lost' novel *Domino Island*, featuring the protagonist Bill Kemp. Michael's original sequel, *Outback*, was published in 2023 as a centenary tribute to Bagley. *Thin Ice* completes a Bill Kemp trilogy.

@mrgdavies
www.mrgdavies.com

ACKNOWLEDGEMENTS

If you're already a fan of Bill Kemp, you'll know that the first name on the list of people I must thank is that of Desmond Bagley. It was this supreme thriller writer whose work I fell in love with in my youth, and whose posthumous novel *Domino Island* I was fortunate enough to be invited to work on by his publishers HarperCollins in 2019. Without him there would be no Bill Kemp, and therefore no *Thin Ice*.

I have had the privilege and delight of being able to maintain a direct link with Bagley's family through Lecia Foston, the sister of Bagley's wife Joan. Lecia and her husband Peter have been a constant source of information, encouragement and even memorabilia about 'Simon', as he was known to the family, and I continue to value their friendship.

The role of HarperCollins in keeping Bagley's legacy alive should not be underestimated. Estates publisher David Brawn has ensured that the novels have remained in print since his early death in 1983, and David has also been instrumental in establishing and furthering my own career as a novelist. I am, naturally, extremely grateful. David's editorial colleague Morgan Springett has offered expert guidance in the development of the manuscript of

Thin Ice, as has Paul Campbell – another fine writer – who supplied superb advice in the early days. My eagle-eyed friend and editor extraordinaire Richard Howarth has been invaluable in the latter stages, while Nigel Alefounder, a Bagley connoisseur, continues to cheerlead relentlessly. Their various roles are all much appreciated, as are those of proofreader Charlotte Webb and cover designer Toby James.

I am also hugely indebted to Bagley fans and readers, and those who have discovered him via *Outback*, for their readiness to welcome my offerings. Whether through direct contact, online reviews, author events or a host of other means, your generosity and warmth has been inspiring.

A novel is a significant undertaking, which I could not possibly have completed without the support, love and practical enablement of my wife Tricia. I can't dedicate every book to you, but you know I couldn't do it without you.

@mrgdavies
www.mrgdavies.com

If you loved this book, don't miss the other Bill Kemp books!

'Like a dream come true –
an undiscovered Desmond Bagley
novel . . . and it's a great one!'
LEE CHILD

Out now.

If you loved this book, don't miss the other Bill Kemp books!

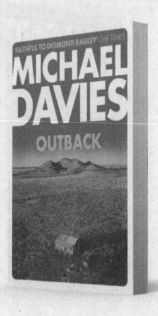

An original tale of danger and death under the blistering Australian sun.

Out now.